Liberated Ladies

Unconventional heiresses...full of big ambitions!

Friends Verity, Jane, Prue, Melissa and Lucy are unconventional ladies with scandalous yearnings and big ambitions—to be writers, painters, musicians—but the only safe sanctuary to exercise their talents is in one of their family's turrets!

They have no wish to conform and be drawn into society's marriage mart, unless they can find gentlemen who value and cherish them for who they truly are...and *not* the size of their dowries!

Read about Verity's story in
Least Likely to Marry a Duke

And Jane's tale in
The Earl's Marriage Bargain

And Prue's story in
A Marquis in Want of a Wife

All available now

And look for Melissa's and Lucy's stories

Coming soon

Author Note

Of the five friends whose stories I am telling in the Liberated Ladies series, Prudence is the one who pays the least attention to living men—the ancient Greeks and the Romans are far more interesting. I could not imagine how she might fall for someone and began to worry that I would never discover the right man for her.

Then she finds herself very much in need of a gentleman—and her friends assure her that Ross Vincent is the perfect answer to her problem because he is very much in want of a wife. So in strolled the Marquis of Cranford, scarred, battle hardened and indifferent to women, and I realized he was absolutely wrong for Prue—and might be just what she needed.

Ross might need a mother for his baby son, but does he *want* all the trouble of a wife? It is just a matter of business they assure themselves and each other. But complicating emotions like desire and love have a way of making themselves felt, and as Prue and Ross began to tell me their story, I discovered that Prue was a much stronger woman than I had realized and that Ross, for all his experience of the world, had a lot to learn about women—especially the one he had married.

I hope you enjoy following Ross and Prudence to their happy-ever-after as much as I did.

LOUISE ALLEN

—

A Marquis in Want of a Wife

HARLEQUIN

HISTORICAL

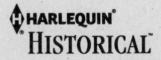

ISBN-13: 978-1-335-50587-3

A Marquis in Want of a Wife

Copyright © 2020 by Melanie Hilton

Recycling programs
for this product may
not exist in your area.

This edition published by arrangement with Harlequin Books S.A.

For questions and comments about the quality of this book,
please contact us at CustomerService@Harlequin.com.

Harlequin Enterprises ULC
22 Adelaide St. West, 40th Floor
Toronto, Ontario M5H 4E3, Canada
www.Harlequin.com

Printed in U.S.A.

Louise Allen has been immersing herself in history for as long as she can remember, finding that landscapes and places evoke powerful images of the past. Venice, Burgundy and the Greek islands are favorites. Louise lives on the Norfolk coast and spends her spare time gardening, researching family history or traveling. Please visit Louise's website, www.louiseallenregency.com, her blog, www.janeaustenslondon.com, or find her on Twitter @louiseregency and on Facebook.

Visit the Author Profile page
at Harlequin.com for more titles.

For the Quayistas, for keeping me smiling through lockdown.

Chapter One

Little Gransdon House, Hertfordshire
—May 1st, 1815

The scent of hothouse flowers still hung heavy in the warm air. The moonlight still sent pearly gleams through the foliage and the distant sound of music from the ballroom still wove its dreamlike spell. And then, like the music of fairyland when the mask of enchantment slipped, it stopped, leaving a silence broken only by the splash of water from the little fountain.

Prue sat up, the bench that had seemed cushioned in swansdown only moments before now hard and cold against her legs. Her head swam, the scent of the forced jasmine was sickly now, warring with the unaccustomed glass of champagne, threatening nausea. 'Charles?'

The man who had laid her down on the bench so tenderly, the beautiful man she loved, who loved her, looked up from ensuring his shirt front was once again perfectly smooth. 'Yes?' He sounded impatient. 'For goodness sake, do something with yourself. Look at the state of you.' He began adjusting the falls of his evening breeches with meticulous attention.

Prue looked down and gasped. Her skirts were bunched up to her waist. One stocking was around her ankle. Her breasts spilled out of the bodice of her gown in wanton abandon and she looked as though she had just... Which she had.

She tugged up the bodice, wincing as she forced abundant curves back into the tight fabric. There were red marks all over the pale skin, the beginning of bruises. She choked back a sob.

'Oh, do be quiet, you silly chit. You asked for it— stop snivelling now it's done.' He turned away, a slender young man, the moonlight gilding his hair, but not before she saw the smile on his handsome face.

'Charles? Where are you going?'

He glanced back; the smile became a sneer and the scales of romance and bedazzlement finally fell from her eyes.

'You told me you loved me. You said—'

'You really are as naive as you look.' He stood by one of the climber-twined columns, pulling off blossom and shredding it on the tiled floor. 'Who'd have supposed Miss Bluestocking Scott would be so foolish? I thought you were supposed to be intelligent. What makes you think a nobleman's son is going to fall for a plain little nobody whose only assets are her bubbies? I wanted to get my hands on them, but it was hardly worth the effort. Still, it won me fifty guineas.'

'You wagered on seducing me?' Merciful anger had her on her feet despite her shaking legs, the pain where he had…he had been. 'You are a cur, an excuse for a man, a coward and I will—'

'You will what, little Miss *Im*prudence? Go crying to Papa? I wouldn't if I were you, not unless you want all of society to know you open your legs for anyone.' He turned away, then said, over his shoulder, 'You stay quiet and my friends and I will keep your little secret. Can't say fairer than that, now can I?'

The Duke of Aylsham's House,
Grosvenor Square, London—May 3rd, 1815

'I will castrate the evil little toad with rusty shears. I will scoop out his shrivelled little bollocks with a blunt spoon. And then I will fry the lot in rancid fat and make him eat them.' Melissa Taverner swirled to a halt in front of the cold hearth and took a deep breath in readiness for the next tirade.

'Richly deserved, but not very helpful just at the moment,' the Duchess of Aylsham remarked with a smile for Prue who was sitting next to her on the sofa. Verity shifted her feet on the footstool and laid one hand on the slight swell of her belly. 'Vengeance can wait. Prue has more practical concerns just now. Has he hurt you at all, dear? I have the most marvellous doctor, utterly discreet and sympathetic. It might be best if you consulted him. I could ask him to come here, you know.'

Prue shook her head. 'Thank you, Verity. But it isn't necessary. I went straight to my room and rang for a hot bath and that helped. I am still a little sore, but nothing else seems to be wrong.' She managed a rueful smile. 'Physically, at least. But I could not think what to do, how to go on with Charles still part of the house party.

'Then I remembered that your letter had been delivered that morning, so the next day—yesterday—I told Aunt that you needed me because of the baby and she said she could see I was worried and hadn't slept properly and I was a good, unselfish girl to want to help my friend. So she let me use the family carriage and said she was going to write to Mama and let her know of my change of plans.'

'How long had you planned to stay with your aunt?' Lucy Lambert, the quietest of all of them, asked. 'Will Mrs Scott object to you changing the plans?'

'It was supposed to be for some months. Aunt always has at least three house parties while the weather can be relied on to be good. Mama thought I was far more likely to meet someone suitable there than at home,' she added bleakly.

'So if I write to your Mama and ask if you can stay with me, and promise to take you out and about to parties and picnics and so on, she won't object, will she?'

'You are a duchess, Verity,' Prue said, with the first flicker of amusement she had felt for two days. 'Mama would not object if you had two heads.'

'Very well. I will beg her to spare you to me. I'll tell her that I am quite well, but sorely in need of female companionship and that I promise to introduce you to all the best people.'

'That has got Prue safely away from that vile man

and she is safe here, but that is no help with the other problems, is it?' Melissa was still belligerent.

'Which ones?' Lucy asked innocently.

'Whether I am pregnant and, even if I am not, what I am going to tell my future husband. If I ever have one,' Prue said. She'd had two nights to brood on that.

'When are your courses due?' Verity was always the practical one.

'In two weeks.'

'That is going to seem like two months,' Melissa remarked with her usual lack of tact. 'If you are, what do you want to do? You wouldn't…'

'No, I would not. I couldn't.' She had thought about it, panicked about it. 'I could tell Mama and I suppose she would send me away somewhere and then we would find someone kind to look after the baby.'

'She is not going to be very sympathetic, is she?' Verity asked. She was well acquainted with Prue's mama.

'No,' Prue admitted. Her nightmare was that Mama would simply spirit away the child and dispose of it with 'suitable' foster parents and Prue would never know what had happened.

'You could insist that Charles Harlby marries you,' Lucy suggested tentatively.

'I would rather marry a viper. A *slug*. To think I believed myself in love with the creature.' She shivered. 'I must have been mad.'

'Ensnared.' Jane, Countess of Kendall, rubbed absently at a smudge of oil paint on the back of her hand and spoke for the first time since the friends had gathered round to comfort Prue. 'He is very pretty, one has to admit. And he has a most ingratiating manner. This is not the first time he has done this to some respectable young woman, I am certain.' She looked thoughtful. 'I could ask Ivo to make him very sorry indeed.' The relish in her voice was in total contrast to her gentle appearance. 'Ivo is *very* good in a fight and this ghastly Charles Harlby creature doesn't deserve something as honourable as a duel. Who is he, anyway?'

'The son of Viscount Rolson. And please do not tell anyone, not even Ivo—I think Charles will keep quiet about it provided I make no trouble.'

'That is blackmail,' Melissa muttered.

'Indeed. But we cannot deal with him effectively just now,' Verity said firmly. 'Prue does not want to marry him—and who can blame her?—so we must deal with the immediate issues: the risk she may be with child and the scandal that Harlby might cause. I know he said he would keep quiet, but I do not trust him one inch.'

'Who would you like to marry, Prue? What kind of man?'

'I did not want to marry anyone until I fell for Charles and now I like the idea even less. But I suppose I might have to, one day, because Mama and Papa are never going to stop nagging and scheming about it. I wouldn't mind so much if it was someone kind who will let me continue with my studies and won't be embarrassed that I'm a bluestocking. Someone with a large library,' she added wistfully.

She looked round at her friends, all worried for her,

all racking their brains to help, and gave herself a mental shake. It was time to take a more positive hand in this. 'I would want a father for my child, if I am carrying one, and I imagine that the sooner I married, the more reasonable the dates will seem. But who would want to marry me? I would have to tell them the truth—I couldn't lie.'

'What do you think about children?' Verity said, not answering her question.

'I'm not...*opposed* to them. I mean, I like them. I just had not thought to have any myself. Before Charles I had thought I would like simply to be a scholarly spinster.' Prue looked up from her intent study of the pattern in the Oriental rug. 'I think children would be interesting.'

Perhaps I am about to find out.

'And would you insist on a good-looking husband?' Verity persisted. 'I know Harlby the Slug is exceedingly handsome.'

Jane put down the sketch pad that never seemed to leave her side and looked intently at Verity. 'Have you someone in mind?'

'Possibly. I have been thinking about an encounter I had a few evenings ago and it has given me an idea... Prue, would you mind if I spoke to someone? Without naming you, of course, but I will have to spell out your predicament. It may come to nothing, of course.'

Prue made an effort to push aside the misery. Verity was always full of schemes, many of them enough to give the Patronesses of Almack's palpitations, but as the wife of that pattern book of perfection, the Duke of Aylsham, she simply glided past criticism with the grace of an accomplished skater on a frozen lake.

'I would be very grateful,' she said. Perhaps some eccentric person wanted a librarian and had no objection to a female one, even a pregnant one.

'Then I will go immediately when we have had our luncheon. Strike while the iron is hot.' She put her feet firmly on the floor and sat up straight. 'There, I expect you all to be my witnesses that I have rested enough to satisfy even the most nervous of expectant fathers. Please do not worry, Prue. Whatever happens, we will look after you.'

'I know. Thank you.' Prue dredged up a smile from somewhere. Her friends would do everything in their power to help her, she believed that totally. She only wished she hadn't been so foolish as to fall for Charles in the first place.

It was all very well for the others to say she had been innocent, unused to the ways of town bucks and their wiles. But she should have seen him for what he was. Or perhaps she had: a nasty little suspicion lurked that she had been too flattered, too much in love with the idea of being loved to listen to her instincts. Foolish indeed. She would do better to stick to her Classical studies, to her books and her libraries. They contained nothing more dangerous than dust and dead spiders.

Ross Vincent leaned on the balustrade at the edge of the terrace and watched his son. Below on the small lawn Jon gurgled happily and waved his rattle at the nursemaid who sat beside him on the rug. They made a pretty picture in the spring sunshine, the rosy-cheeked child and the equally rosy, plump girl with her clean white apron and her ready smile. She was the perfect nurse for a motherless babe. But not a mother.

Society would call it shocking that he should be thinking of remarrying barely six months after the death of his wife, but Jon was able to sit up now, had begun to babble. He recognised people, knew everyone in his happy little world. His latest words were *Dada, Mama, Gugu*—although those seemed to be applied indiscriminately to his father, his nurse and his toy dog.

Jon needed a mother before he realised he was without one, but how the devil was a man to find a wife when anyone he approached—if they were well bred and respectable—would be shocked that he should do so while still in mourning? And how to judge character? He had hardly made such a good fist of it the first time around. Lady Honoria Gracewell, daughter of the Earl of Falhaven, had been pretty, accomplished, exceptionally well connected and apparently delighted to wed a marquis, even one with his shocking background, his looks. *Apparently.*

But there might be hope if the eccentric Duchess was right. Why on earth he had let his guard down so comprehensively at the Hendersons' soirée he could not imagine, unless the woman was a witch and could read minds. She had moved smoothly from murmured sympathies about his wife to warm enquiries about his son and within ten minutes had him on his third glass of champagne and spilling out his desperate need for a mother for Jon. Champagne of all things, he thought bitterly. And him able to drink a privateer crew under the table on rum any day of the week.

Then she had arrived on his doorstep yesterday afternoon, pretty as a picture in a Villager hat and pearls that made him blink, and announced that she had just the wife for him—provided, that was, he would accept the possibility of a second child who was not his. When he had not replied immediately she had informed him coolly that the possible pregnancy was no fault of the lady in question who was of impeccable morals and behaviour and who had been deceived and betrayed.

The Duchess of Aylsham was a force of nature, he decided, and there was no more shame in giving way to her than to a hurricane or the changing of the tides. Although after a night to think it over he was having his doubts about the wisdom of this and his imagination was producing one disastrous scenario after another. But it was too late now; he had given his word and the Duchess's friend was due at any moment.

'The young lady you were expecting, my lord.' Finedon, his new butler, was a considerable improvement on the one he had inherited along with the title, Ross acknowledged. Hodges had never recovered from the shock of discovering that his master's grandson was a privateer and would visibly flinch if Ross raised his voice above genteel conversational tones.

'Show her out here, if you please.' He straightened, but did not turn fully to face the woman who was making her way across the terrace towards him. He had no desire to frighten her before she even had a chance to open her mouth. That would happen soon enough.

Not a beauty, was his first thought. But then neither was he. Ross thought her face pleasant and open, her expression more used to smiling than frowning. Blonde with blue-grey eyes, he saw as she came closer, apparently composed despite the length of the walk to his side. And a very fine figure, currently modestly covered in a modish gown. Or modish as far as he could tell—ladies' fashions were one of his gaping areas of ignorance.

Slim, except for her bosom which he could now see was rising and falling with the agitation she was managing to keep from her face. Ross swallowed. Yes, that was definitely her finest feature. He got his imagination under control and waited.

'My lord.' Her curtsy was absolutely correct, her voice soft and pleasant, and he managed to keep his gaze on her face and not the lavishly distracting curves lower down.

'Madam.'

He did turn fully then, watched her eyes and saw them widen, heard the soft sound that escaped her. But she stood her ground.

He did that deliberately to see how I would react.

The scarring was savage, as though something with talons had clawed at his face, dragging its way down through the right eyebrow, down the cheek, catching the corner of his mouth.

He had made her nerves flutter from the first glimpse of him, simply because of his size, as he stood there like a rock gazing down into the garden. He must have been well over six feet tall, with broad shoulders, a deep chest. He looked as though he could fell trees and then haul the trunks without breaking a sweat.

Then she had seen that he was not a handsome man and that had been somehow reassuring. Mid-brown hair, unfashionably tanned skin, an undistinguished nose not improved by being broken once or twice, heavy brows to balance a strong jaw and unsmiling mouth. If Verity had wanted to find her a complete contrast to Charles, she could not have done better.

Verity had told Prue that he was a recent widower and nothing more. Now she wondered what this man might have to smile about, with his wife lost to fever only months before and a face he clearly expected people to flinch from. The brown eyes held hers, assessing, judging.

Not cruel, Prue thought. *Not unkind—just unreadable. Cold.*

She knew what it was like to have people make assumptions based on how you looked. Men stared at her bosom, the fact that they were mentally licking their lips all too plain to see. However modestly she dressed, women assumed she was casting lures and men assumed they had licence to leer and expected her to be flattered by the attention. When she was not they were unkind, dismissive or rude. But having a bountiful figure was nothing compared with what this man had endured. The pain must have been appalling, the fear that he might lose his eye, ghastly.

How did a lord come by such a wound? she wondered. And what kind of lord was he, anyway? Verity had been exceedingly discreet and Prue had not known he was one until his butler had announced her.

He expected her to shriek or recoil, she assumed. Instead Prue folded her hands neatly in front of her and waited. He narrowed his eyes at her and went from merely dour to downright sinister. She swallowed, kept her composure and wished she could sit down.

Then there was a gurgle of laughter from the garden below them and the left-hand corner of his mouth lifted a fraction, the right still dragged down by the scar.

The relief at having his intent gaze removed was almost physical. 'Is that your son?'

They both looked down to the lawn where the baby was crowing with laughter now as he batted gleefully at a toy his nurse was holding out to him.

'Yes. Jon.'

'He sounds so happy.' Prue waved until the child saw the movement, laughed and waved both his hands in return, fetching the nursemaid a blow on the chin. 'I am so sorry!' Prue called down and the girl smiled back. 'You have a good nursemaid for him.'

'You know about such matters?'

'Nothing at all. But I know a cheerful, kindly face when I see one and he is clearly happy and thriving.'

His Lordship grunted and turned away from the edge of the terrace. 'You have strong nerves, madam.'

'My name is Prudence. Prue. You think so because I dare come to a man's home alone?'

'I mean because of this.' He lifted his right hand to touch his cheek and she almost flinched then. The back of his hand was covered in a black design of a great claw, its talons extending down each finger. *Tattoo*, they called it. She had read about the practice in the writings of Captain James Cook about the South Seas, but she had never seen one.

'It was a shock,' she admitted. 'I do not like to consider how dreadful it must have been to endure a wound like that. Who did it?'

'A bird. An eagle someone had trained to attack.'

'Goodness, I had no idea you could do that.'

'He was a Swede—more a pirate than a privateer. They train golden eagles to bring down deer.'

She could only guess at the power of a bird that could do that. 'You killed it?'

'Why should I? It was a weapon.' Those deep brown eyes locked with hers. 'I killed its master.'

The country was at war. Perhaps he was a soldier, although which Frenchmen fought with live eagles? She was not going to meet his expectations and recoil. 'And showed your respect for the weapon with a tattoo?' Prue gestured towards his hand.

'It seemed like a reasonable distraction while I was healing. One of my crew has the art.' He shifted away from the balustrade. 'Would you care to sit, Miss Prudence? We have more important things than scars to speak of.'

There was a table set out in the sunshine with two chairs, and Prue followed him, wondering about that reference to a crew. He was a sailor? A naval officer? But he was a lord of some kind.

She sat in the chair he held for her, waited while he settled in the other with that ruined cheek towards her.

Testing her, she supposed. Well, she had recently seen worse things on a man's face than the ridge and furrow of white scar tissue. She had seen betrayal and scorn and petty triumph. Honest injury was a clean thing in contrast to that.

'I am looking for a wife in order that my son does not grow up without a mother,' he said without preamble. 'And I need to find him one before he realises the lack. The Duchess thought you might be interested.'

Prue found she was not put off by his plain speaking. At least she would know where she was with this man. 'Will you tell me your name, my lord? As you must realise, I am in no position to gossip.'

'Ross Vincent, Marquis of Cranford. Ah, I see that I have finally succeeded in shaking that remarkable composure.'

'You are a *marquis*?' He nodded and she made herself think. 'Two years ago—I remember reading about it in the newspapers. *The Privateer Marquis? The East End Aristocrat*, they called you.'

He nodded, waiting.

'And you want to marry *me*?'

'Not necessarily,' he said coolly. 'But I think you might very well do.'

Chapter Two

Lord Cranford had done more than shake her composure. He had deliberately shocked her and then insulted her with faint praise—the thought of walking straight out the way she had come in was exceedingly tempting.

Prue knew perfectly well that act of rebellion would do nothing but salve her pride for a moment. Worse, it would throw away the lifeline that Verity had found for her. It would not be sensible and sensible was one thing she knew herself to be. At least, she admitted ruefully, when it did not concern smooth-talking, good-looking young gentlemen with the morals of tomcats.

This man, who was certainly not smooth-talking, definitely not good-looking and not particularly young either—late twenties, early thirties? she wondered—was looking for a wife in order to give his son a mother. That, at least, was an attractive motive.

'You do not know me, or anything about me, other than that I am not a virgin and I may be carrying another man's child.'

He shrugged. 'I trust the Duchess. Your past does not concern me and I have an heir. You may be assured that I would never treat the child as anything but mine.' When she frowned at him, trying to puzzle him out, he glowered back. 'I am not interested in marrying again for the sake of it. If you are anxious that I will want to bed you, you need not be. And do not direct that prissy look at me, madam. I would be faithful. I find I have lost my appetite for...that sort of thing.'

'And when you get your appetite back?' she retorted, rattled by the frankness.

Prue thought for a moment he was going to laugh, then the heavy dark brows drew together. 'I keep my promises, honour my vows and I have no desire to bed a woman who does not want me. Your friend the Duchess told me a great deal about you—good gentry family, a bluestocking who lost her head over a plausible rogue, a loyal friend. An intelligent, kind woman. And a stubborn one in a quiet way. That last I can believe very easily.' He stood up. 'Go and see what you make of my son and what he makes of you.' When she did not move he added, 'Or leave and we will forget this meeting ever took place.'

'That seems fair.' At least he was straightforward, this privateer turned marquis. He followed as far as the top of the steps, then stopped, leaving her to make her way down to the nursemaid and child on the rug.

Prue smiled at the girl. 'Please, do not get up. I will sit down.' She sank on to the rug. 'This is Jon, is it not? And you are?'

'Maud, madam.'

The baby waved his well-sucked toy at her and gurgled. Prue took hold of one of the toy dog's soggy knitted legs and tugged gently. Jon laughed and pulled back.

'That is fun, is it? Shall we see if I can pick you up without dropping you?'

He was a surprisingly solid weight in her arms, sturdy and warm. Prue jiggled him a little until he felt secure to her, then stroked one hand over silky dark hair. 'You have your papa's eyes, haven't you?' And by the size of him he would have his father's height one day as well. Her words won her another happy gurgle and a huge gummy smile.

What would that man watching them look like if he smiled properly? Would those dark eyes warm as his son's did? One thing was certain; his smile would show a lot of teeth. Big, sharp teeth.

Jon's smile turned into a look of extreme concentration and Maud reached for him. 'I think His Little Lordship is going to need changing at any moment, madam. Shall I take him?'

'Yes. Please.' Prue thrust him into the capable arms. Dribbles were one thing, but she thought she would need to work up to anything messier. But despite her instinctive recoil she felt a pang at relinquishing his compact little body.

Maud stood up. 'I'll just take him inside now, madam. Wave goodbye to the nice lady, Jon.' She waggled his hand until he got the idea, beaming back at Prue over the girl's shoulder as she carried him away.

A long shadow fell across the rug. 'Well?' The Marquis had come down to the lawn without her realising and was now looming like an oak tree, shutting out the sun.

'Well what?' Prue retorted inelegantly as she sorted out her skirts, ready to rise. 'He is a charming child. Friendly, happy. He seemed to like me.'

To her surprise Lord Cranford sat down beside her, long legs crossed tailor-fashion. 'Well, will you marry me?'

His breeches stretched tight over muscled thighs; his booted feet took up a lot of the spare space. Melissa recounting a naughty saying about the size of a man's feet in relation to other parts of his body flashed into her mind and she blushed.

'I do not know. I have hardly had a chance to consider it. Consider you. Um…us.' She felt flustered and inarticulate and she was not used to that. On the other hand, it was almost a welcome relief from the blank misery she had been feeling for the past days.

'Then consider this. I require a wife who will be a good mother to my son, who will act as my hostess when I choose to entertain, who will manage my household. Households,' he corrected himself. 'I will give you a generous allowance. I will accept the child you may be carrying as my own. I will be faithful to you.'

So they were down to negotiations, were they? She was capable of plain speaking, too. 'I want time to study and a library. An allowance that will enable me to add to that library as I wish. I need to attend lectures, visit exhibitions. I must be free to visit my friends and have them visit me.'

Prue bit her lip, wondering how to address the two questions that were at the front of her mind, then decided to simply ask. 'Did you love your wife?'

'No.' The answer rapped right back at her without hesitation. 'When, against all probability, I inherited the title I understood that I needed a wife and an heir. Honoria was suitable and eager to become a marchioness.' He shrugged. 'We had nothing in common and we went our own ways most of the time. We could have continued like that for ever—I did not wish her dead, if that is what you are asking. She insisted on attending a party at Vauxhall despite rumours of cholera cases and caught the disease.' His lips thinned even further. 'It killed her.'

His face was completely expressionless. In any other man that would have been a sign he had something to hide, but with this one? It appeared to be his normal resting expression.

'Poor lady,' she said, meaning it. One more question… 'Are you still a privateer?'

'No, I am not. And I wish I still was.' He watched her face, his own disconcertingly unreadable. 'You do know what the difference is between a privateer and a pirate, I assume?'

'Of course. When I read about you at the time when you inherited the title I realised I was not quite clear, so I researched the matter. Pirates are the footpads of the sea. Criminals. Privateers are independent captains who carry a letter of marque from their government allowing them to harry and attack the shipping of nations they are at war with. In your case that was the

French and their occupied countries. I imagine it is a very profitable occupation, if a risky one.'

'It can be both. Any more questions?' Prue shook her head. 'Because I have three. What is your name?'

'Prudence Scott from Dorset. You may find us in the *Landed Gentry* if you care to look.'

'How old are you?'

'Twenty-three. And my father, who is terrified that I am on the shelf, would be transported with joy to have a marquis propose to me.'

Mama will faint with delight.

'And who was the man responsible for putting you in this predicament?'

'Why do you ask?' The dark brows drew together, his expression making it quite obvious what the answer would be: violence. 'I will not answer that. Not because I wish to protect him, but because I want to forget him and I do not want you doing whatever it is you are considering,' she finished saying in a rush.

'You can read minds, Miss Scott?'

'I have observed the behaviour of gentlemen and the fact that, for your sex, violence often appears to be a reasonable solution to problems.'

'Very well. If you have no further questions or stipulations, will you do me the honour of accepting my hand, Miss Scott? Do I have your permission to approach your father?'

'Yes, I will and you may.' What was she thinking of? She never did anything without thinking it through, researching it, considering options and alternatives. Except, it seemed, when it came to men. She did not normally rely on instinct, but it was instinct that was telling her to trust this dour, dangerous-looking man. Instinct and trust in Verity's judgement and a blind faith that the father of that happy child could not be a bad man. Not if he was so desperate to find his son a good mother to love him.

Loving baby Jon was unlikely to be difficult; loving the Marquis of Cranford would probably be impossible. But then he did not want her love, did he? Any more than she wanted his. Security, a safe haven, that was all she asked.

'I will write to my parents this afternoon.' She dug in her reticule. 'Here is my card with their address in Dorset.'

'Thank you.' He glanced at the pasteboard rectangle. 'I will be away from London for several days. I am sure Mr Scott will wish to examine my proposals for the settlements with great care.'

I very much doubt it. He will be too busy dancing a jig of joy at having me settled.

Lord Cranford stood and held out his left hand to help her to her feet. Her own slim fingers, with the inevitable ink stains, were swallowed up in his grip and he pulled her up with such ease that it took her breath. He was strong, hard, lean despite the impression of bulk that his big frame gave.

Prue tugged, but he held on to her hand. 'You manage the appearance of remarkable composure, Miss Scott, yet your pulse is hammering like the heartbeat of a trapped rabbit.'

'I wonder why that might be, my lord?' she retorted.

'I have just agreed to marry a total stranger, a privateer, who has just demonstrated that he is strong enough to snap me in two.'

He reached out with his right hand and touched her cheek, the long fingers with their talon tattoo remarkably delicate and sensitive on her skin. 'I do not mistreat women, Prudence. You do not love me, you do not like me, but you need never fear me.'

It was a statement delivered without the slightest effort to charm or coax and for some reason that convinced her as soft words never could have done.

'Very well. You will find me at the Duchess of Aylsham's house in Grosvenor Square. I am staying there for the foreseeable future.'

'The foreseeable future, Prudence, is about a week. I will arrange for a special licence so that we can be married as soon as I return from Dorset. I imagine your parents will wish to travel up at the same time. We can be married here.'

'We will be married at Grosvenor Square,' Prue stated, crossing her fingers that Verity would agree. 'In the respectability stakes the most perfect duke in England trumps the Privateer Marquis, I believe.'

'Very well. I will have my secretary arrange your allowance, make sure you have access to it urgently.'

'That is very generous.' She straightened her bonnet. 'What if I change my mind?'

'I do not believe you will, Prudence. That would not be…sensible, now would it? And I suspect that you are always sensible. Nearly always.' Lord Cranford crooked an arm. 'Do allow me to show you out. Your carriage is waiting, I imagine.'

At least he says sensible *and not* prudent *as Charles did when he was warning me to be careful*, Prue thought. *A man who can resist that obvious play on my name must have* something *to be said for him*.

This was going to be her husband, she thought, borne on a wave of unreality through the back door into the hall of what seemed to be a rigidly tidy house.

My husband, my home.

He was a marquis, so there must be more properties besides this one on Hanover Square. It still did not seem real—perhaps she had fainted in the conservatory, hit her head. She would wake up in a moment surrounded by shrieks of outrage and find herself the scandal of the year.

'I said I would marry him,' Prue said.

Verity nodded; her husband, Will, steepled his fingers and regarded her over the joined tips. Lucy murmured something, Jane smiled.

Of course, Melissa scowled as she had done ever since Prue had revealed the name of the man in question. 'Are you certain? The man was the next worst thing to a pirate and he was brought up in the slums, by all accounts.'

'He is well spoken, there is nothing wrong with his manners, as such, and he appears intelligent.'

'What do you mean, *as such*?'

'His manners are conventional—his manner is not. He is alarmingly frank. He makes no effort to dissemble, to put a good face on things. He made not the slightest attempt to charm me or make me like him. It is not to shock—I think he is merely impatient of hypocrisy and deception. But I do trust him. I think he is honest, even if he cannot be said to be restful company.'

Prue saw Verity was nodding. 'What do you know about him, Will?'

The Duke lowered his hands. 'They say he is a courageous fighter and, unusually for a privateer, loyal. There are no reports of his ships picking off the occasional British merchantman, for example. He has the reputation of being a hard man and a secretive one. He certainly does not trouble himself with society.'

'Probably because everyone is horrible to him because of his upbringing,' Lucy said in her soft voice. 'I read about it when he inherited and Mama was very shocked to hear about him. But I expect he told you all about it.'

'No, he said nothing and I did not like to ask.'

'Well…' Lucy sat up as though to give a report. 'Let me get it straight in my mind. His grandfather had two sons: Peter, the elder, and John, who is this man's father. Peter married and had two sons: George, the heir, and Frederick. Both married although only George had children—a boy and a girl.'

'Four people, plus his own father, between Ross Vincent and the title,' Melissa observed.

Lucy nodded. 'John, his father, was a big man who was a very keen follower of pugilism and bare-knuckle fighting. And, reading between the lines, he was always in trouble with his father, the old Marquis, for mixing with rough company at fights. And then he fell in love with the daughter of one of the bare-knuckle fighters and wanted to marry her.'

'His father must have been outraged,' Prue said.

'It gets worse,' Will said, picking up the story. 'The fighter in question was the disgraced son of a baronet, so there was that scandal in the background as well. His daughter was a tall young woman, almost as tall as John Vincent, and quite capable of holding her own in that tough company. But by all accounts she was an honest, intelligent young woman and she was not going to become a gentleman's mistress—it was marriage or nothing.'

'So he wed her despite his father? I can admire that,' Prue said.

'But he paid a hard price for it. John was cut off without the proverbial penny. They ended up in a very poor part of the East End, near the river. John earned what he could by everything from labouring, to writing letters for the illiterate, to teaching foreign traders some English. He schooled his own son as well and the boy had a dual life—running wild with the children on the docks and getting an education and behaving like a young gentleman at home.

'Then his parents died in one of the fever epidemics that regularly sweep the slums and he ended up working the sailing barges on the river. Where he found the money to buy his first ship, I have no idea,' Will said with a frown. 'But by the time he was twenty, in eighteen hundred and seven, he was master of a brig. He armed it, got himself a letter of marque and went to sea as a privateer. He bought more brigs and I imagine he might well have continued as one, trading up to more and bigger ships. With peace he could have become owner of a merchant fleet.'

'But then it happened,' Lucy said, clearly bursting to continue. 'The old Marquis fell ill and George, the elder son of Peter the heir, and his family, were driving up to Leicestershire to the deathbed and the carriage overturned on a hill and they were all killed. That was dreadful enough, but then Peter had a heart attack on hearing the news. That left his childless son, Frederick, as heir. The reason that Frederick was childless was because, although married, he was deeply in love with another man's wife.' She broke off, blushing.

'Bad enough, you might say,' Will continued. 'The gossip goes that his own wife nobly offered to put all that aside and resume marital relations for the sake of obtaining an heir. Frederick went off to his mistress to renounce her—and encountered her husband who had been blissfully unaware of the affaire until then. He challenged Frederick, killed him and the shock finally carried off the old Marquis, leaving Ross Vincent as the sole heir.'

'Oh, my goodness,' Prue said blankly. 'No wonder he seems so very self-contained and capable.' Or antisocial and as hard as teak, if she was not to be tactful about it.

'Does that make you reconsider?' Verity asked. 'Perhaps I should have told you more about him before arranging the meeting.'

'I am not certain.' Prue tried to think it through.

'I think it was better that I went without any preconceptions. On the one hand he has had a very difficult childhood and he must be finding his present position difficult to adjust to. He is very different from any type of man I have ever encountered. But he has had the example of a loving family home—at least, one assumes it was—and he is certainly a man of ambition, one who works hard. And he loves his son.' She took a deep breath. 'And, when I think of the alternatives, I am going to trust in my instincts—and yours, Verity—and marry him.'

Chapter Three

Grosvenor Square—May 13th, 1815

Ross set his teeth and reminded himself not to scowl, or look at the clock, or pace. He was a happy bridegroom, even if he was scandalising society by marrying when he should be in mourning and infuriating it by not providing more gossip in the form of a thoroughly unsuitable bride for a marquis.

The East End Aristocrat might at least give them some sport by marrying a Billingsgate fish girl; the Privateer Marquis could have had the decency to come back with a female buccaneer for the scandalmongers to salivate over. Taking a pleasant young lady from an undistinguished gentry family as his wife was downright unimaginative and inconsiderate of him. How gratifying.

Next to him Simon Lester, his second in command from his privateering days and now manager of his trading business, stood stock-still. He'd be focusing on not fidgeting in unaccustomed silk breeches, swallow-tail coat and high neckcloth, Ross guessed. The ring was safe in his pocket which meant that Simon had nothing to do, no crew to shout at, no one to shoot at, so he was at a loss and miserable.

'She's late,' Simon muttered out of the corner of his mouth. 'Am I supposed to go and roust her out?'

Ross shook his head. 'The bride is supposed to be late. You are only responsible for getting me here on time, conscious and reasonably sober.'

At least he had gone through this once before, although with a rather more respectable best man at his side. Honoria's mama had approved of his choice of a distant cousin who was an earl. It was about the only thing she had approved of, other than his own title.

'Enem— Here we go.'

Ross almost cracked a smile then. *Enemy in sight* was what Simon had begun to say. Then he saw his friend's jaw drop. 'What?' He turned to look at the double doors that led to the hall from the great salon of the Duke of Aylsham's town house where they waited.

He had met Miss Scott—Prudence—four times since that first encounter in the garden. Once to call to say her father had given his permission for the match and that settlements had been agreed. Once at a very formal and stilted dinner party when his future in-laws arrived in London, and twice to agree the details of the wedding itself. That had merely been an exercise in agreeing to whatever the Duchess and Prudence's three other unsettlingly unconventional friends had decided upon.

On every occasion she had been neat, respectably and appropriately gowned, pale in the face and subdued. Pretty enough, he supposed, and subdued out of anxiety about her immediate past and her impending future.

Now she stood in the doorway, her hand on her father's arm and all Ross could think was, *Venus*. Curves. Curves that were no longer bundled under too-pale clothing that only drew attention to them. Curves that were gowned in shimmering ivory silk that dipped at the neckline to show soft, glowing skin. Her hair was dressed with one curl brushing her neck, no longer appearing a nondescript blonde, but dark honey now it was no longer contrasting with washed-out pastels.

As he watched her, along with the other fifty people in the room, he saw the colour come into her cheeks at the attention. Then Prudence bit her lower lip.

The rush of arousal was so unexpected, so total, that Ross turned sharply to face the front while he pulled in air, willing his body into submission. He had been celibate for over a year and it had been no struggle. Nor had it been deliberate. He had simply not wanted a woman. There had been too much to deal with, too much not to think about. Now he wanted this one, the one he had promised not to bed. Ever.

It will fade, he told himself as the pianist and harpist at the back of the room launched into something he assumed was suitably bridal. It was only lust and a man at sea for weeks at a time learned how to deal with that. Lust and surprise.

There was a rustle of silk, a breath of jasmine and Ross looked down to find Prudence by his side.

She is so small, he thought. *I could snap her in two and yet she does not seem afraid of me.*

Why not? Other women found his size intimidating and he knew they saw nothing in his looks to compensate. Yet his new bride was not repelled by looks or size or even by the scars or the inking on his hand. Either Prudence was a fine actress or she was braver than many of the people who encountered him, including his crews.

'Dearly beloved...' The Dean, who the Duke— 'Call me Will, won't you?'—had produced, was some kind of distant cousin. He certainly added gravitas to the occasion. Ross made himself concentrate, putting aside memories of the other wedding in St George's. This was a matter of business—Prudence needed a husband, he needed a mother for Jon and that was all there was to it.

She was intelligent and had no illusions about what she was agreeing to, so he could not hurt her heart, her emotions, if all he did was simply behave decently to her.

Act as though she is my sister, living in the house to help with the child, Ross told himself. Yes, that was it: a sister.

Simon nudged him, handing him the ring, and he took Prudence's left hand in his, soft and warm and pale, swallowed up in his hard, brown grasp. With his right hand he slid the ring on her finger and felt the flutter of her pulse, heard the little sigh she gave.

Relief, anxiety, regret? There was no time to ponder that now. The Dean raised his voice. 'I now pronounce you man and wife.'

There was a ripple of whispers from behind him, the sound of his new mother-in-law sobbing happily into her handkerchief. She flinched every time she looked at him, but it was clear that to have her daughter married to a marquis, however shocking, was an ultimate happiness.

Ross looked down at his wife. 'Well, Lady Cranford?'

'Very well, my lord.' Prudence was pale again, but her smile was serene, even as the light flickered and danced on the diamonds that draped across her bosom, hung at her ears. She was trembling, he realised as he turned and she tucked her hand into the crook of his arm.

'There, that's done,' he said as they stepped out into the hallway. 'The wedding breakfast is likely to be a trial, I have no doubt, but then we can get back to Hanover Square and some peace and quiet.'

'Yes, of course,' Prudence agreed. Something in her tone made him glance down. Her chin was up, her lips curved into a smile, yet her grey eyes were stormy. He had thought them blue.

Was she angry about something? 'I hadn't realised that your eyes were grey,' Ross said.

'Why should you have?' She cocked her head to one side. 'Yours are brown, very dark. I noticed those at once. Very good eyes for keeping secrets.'

'Prudence, what is wrong?' They were close, as

close as he had been to men who were trying to kill him, men he was trying to kill. Watch their eyes, his father had taught him. Do not worry about what they say, the moves they pretend to make. Watch their eyes. But her gaze slid away, evading.

'Wrong? Nothing. Whatever should be wrong?'

'I do not know.' The volume of sound behind them increased. 'Hell, everyone is coming out. We will speak of this later.'

It was not quite everyone, but it was Mrs Scott with the Duchess of Aylsham and Prue's three other friends at her heels and that was more than enough.

'We have come to borrow your bride,' the Duchess said.

'Of course. Provided you return her.' He could say all the right things when he had to.

Ross caught the glint in the eye of Melissa Taverner. The other three—the Duchess, Lady Kendall and Miss Lambert—seemed prepared to accept him, if only as a necessary evil, but Miss Taverner looked like a woman who kept blunt scissors handy to deal with any male who displeased her.

He returned her stare with an inclination of his head. *I acknowledge your distrust and I will tolerate it for the sake of your friendship with my wife. But only so far.* Her friends might have arranged this match, but that was where their interference ended.

Miss Taverner narrowed her eyes, then, apparently satisfied for the moment, turned to follow the other women up the stairs, leaving Ross to accept the congratulations of the guests.

* * *

'I still cannot quite believe it. A *marchioness*.' Mrs Scott perched on a chair in the best guest bedchamber and fanned herself feebly with her hand.

She had been murmuring the same thing for the past five days, ever since she and Prue's father had arrived post-haste from Dorset almost incoherent with shocked delight.

'I had quite given up on you ever finding *any* gentleman acceptable.'

Prue, submitting to a thorough re-pinning of her coiffure by Verity's formidable lady's maid, Field, did not dare nod. 'Yes,' she agreed. 'So had I.' Her pulse was racing and it was difficult to keep her hands steady as she soothed down her skirts.

'Of course, we had no hopes of a duke.'

Prue refrained from pointing out that there were no available dukes to be had just at that moment, Verity having captured the last single one between the ages of seventeen and sixty-five. Lucy jumped up and rescued a pearl-studded comb that tumbled free. Prue could hear her stifled giggle and she looked up, seeing her reflection in the mirror.

That was what was wrong with her: she was angry. Angry with Ross, she realised. This was not nerves— or not entirely. He wanted this over, done with. Their wedding day was nothing more than an inconvenience that he had to go through to acquire a wife and he was making scant effort to conceal the fact from her.

'And even earls and viscounts seemed elusive and I still cannot quite understand how dear Jane here came to catch… I mean, *meet*, Lord Kendall. We would have been delighted with a baron, or even a baronet, for Prudence although *they* are not of the peerage of course, but a *marquis*…'

Prue let the gentle, happy murmurings pass over her and pretended to concentrate on whisking the powder puff over her nose and cheeks. Was she being unreasonable? Theirs was a business arrangement and it would be hypocritical of either of them to behave as though it was anything else. But surely Ross could have at least pretended it was something other than a thoroughgoing nuisance to go through the ceremony with her?

She had to hide how she felt, keep her feelings from showing. A fairy-tale wedding was just that, a fantasy. What happened afterwards was what mattered. Now she must concentrate on looking the part and behaving like a marchioness.

Prue studied her reflection as she might have considered a page of Latin from an unknown text. Was that the image of a lady of the aristocracy? She was still not used to how she looked in this gown. Verity's favourite modiste had deemed it suitable for a wedding and, as her own mind had become a complete blank when she was asked what she would like, she had simply agreed with whatever was proposed.

'Marchioness,' Verity had stated when she detected the first signs of mutiny and so Prue had meekly endured the endless discussions about style and fabric and trimmings, the measuring and the fittings. When she had seen it she realised that she could hardly object that she would be much more comfortable in something simple, not when it had been Verity's gift, so she had concentrated on not trying to pull up the edge of the bodice every few minutes.

It still seemed like a dream, a waking dream. The real night-time dreams were haunted by Charles Harlby's sneering face, or, almost worse, the sweet false smiles he had lavished on her while she fell in love with him.

During the hurried preparations Prue had told herself she was feeling so disorientated because she was spending all her time in a flurry of feminine family and friends and not quietly in a library studying, thinking about her next translation project, or, given the luxury of a London stay, looking forward to a lecture from some leading scholar, or a visit to the British Museum to view the latest antiquity.

But the ceremony was over now. The die was cast and she was married. Everything would be fine when today was over and she could create her new routine in her new home.

'You can breathe, my lady,' Field said.

'Oh. Er…yes.' *My lady.* That was her. Had she been holding her breath? She certainly felt a little dizzy.

'That looks perfect, Field,' Verity said from her perch on the end of the bed. 'Thank goodness you are not setting out on a long wedding trip today, Prue. The rain just seems to get worse by the hour.'

'It is so terrible, the farmers are suffering badly at home.' Her mother forgot to think about the wedding for a moment. 'I do not know what the world is coming to! The Corsican Monster on the loose, the weather so frightful, income tax not being abolished this year as they said they would—and now the poor King is dreadfully ill. Thank goodness I know you are safely married, dear. How frightful if the King were to die. I am certain a marquis would be expected to go into Court mourning for *weeks*.'

Prue was not certain how her wedding would be much protection against flood, the threat of the French or the income tax, but amusement at the thought helped lift her mood a little as she submitted to Field's minute adjustment of neckline and petticoats.

'There we are, my lady.' The abigail stepped back and gestured to one of the maids. 'Maria, make certain the jewellery box is fastened securely and put with the rest of Lady Cranford's luggage.'

The girl laid a blue morocco leather box on the dressing table and opened it. There was a sigh from several female throats. Lord Cranford—*Ross*, Prue reminded herself—had presented her with a pearl and diamond parure as a wedding gift and even she, resolutely sensible about glitter and sparkle, had been caught by the glamour of it.

'Now, my lady, let us just review. You are wearing the earrings, the necklace, two bracelets and the hair pins,' Field pronounced, checking the various empty indentations in the fitted box. The tiara, deemed unsuitable for a late-morning wedding, remained along with a longer version of the necklace and another pair of earrings. 'Excellent, everything is there.' Prue could only be glad that the abigail did not feel it necessary to check over the other, very worn box that contained all the other pieces that Prue possessed—a locket, a gold chain, some simple pearl earrings and a strand of amber beads.

Five minutes later Field said, 'There, now, Lady Cranford. You are quite ready to go down again. If you will just look in the long glass.'

Prue stood up obediently and made her way to the cheval glass. She should be more assertive with staff now, she knew that. She must stop blindly following everyone else's direction, decide what she wanted— And then she saw her full reflection again and the thoughts fled. They had put her in front of the glass before she had gone downstairs for the ceremony, but she had not focused; it had all been a blur.

Now the Marchioness of Cranford stared back at her. The figure in the gown of soft ivory silk must be her because it could not be anyone else, but in this version of Prudence Scott her bosom seemed all in proportion. Curvaceous, yes, but right, somehow. The neckline was, she had protested, shockingly low, but now she saw that revealing instead of muffling the offending area of her body actually made it a harmonious part of the whole. The rich ivory was a revelation, too. Mama had always insisted on white or the palest of pastels, but the colour suited her, made her seem rosier, warmer, more definite in a way she could not quite define.

The sparkle of gems was almost the most difficult thing to come to terms with. These were not borrowed, not paste. These were the jewellery of a marchioness and she had to begin being that person. She owed it to

Ross, however indifferent he seemed to be to the title and status. That was part of the bargain she had made to save herself.

Prue blinked, looked away from the unfamiliar self in the glass and saw her mother was dabbing at her eyes. Verity, Lucy and Jane were beaming, and even Melissa looked grudgingly admiring.

Time to begin asserting herself now. 'Shall we go down?'

Chapter Four

'That went well, I think. You are not too tired, I hope?'

Too tired for what?

Prue felt a stab of apprehension, then reminded herself that Ross had said that he did not want, or expect, to share her bed. How long that would hold, she was not certain. He had said he would keep his promises, but it had not been a promise, exactly, simply a statement that, at present, he had no taste for what she had once heard described as *bed sport*.

'A little tired,' she admitted. 'It was an early start because Verity's dresser was so adamant about all the things that had to be done to my hair.' It felt so securely looped, braided and pinned that she wondered if she would ever be able to untangle it, but presumably her own new dresser would have the knack. 'What time is it?'

'Just after eight when we left. The sun will be setting soon.'

Her new husband—and what an uncompromising word that was!—sat beside her in the carriage, but as she was on the far left-hand side and he the right, there was considerable space between them. Despite her fervent hope that she would sleep alone that night, Prue did rather wish he would hold her hand, just for some moral support.

Foolish, she chided herself. No one had held her hand from when she was about ten years old until Charles and look where that had ended. But Ross's hand remained relaxed on the seat between them. She only had to let hers slide with the motion of the carriage and they would touch.

But he was what she needed moral support for, so it was futile to expect him to provide it. Prue folded her hands primly in her lap as the carriage crossed Bond Street into Little Brook Street. 'You will have missed Jon all day. I imagine he will be fast asleep now.'

'Yes.' Ross turned his head against the squabs and, out of the corner of her eye, she could tell he was looking at her. 'He sleeps soundly. We could look in on him.'

'I would like to do that.' It would be a beginning. She must learn the child's routine, the pattern of his days, so she could fit her own life around him.

'We have not had time to properly discuss the management of the house,' Ross said, his tone businesslike, as though in conversation with a member of his staff, Prue thought with a flash of resentment.

'I will meet with your housekeeper in the morning. I am sure we will soon work out the way of it together.'

'Very well. You will hire any additional staff as you see fit, organise the house as you wish. I would ask only that you leave my study and my bedchamber as they are.'

Surprised, Prue twisted on the seat to look at him. 'You mean I may order redecoration, rearrange the furniture?'

'Order new if you wish. Change the staff, with the exception of Finedon and my valet.' Ross shrugged. 'You have only to speak to my secretary. He will be at your disposal.'

'He will? I would have thought that a marquis had a great deal of business to transact—correspondence, estate affairs, political matters—and that would keep his secretary too busy to worry about my concerns.'

'I have competent agents in place to deal with the estates. I am known as unsocial, so the invitations I receive are easily dealt with and I do not sit in the Lords.' There was a hint of sardonic humour in his voice as he added, 'Politics and politicians bring me out in a rash.'

Prue bit her lip. That exactly summed up her feelings as well, but she felt she ought not to encourage him in so radical a view. 'I suppose you sold your ship when you ceased to be a privateer.'

'Why should you suppose that? I still hold my letters of marque—my four ships are still at sea. Only now we are at peace, the cannon are cold and all the cargos are paid for in coin and not in gunpowder and blood. I suppose I should have warned you that I am still a merchant and that, as my wife, you are now tainted with the stench of trade.'

'I have no objection to that,' Prue said coolly, refusing to rise to the slight jeer in his tone. 'Trade is the wealth of the country. But we are not going to remain at peace much longer, are we?'

'There is still opposition in Parliament against a declaration of war, but I think it inevitable. They are sending troops over the Channel in their thousands.'

'And when we are at war, will you go to sea again?' There was an unpleasant hollow in the pit of her stomach. War was bad enough, but she had not thought to find herself married to someone who would be taking up arms.

'My captains are competent.'

'That does not answer my question.'

'Rest assured that if I do and the French get the better of me, you will find yourself a very wealthy widow.'

'Then you had best assure yourself that I will be a suitable stepmama to Jon before you risk your neck in that way,' she replied politely.

Ladies do not smite their new husbands over the head with their reticule, whatever the provocation.

'I assure you I have every intention of doing so.' The light was failing, but she thought she detected a hint of his twisted smile as the carriage came to a halt. 'Are we having our first married argument, Lady Cranford?'

'I believe this is what you sailors call taking ranging shots, is it not?' Prue gathered her reticule, straightened her bonnet and took a firm hold on her temper. 'Naturally, you will do as you see fit, my lord.'

'Of that you may be certain.' He handed her out as

the door of the house opened. 'You have met Finedon, of course.'

'Yes. Good evening.'

'My lady.' The butler bowed as they entered the hall. 'Your trunks arrived this morning, my lady, and have been unpacked. Shall I ring for Hedges?'

That was Tansy, her new dresser, selected for her by Verity and, thankfully, rather less imposing than Field. Her name made Prue think of the countryside, which was cheering.

'Thank you, Finedon. Tell her that I will go to see Lord St James first.' It seemed ridiculous to lumber a baby with a title, she thought, but that was how things worked and she must accustom herself to the fact that little Jon was a viscount, even if it was only a courtesy title.

She began to follow Ross up the stairs, then realised that if she was carrying a child now, then that baby would have a courtesy title as well. How easy it had been to forget the possibility of a child once the fear of bearing it and having to give it up was gone.

'My lady?' Ross was formal in Finedon's presence.

'I tripped.' She laid one hand protectively on her stomach, then took it away before he noticed. Time enough to test the reality of his promise to accept another man's child when she was certain she was carrying one.

'Another flight, I am afraid. You are tired. I suggest you retire when we have seen Jon. You could have supper in your suite.'

'You do not require my company this evening?' She was so taken aback that she blurted out the question.

Ross stopped on the landing and waited for her to reach him. 'I do not require you to do anything except be a mother to Jon. I had thought I had made that clear.'

She made a non-committal sound. He had made it clear he would not require her in his bed, that was all. Nothing had been said about leading separate lives. If he thought that she was going to flit about the house like a ghost, keeping out of his way so that he could carry on being a comfortably single man, then Lord Cranford could think again. They were both entitled to their own lives, of course, but they were married now and *both* of them were going to have to make concessions if she had anything to do with the matter.

Then Ross opened a door and Prue followed him into the nursery and promptly forgot to be irritated. Maud, the nursemaid, stood up from her seat where she was stitching next to a lamp to supplement the failing light and bobbed a curtsy as Ross trod softly over to the crib.

Prue joined him, watching as he stroked his hand over his son's silky dark hair, then cupping the little head for a moment, the inked talons suddenly appearing protective instead of threatening. Whatever else this man was, he was also a loving father and that warmed her heart, giving her some hope that they could create some sort of family together.

Then Ross stepped back, his eyes dark and brooding as he watched her hesitate. Children, especially small ones, were a mystery to her. Would her unfamiliar touch wake Jon or would another caress somehow reassure the sleeping child? But Ross seemed to expect it of her, so she leant over the crib, tucked the knitted blanket more securely around the child and stroked her finger down his cheek.

'So soft,' she murmured and realised that she was smiling.

Ross nodded to Maud, then held the door open, clearly waiting for Prue, so she gave Jon one last look and followed Ross out on to the landing.

'It is difficult to believe that someone that small and tender will grow up to be as large and hard as you.'

'His mother was not much taller than you are. He may take after her, not me.'

'True,' she agreed, determined to be peaceable, this first night of their marriage.

'I will show you your suite,' he said, leading the way down one flight of stairs, then paused on the landing, hand on the ornate wrought-iron balustrade, waiting for her.

So formidable, so unyielding, she thought as the dying light through the stair window caught him. *So hard. Jon needs a father who can unbend a little and I would rather like a husband to laugh with occasionally. I should not try to change another person to suit myself, but perhaps, just perhaps, there is more than flint beneath that weather-beaten skin if I can find it.*

At least there was no inconvenient sensual attraction. Perhaps Charles had cured her of that or perhaps her deceitful lover was the physical type of man she desired and large, battered, intimidating males would never cause unseemly flutterings. She hoped so.

'These rooms have been redecorated and refurnished. However, if there is anything you wish to have changed, please give orders for what you want.' He stood just inside the door, well back so Prue could walk into the sitting room without brushing past him.

It was elegant, with panelled cream walls, deep blue hangings, chairs that looked comfortable, although it felt unlived in. Then she realised that she could smell fresh paint and the fabrics at the window were crisp and new. This had been his first wife's suite and Ross must have ordered it redecorated as soon as she had agreed to marry him.

Tactful, was her first thought, then, *Cold-bloodedly practical.*

Perhaps not—perhaps he had loved his wife too much to have a reminder of her in his new wife's chambers. But he had said he had not loved her...

Prue gave herself a little shake as a door to her right opened and her new dresser came out and curtsied. 'What a lovely room. Good evening, Hedges.'

'My lady. My lord.'

She turned and smiled at Ross, held out her hand. 'Thank you. I will be glad of the opportunity to rest.' Instinct stopped her from bidding him goodnight, although she supposed the staff would realise soon enough that the Marquis was not sleeping with his wife. It was impossible to keep that kind of thing from the servants. What would they assume? Then she realised that if she was with child then they must at least make some show of sharing a bed, if only for a few nights. Perhaps for the next few days the staff might assume he was showing consideration to a blushing bride.

Ross took her hand and she felt the calluses that she had noticed when he had slipped the ring on her finger. Did he really haul ropes with his men still?

'My lady.' He raised it to his lips, breathed what might pass as a kiss over it, then released her.

Prue found herself alone with her dresser. Tansy Hedges was about the same age as she was, a neatly dressed brunette with blue eyes, a wide mouth and the air of having just stopped smiling.

'Hedges—' Prue stopped, uncertain what she had been about to say.

'My lady?'

'I have never had a dresser before, Hedges.'

'I have never been one before, my lady, but I suppose that between us we will manage well enough.' The smile peeped out.

'I expect we will. I will call you Tansy when we are alone and you can say *ma'am* instead of *my lady*, if you must, although I am more than happy if you say neither.'

'That would suit me very well, ma'am, thank you. I can have hot water here in just a moment.'

'I think…' She must not dither and look for helpful suggestions She was mistress of this household now. 'I think I would like to wash and change into something less tight-laced, and then have a light supper here.' She had books and she had never felt lonely before in the company of a book.

'Of course, ma'am. All your clothes have been un-packed and pressed and I have just the thing for a comfortable evening.'

'My other things? My books, for example?'

'Everything is here, ma'am, except the books. All those crates have gone to the library.'

'Yes, of course, thank you. And the library is where, exactly?'

'On the ground floor, just below this suite. Mr Finedon asked His Lordship whether he wanted one of the footmen to put all the books on the shelves and His Lordship said not to. That it was probably more than his life was worth to touch them.'

'He did?' Either her husband had a sense of humour buried so deep she had been unable to notice it so far or he thought she would prove to be a terrible nag.

'Yes, ma'am. Mr Finedon was quite worried about it yesterday evening because he had hoped you wouldn't be, um…' Her voice trailed off.

'Difficult?'

'Yes, ma'am. And I said I was sure it was only His Lordship's little joke and Mr Finedon said that His Lordship does not make little jokes.'

'You may tell Finedon that I have no intention of being difficult, but that I am exceedingly fond of my books and I expect His Lordship merely wanted them taken care of.'

'Thank you, I'll do that if he says anything again. Only I have to watch my place now I'm with the senior servants, being your dresser. When I go to the room afterwards—Mrs Tredwell's parlour, that is—for tea after dinner in the hall I can tell they don't want me getting above myself.'

'You outrank all the female staff except Mrs Tredwell, Tansy. If you show that you expect to be treated like that, but are not demanding, then I am sure they will soon relax with you.'

'Thank you, ma'am. Look, here is the nightgown and robe I thought right for this evening.'

That was what came of allowing her friends to go shopping on her behalf. When she had replied to their anxious enquiries that she had no time for more than the wedding gown fittings and a few extra pairs of silk stockings and gloves and she could shop for clothes after the wedding, Jane and Verity had exchanged glances and announced that they would take care of the essentials.

Indecently gorgeous lace nightgowns apparently came under the heading of *essential*. This one was a soft raspberry pink trimmed with cream and appeared to have very little bodice and even less back. The robe, thankfully, looked as though it would at least cover her decently. In a heavy cream silk with pink lacings to match the gown, it draped elegantly from Tansy's hands.

'Yes, that will do very well.' Most new brides would be expected to wear something like that for their wedding night, she was sure, and it was pretty, even if only she and Tansy would see it. 'And now I am dying for you to remove all these pins from my hair!'

Chapter Five

A light supper of poached salmon and green peas followed by a fruit fool with almond crisps was exactly right. With nothing on under the nightgown her ribs were blissfully unconfined and her hair was brushed out and loosely plaited.

'You only have to pull the ribbon and shake it out when you want it loose, ma'am,' Tansy had murmured, turning a trifle pink.

For a moment Prue had no idea what the girl was blushing about, then she realised that she expected her mistress to retire to bed with her hair flowing around her shoulders to wait for the Marquis in suitably virginal glory.

Prue had dismissed her for the night and now, with nothing to do but explore her suite—sitting room, bedchamber and dressing room—she was bored. There was not a single book in the rooms. Not even a small bookcase. Changes would have to be made tomorrow, but for tonight, what was she supposed to do with herself at half past ten?

Say her prayers and go to bed, she supposed, fidgeting about the sitting room.

Or find a book. She could hardly send for a footman and a crowbar at this time of night, but the library must have books on its shelves, journals she could borrow.

Silent on slippered feet, her robe securely fastened over the shocking nightgown, Prue opened the door and looked out, then stepped into the corridor, illuminated with lamps at either end.

There was no one in the hall, no sounds as she hesitated at the foot of the stairs, getting her bearings. The library was under her rooms, she recalled, counting. Which meant that this must be the door. She opened it, expecting darkness, but one of the lamps that were scattered through the house was burning on a side table and another stood on the mantel shelf.

The lamplight cast a soft glow over the books and the mahogany of the shelves and tables. So many books. With a happy sigh she picked up the lamp from the table and began to wander along the shelves.

The section nearest the end of the long library table had an atlas stand and a globe. A pile of books with paper markers sticking out were on the table and when she looked at the titles in the nearest bay she found they were about politics and geography, economics, statistical tables and sailing. This was, surely, Ross's working collection.

She left it and moved on, puzzled now. The rest of the books seemed to be arranged in any order except one that made sense. On one shelf they were ordered by size, on another some lovely examples of binding were grouped together and there was even a section that was arranged by colour. In one place Classical authors rubbed shoulders with novels and books on wildfowling. In another she found the lives of the early church fathers next to Hoyle's *Games*. It was enough to give any self-respecting scholar acute indigestion.

'This is appalling,' she muttered, plucking *The Recluse of Norway* from between Grime's *Latin Primer* and *A Voyage Among the Scottish Isles* and then having nowhere to put it.

'Why not send for more lights?'

Prue dropped the novel, said something unladylike under her breath and turned. 'I did not know anyone was in here.'

Ross stood up from the deep armchair where he had been brooding in the gloom on the likely consequences for trade of the outbreak of war and took the four strides across the room necessary to pick up the fallen book from the carpet. 'You disapprove of fiction?' he asked after a glance at the title.

'I do not. I was commenting aloud on the organisation—if that is what it can be called—of this library. I apologise if it is your personal system, although *system* is hardly the word.'

Prudence certainly said what she thought, Ross decided. After Honoria's hints and sulks and little mysteries this was a refreshing trait in a wife.

'I would not have said anything about it if I had known you were there,' she added.

And she had good manners, too. He shrugged. 'I do

not see why not. It is just as much your library as mine
now. As for the state it is in, you must lay the blame on
my grandfather, I assume. When I inherited I pulled
out everything that was of use to me, added my own
books to it and ignored the rest.'

'Then I may set it in proper order?'

'You may paint it green and hang gold tassels on it
for all I care, provided you leave that bay alone,' he said
impatiently. He gestured towards his books and she
turned, bringing the scent of scented soap and warm
woman to his nostrils. The skirts of her robe flipped as
she moved, providing him with a glimpse of raspberry-
pink lace and bare ankles in little pink morocco slippers beneath.

Ross caught his breath as she looked over her shoulder at him, eyes bright with an emotion he recognised.
Desire…

There was a breathless silence, then, 'I may? Do as
I choose with it, I mean? Oh, thank you. It is so much
larger than Papa's library at home, almost as large as
the one in the Duke's London house.'

Yes, it had been desire, but for his books, not for
him. That was a relief. Unflattering of course, to be
of less interest than shelves of dusty tomes, but then
his self-esteem was not in need of bolstering and he
had made it quite clear to her that he would not trouble
her in that way.

Which had been a perfectly reasonable reassurance
to offer her and nothing but the truth when he had said
it. Ross went across to the atlas stand and shut the big
volume with a thump. Had been the honest truth until

Prudence had walked towards him in that ivory silk wedding gown and then had come and twirled in pink lace right under his nose, damn it.

At least it was reassuring that he was still functioning in that area, he supposed. Ross stared unseeing at the globe and acknowledged that he had begun to worry at the back of his mind about the fact that nothing and no one had seemed to stir the slightest hint of lust since Jon's birth.

So now he had the welcome reassurance that his virility was undimmed and the damnable realisation that he had promised Prudence that he would not expect to bed her. Which left self-control, he supposed. Self-control and hard work and, hopefully, the opportunity to take some French shipping once the government and Parliament stopped flapping about like a collection of wet hens and declared war.

Scuffling sounds behind him reminded Ross that he was not alone. Prudence was scanning the shelves, lamp held high like some minor Greek goddess as she pulled another book out and added it to a tottering pile.

'May I take these up to my room?'

Ross made a sweeping gesture. 'As I said: your library, your books.'

She put down the lamp and tried to pick up the pile in both hands, wedging it under her chin.

'Let me. Surely one is enough for tonight? The rest can go up tomorrow when we have found a bookcase for you.'

He reached for the pile she held on to as they tipped, then he had most of them in his hands and the memory of the slide of silk over lush curves tingling at his fingertips. They stared at each other over the books, Prudence's cheeks pink, her eyes wide and startled.

Damn, damn, damn...

Ross put the volumes he held on the table and returned to his chair. It seemed the least threatening thing he could do. Certainly wrestling the volumes she was holding like a shield away from her, and then exploring beneath the folds of cream silk, was not. 'You can manage those few, I imagine?'

'What?' she said, breathlessly. 'Oh, yes. Goodnight.'

'Goodnight.' Ross did not look round.

He said he wouldn't...that he didn't want to...

Prue caught up the skirts of the robe in one hand, clutched the three books she had been left with tighter to her chest and made herself walk calmly across the hall, up the stairs and into the sanctuary of her sitting room.

Ross had said that he had lost his appetite for *that sort of thing*. It seemed he had found it again if the intensity in those dark eyes was anything to judge by. He had not intended to touch her, she realised that. But he had and for a moment she had wanted to drop the books and step forward so those big hands would slide along both sides of her breasts. She shivered, felt the heat of that glancing fingertip touch through the silk all over again.

The books made a dull thump as she dropped them on a side table and little puffs of dust escaped from between the pages. She should go to bed, take whichever of them looked the most challenging—after dusting it—and read until she fell asleep.

But she did not want to face the bed. It conjured up too many images in her mind, too many questions.

Did she really want her husband in that way? She knew now that caresses, however pleasant, led to a reality that was far from enjoyable. But that had been Charles, who had not cared for her, or about her, at all. He had only wanted to take and take until he had satisfied his own needs.

Verity and Jane clearly loved their husbands—and loved what went on between them in the bedchamber, there was no mistaking that. So it must depend on the man and on one's feelings for him. *And his for you*, Prue reminded herself.

Verity and Will, and Jane and Ivo, had known each other before they married and in Will and Verity's case had certainly been in love. It had taken rather longer for the other couple, but at least they'd had a relationship first. Ross had no reason to have more than mild liking for her. Liking and enough trust to believe she would be good to his son.

He wouldn't be careless or intentionally unkind, she was certain of that. Prue curled up in the armchair and tucked her skirts around her feet. But he was very big, very dour. She was not at all sure she wanted to lie with a man who never laughed.

Prue came down to breakfast the next morning after taking some trouble to thoroughly rumple the bed on both sides. Whether that was sufficient to fool Tansy she had no idea, not having any experience in observing marital beds after lovemaking.

Church bells were ringing and she realised with a guilty start that this was Sunday. What was the household routine? She should have asked Tansy.

Then she saw that Finedon was passing through the hall. 'Good morning, my lady.'

'Good morning. Finedon. What are the arrangements for the servants to attend church?'

'Most of the household attends morning service which is at half past ten at St George's. Those who remain on duty go to the evening service. There are three non-conformists in the household and they have a meeting house just beyond Golden Square.' He gave what Prue suspected was a disapproving cough. 'Your Ladyship may have *views* on the employment of those of a Methodist persuasion.'

'None at all. If they perform their duties adequately, their beliefs are no business of mine,' she said firmly.

'Very good, my lady. The breakfast room is through here, my lady.'

Ross rose to his feet as she came in. 'Good morning.'

'Indeed, it seems so. Tea, if you please,' she added to the footman. 'And some toast, nothing else.'

'That will be all, Michael,' Ross said when the tea pot had been delivered and the toast rack filled. 'You appear to have some observations to make, Prudence,' he added as the door closed behind the man.

'Not at all. I was going to ask which church you prefer to attend on Sundays.'

'I do not attend church.'

She might have guessed. 'You will have no objection if I attend morning service at St George's? Hedges can accompany me.'

'No objection at all.' Ross passed her the butter. 'Jam? There appears to be blackcurrant or strawberry this morning. You are a devout churchgoer?'

'Blackcurrant, please. And, no. I have no claims to devotion, more to a sceptical spirit of enquiry. But it is a social as well as a spiritual obligation to attend the Established church, is it not? And I find a good sermon intellectually stimulating, whether I agree with it or not.'

'What a very shocking attitude in a young lady. My second cousin the bishop would be outraged.'

'You may have no fears that I will infect Jon with a spirit of scepticism. He may make up his own mind on the matter when he is old enough. I thought to take him and his nurse down to Green Park after church if this sunshine continues.' It had, in truth, only just occurred to her and now, seeing a frown gathering on Ross's face, prepared herself for a tussle.

'You will need the carriage. I will have Maud and Jon come to collect you after the service. Hedges can walk back as she would have done so anyway.'

'Thank you.' They were very formal, but she supposed that would wear off with time and a growing familiarity with her husband. And thinking about familiarity, there was, thankfully, no heat in the unsmiling gaze he fixed on her now. Her dreams had been somewhat troubled by the memory of those dark eyes, the little tug of rough fingertips on the silk of her robe.

'Is that gown new?' He was regarding her with clear disapproval.

'No. I bought it last Season. Why?' Prue squinted down at herself. Surely Tansy would not have let her come down in something that was stained or torn. 'It is very suitable for attending church, I believe.'

'It is very suitable for a nunnery. I do not pretend to know anything about female fashion, but I know when I see something dowdy. Have you not bought a new wardrobe? I thought I had given you sufficient funds, but if not—'

'You know, it is really difficult to know in what order to address that! I had about one week to prepare for the wedding—how on earth could I buy an entire new wardrobe in that time? And this is not a nun's habit, it is a perfectly—'

'Hideous garment,' Ross concluded for her. 'You have a very fine figure, so why truss it up in a dark blue sack as though it is something to be ashamed of? Take the Duchess of Aylsham with you and visit some modistes—she has excellent taste. Otherwise I will escort you myself.'

Prue considered throwing the jam dish, dismissed that as unfair to the servants and settled for a sweet smile. 'Thank you, Ross. I do appreciate that. I would be delighted to have you accompany me.'

And that would have wiped the smile off your face if you had been wearing one.

But of course he was merely as sardonic as usual. It had made him thin his lips a trifle, though.

'I am entirely at your disposal. Shall we say tomorrow morning? I will welcome the opportunity to discover which French imports the dressmakers of London are most in need of so as to be beforehand when the French situation is under control again.'

Oh! Tit for tat, my lord, and a point to you.

She had been hoping to pay him back for his remarks by making him twiddle his thumbs in an endless succession of shops. As for Ross's remarks about her gown and her figure, to say nothing of the implication that her own taste was so bad so that she needed guidance, she would not lower herself to retaliate.

'Thank you *so* much. I will send a note round to Verity and ask her for a really comprehensive list of recommendations. I think we should take in milliners and cordwainers and haberdashers as well.'

'I will remember to have a good breakfast,' Ross said smoothly. 'And now, if you will excuse me, I have matters to attend to. I will speak to Finedon about the carriage.'

Prue demolished another two slices of toast and drained the teapot. Really, being married required a great deal of energy, if only to control one's temper. What next? Jon, of course. Maud ought to have him bathed and dressed and breakfasted on whatever babies ate for breakfast at his age.

She found Maud tidying the nursery, Jon in the arms of a plump woman who was nursing him at her breast,

and realised that she should have known he needed a
wet nurse.

'Good morning, Maud. No, do not get up, Mrs—'

'Mrs Goodnight, my lady. My husband, Robert, is
His Lordship's coachman and we live in the mews.
Handy for His Little Lordship,' she added with a
chuckle. 'My Rosie's not a big feeder and I've always
got a good supply.'

'Er…excellent.' Prue couldn't help but feel that was
rather more information than she was ready for. 'Maud,
I thought if this sunshine holds we might take Jon for
an airing in Green Park. His Lordship will send you
and Jon in the carriage to collect me after the service
if you think it will fit in with his routine.'

'That would do nicely, my lady. He'll take a little
feed and be all changed and ready. I expect he'll sleep,
but that doesn't matter.'

Mrs Goodnight stood up, rested the baby against
her shoulder and patted him on the back until he produced a satisfactory burp. 'There you go, my lordling.
Back to Maudie.'

'Look who's here to see you,' Maud said, holding
him so he could see Prue.

He cooed and waved his little fists and Prue waved
back at him.

'There's a clever boy, saying good morning to your
mama—' She broke off. 'Oh, I do beg your pardon,
ma'am. That just slipped out.'

'You were quite right, Maud. Come to Mama, Jon.'
She held out her arms and took him, gurgling and wriggling. It felt strange to say it, but good, too.

'Oh, do be careful, my lady. He might— Oh, dear, and all down the front of your gown as well.'

'No need to worry, Maud. I have it on good authority that this gown is a disaster. But you had best take him back if I am to change in time before church.' Prue handed Jon to her, touched despite herself at how pleased he had been to see her. But then he was a cheerful child and probably would have greeted the chimney sweep with as much enthusiasm.

Your father must have some light in him somewhere if he made you, she thought, suddenly prey to nerves and an unpleasant feeling of loneliness.

Chapter Six

Tansy bundled the soiled gown away, nodding enthusiastically when Prue said she could have it to cut up, or alter and do as she liked with if she could remove the stain. 'The leaf-green walking dress with the darker green pelisse, ma'am?' she suggested. 'It isn't as serious and Sunday-like, but it is much more flattering.'

And it would be more fitting for a marchioness, Prue reminded herself as she unfurled her parasol on the steps and set off around the Square with Tansy one step behind. How long was it going to be before she was used to that? Rather sooner than she became accustomed to her husband, she suspected.

Despite its name, St George's Hanover Square Church was not actually on Hanover Square but a short distance from it along George Street. Carriages were already passing them and other churchgoers, lured out by the bright sunshine, were converging on the church's pillared portico from the fashionable streets and squares all around.

Prue furled her parasol as they reached the steps and kept a pleasant smile on her face, feeling suddenly very exposed, certain she was being stared at and scrutinised. There was no one she knew in sight—Verity and Will often attended the Chapel Royal at St James's Palace—and although there had been a fashionable crowd invited to the wedding she could not say she was acquainted with any of them. In fact, the entire day had passed in a blur. All she could do now was be alert for anyone showing signs of recognition and hope she could bluff her way through an exchange.

And Ross, not being a churchgoer, would not have paid the rent on a pew either, so they would have to sit in the unallocated ones at the back.

'Good morning, madam. May I assist you?' It was a black-clad verger, politely attentive to an unfamiliar face. 'If I might enquire your name?'

'Lady Cranford,' Tansy said before Prue could ask why he wanted to know.

'Of course, my lady. I do beg your pardon. The Marquis's pew is just along here.'

He closed the door on them, leaving Prue feeling considerably flustered. 'Lord Cranford did not tell me the family had a pew here,' she murmured to Tansy as they rose from their knees and waited for the service to begin.

'Perhaps he does not know, my lady. I guessed there might be, because of this being the nearest church to the house, and Mr Finedon told me that this is the one the staff attend.'

* * *

The service proved soothing in one way, but the sermon was both dull and lengthy and allowed far too much time for brooding. The past days had gone in a blur and Prue wondered if she had thought about anything coherently from the moment she had realised in the conservatory just what Charles was and how she had let her heart betray her.

The practical part of her brain had taken over: get away, go to her friends, agree to this marriage. She had assessed the benefits—safety for a child if she was carrying one, protection from scandal, freedom from the restrictions of home, a husband who appeared willing to tolerate her work—and what she could give in return, her care for Jon. She had been too anxious, too tired, to fret over practicalities.

But now, amid the scent of beeswax and polish, perfumes and the hint of rather too many warm bodies in close proximity, she had the space to feel. There was the ache over her lost love, unreal though it had been. There was anger at Charles's cynical betrayal. There was the anxiety over whether he might do or say anything now she was married and how Ross would react if he did.

And then there was the realisation that she was indissolubly linked to a silent, unsmiling man with a present he showed no signs of wishing to share with her and a past she could barely comprehend. A man for whom, against all reason, she felt a tug of physical attraction. And she was totally in the power of this virtual stranger. Yet oddly, of all the things she was afraid of—Charles, scandal, finding that she was with child, failing to live up to her new exalted rank—Ross Vincent, Marquis of Cranford, was not among them.

That probably showed how poor her judgement was, Prue thought as the congregation stood for the end of the service. Her stomach was full of butterflies and she realised, with horror, that it would not take much to have her in tears.

Chin up. Smile.

She led the way out of the box and was immediately aware of being watched. Several elegant matrons gave her a slight bow which, startled, she returned. Others smiled politely or nodded. The verger must have been passing on the interesting intelligence that the new Marchioness had attended church—and without her husband. Although if they knew Ross at all, that would hardly come as a surprise to any of them.

And there he was, lounging in a very elegant landau with the roof folded down and looking thoroughly piratical as he surveyed the congregation coming down the steps or stopping to talk. And in many cases, stare. The presence of a nursemaid holding a baby seated opposite him merely made him look even more dangerous by contrast.

A wolf with a lamb between its paws, Prue thought rather wildly.

When she hesitated between the columns Ross saw her, stood up and bowed, causing a little flurry in the onlookers as he descended, waving away the groom and holding the door for her.

'Thank you, Hedges. I will not be needing you until

just before luncheon.' Prue was really quite pleased at how composed she sounded. 'My lord. Thank you.'

She saw as she sat down that the baby was asleep, so she merely smiled at Maud as she settled in the forward-facing seat.

'A good sermon?' Ross enquired as he sat beside her and signalled to the coachman to set off.

'Dull, I am afraid. Did you know we have a pew at St George's?'

'I did not and I admit that the existence of one was not a question that had been on my mind. I trust you will get full value for all the time I have been paying to keep it empty.'

'I'm afraid one service a week will make it an expensive indulgence.' The landau which had looked so spacious from the street felt strangely cramped now they were sitting so close. Prue made a business out of opening her parasol and setting it just so.

'Nonsense. One must be seen. Or, rather, *you* must be seen. At least one of the Patronesses of Almack's attends St George's, I am told. Lady Jersey, possibly. I heard her husband is a church warden, which seems improbable. I do know that there's a box at the opera I am paying rent on, and one at the Theatre Royal. I may make some use of those.'

'I have never been to the opera at all before, nor to the theatre in London.'

'Look at the news-sheets, decide what you would like to go to and I will take you if I can. Church is one thing, but you cannot go to the theatre alone.'

'I had not intended being a nuisance.' She tried not

to sound defensive, but there had been a slight edge
to his tone.

'You would not be, Lady Cranford, I assure you,'
he said with such politeness that Prue did not believe a
word of it. No, entertaining his new wife had not been
in the agreement.

She wondered what his reaction would be to a demand to be taken to Astley's Amphitheatre, given that
he had so politely offered in front of a witness. It was
very tempting. Then she realised what he had said
about St George's. 'Almack's?'

'You will naturally wish to attend and therefore require vouchers.' Her expression must have been very
revealing because he added, 'You will want to go with
your friends.'

'Not with you?'

'I do not require you to go to sea in one of my ships
and, in return, you will not require me to squire you
to balls, masquerades, breakfasts or whatever other
nonsense the Season involves.'

'I would enjoy going to sea, I think.' Prue took advantage of the carriage slowing for the turn into Bond
Street to raise her parasol higher. It was pale green and
buttercup yellow and decidedly frivolous for a Sunday,
but she felt a sudden need to twirl it defiantly. 'I have
never been on board a ship.'

'Well, I have done my share of balls, masquerades
and suchlike nonsense and I enjoy them as much as you
would enjoy a storm off the North Foreland at night.'
That uncompromising mouth was set in a firm line and
she realised that he was not teasing her. The previous

experiences must have been with his first wife. Was he simply thoroughly antisocial or did he not want to be reminded of her? Was he still in love with her, despite what he had said? That would explain his promise not to bed Prue—it might feel like a betrayal of the other woman and he had lied to spare Prue's feelings.

She would have to discover more about the first Lady Cranford. It was not that she wished to pry, but how could she live in the same house, become a second mother to a child, if she knew nothing about the past? She did not even know the poor woman's name.

The pretence of finding the right angle for her parasol gave Prue the excuse to shift on the seat, see Ross's face more clearly. It was six months since he had lost his wife—no wonder the man did not smile, let alone laugh. Not if his heart was broken and he felt he had to hide the fact.

'What is wrong?'

She should have realised that this was someone used to command, to managing a tight-knit crew. He would be skilled at reading expressions, watchful for changes of mood. But Maud was sitting there and, even with her attention apparently all on Jon in her arms, this was no place for even the lightest attempt at probing.

'I am wondering if this parasol is unsuitable for a Sunday.'

That was frivolous enough to deflect his curiosity. 'It looks adequate to me,' Ross said dismissively as the coachman turned the pair out into Piccadilly. 'I told Robert to stop by the reservoir. Jon might like the ducks.'

Jon did. He woke up, full of energy and ready to be entertained by the fowl that were already clustered by the edge of the long strip of water where other excited small children were throwing crusts for them.

'I will take him,' Ross said to Maud. 'Take a little time for yourself while we walk.'

The child went willingly, burbling, 'Dada, Dada', as he landed in Ross's arms.

'Now there's a clever lad.' Ross did not quite smile, but his expression certainly lightened.

It promptly darkened again as Jon twisted in his grip, waved both clubby fists at Prue and said, 'Dada!'

Prue stifled a laugh. 'I think he is still trying out sounds. Look, Jon—ducks. Quack, quack.'

Ross rolled his eyes, shifting Jon more securely in his arms. 'Shall we walk?'

'Certainly. The air is fresh today. The view of West-minster Abbey is beautifully clear.' They strolled to the end of the reservoir, turned and began to follow the southern bank. 'The service must have finished at the Chapel Royal—look how many people are coming into the Park from the Palace end.'

'Good God, what has that woman got on her head? From here it looks like an entire ostrich. Can you take Jon?' He thrust the baby into her arms and removed a notebook from an inside pocket. 'If plumes are com-ing into fashion to that extent, then I can release some of the ones from the warehouse.'

'I will ask Verity—she is sure to know. Ostrich plumes come from Africa, do they not?'

'Yes.' Ross had finished his note and put the book

away. 'North Africa through the Mediterranean or from the south, which is a much longer and more dangerous route up the west coast of Africa. But one of my ships took a Dutch trader that was stuffed with the things, just at a moment when no one seemed to be wearing them.'

'Except for Court events. Plumes are still compulsory for that, are they not they? Perhaps we can bring them back into fashion generally. Feather fans, feather parasols…'

'You see yourself as a leader of fashion, Prudence?' He retrieved Jon from her and pointed at a hopeful-looking duck. 'Quack?'

'Ook.'

'Close enough. Clever boy.'

'I most certainly would have no influence on fashions, but I will suggest it to Verity. It would amuse her to have everyone decked out in plumes like an entire flock of ostriches.'

'You are a marchioness, you would influence others if you cared to.'

'I do not and all I have is the title. We will not be active socially, you tell me. You are not in government. I am not establishing a *salon*.'

'You could if you wished.' When she looked at him quizzically he shrugged, making Jon laugh. 'I thought that bluestockings liked nothing better than to have reading circles, salons, intellectual discussion tea parties. What do you intend to do with yourself this afternoon?'

'Speak to the housekeeper, then write letters—there

are still people to thank for wedding gifts and I must write to Mama and Papa so there is something soon after they arrive home. Then I have work to do.'

'Are a pile of correspondence and household matters not work?'

'Those are duties and social matters. No, I mean my translation.'

'The Duchess said that you were a scholar. She did not say of what.'

And you were not interested enough to find out, she thought with an inward sigh. Or he thought it was some minor pastime, that she read a little light poetry in Italian, perhaps.

'The translation of Greek and Roman literature mostly, although I am interested in the history of those civilisations as well. And the Egyptians are fascinating, of course. But no one can read their writing, so that is just something I read about. At present I am translating a selection of poetry from both Greek and Latin. I almost have enough for a volume of it and plan to have the original printed on one side of the page, my translation on the one opposite. I am not a poet, but I hope to make the English read well, not simply be a straightforward rendition of the words.'

'And you seriously intended to publish it?'

For a moment she thought Ross was going to object. His right to control her work had not been part of their agreement, but she was all too well aware of the authority a husband could exert if he put his mind to it.

She had survived parental disapproval by meekly agreeing with everything Mama said about bluestock-

ings and husbands—the lack thereof—and quietly carrying on with her work whenever she could. It had
been frustrating and limiting and this marriage had
appeared to be an escape from that subterfuge. Now
she was prepared to fight for the right to do what she
wished in her own time. 'Certainly, I do. I had thought
to approach Mr Murray.'

'You set your sights high,' Ross said coolly. 'The
most fashionable publisher in London, or so Mr Murray himself would have us believe. Lord Byron and
Walter Scott are published by him, I believe.'

'And a great many less exalted authors as well,' Prue
retorted crisply. 'I would do so under my maiden name,
of course,' she added, in the thought of offering an
olive branch. It was no great matter to her under what
name her work was published. 'Or *By A Lady*, even.'

'Why the desire for anonymity? Are you ashamed
of your work or simply lacking in confidence in its
quality?'

'Am I— No, of course not. It is just that there seems
to be a convention about female authors, especially
married ones, and I assumed you would object.'

'I imagine it would sell better under your married
name because that would cause quite a little stir in
polite circles. Most of society probably assume I can
barely write my own name, so the idea that my wife is
a scholar would arouse plenty of talk. Murray would
like that, don't you think?'

'Use your title to sell my work? Have Murray accept
it because he thinks it would cause a little sensation,
regardless of its quality? Or perhaps because he wished

to curry favour with a marquis?' Prue stopped dead in her tracks. 'I have never been so insulted!'

'Really? What a very restricted life you must have led if that is the worse insult you have experienced.'

Ross came to a halt and regarded her. It must be how he would consider a strange sea creature encountered on a voyage, she thought, bristling. 'Do you not consider the actions of the gentleman we do not discuss a worse affront to you?'

'Of course I do.' Prue realised she was within an inch of stamping her foot. 'I meant towards my work.'

'I was going to suggest,' Ross said mildly, 'that you submit it to Murray first, then, when he has accepted it and you are discussing terms, you produce your title as a bargaining ploy. No, that is not edible.' He freed the brim of his hat from his son's grasp. 'Nor do the ducks want it.' He looked back at Prue, still standing stock-still in the middle of the path. 'You disagree?'

'No, not at all! But I thought you were going to try and forbid me. Are you not concerned about your name?'

'If you mean my title, no, not particularly.' He shrugged. 'No one bearing it showed any interest in me—why should I value what they protected so fiercely? Half of my blood comes from my mother and they thought her inferior stock, not suitable for breeding with the exalted Vincent line. The title itself is a confounded nuisance most of the time. Let us make use of it where we can.' A faint, sardonic twist that was the nearest she had seen to a smile ghosted across his lips. 'I was plain Mr Vincent and you were plain Miss

Scott for most of our lives. We may as well enjoy the benefits of the Cranford connection.'

When she did not move Ross said, 'What else is troubling you?'

'Most men would not wish their wife to do such a thing. Most would not approve of her spending time in study, let alone publishing the result commercially.'

'I am not most men. And you are not my property, Prudence.' She opened her mouth and Ross held up his hand. 'No, before you lecture me on the legal position and how you might as well be my slave, my chattel and so forth, let us take that as said. You are, I suppose, in the position of a business partner. Our enterprise is raising this child and I fail to see how publishing poetry is going to interfere with that.'

'What if I am wrong and it is dreadful poetry?' She fell into step beside him again, her feelings a not unpleasant mixture of surprise, shock and cautious optimism.

'Then Murray will not take it,' Ross said, making her laugh. 'And what was amusing about that, might I ask?'

'The fact that you took no pains to sugar-coat your opinion. It is refreshing.'

'It is the truth and it is usually better in the long run to face the truth and not pretend things are other than they are.'

That was said with a lack of emphasis that had her turning slightly to study his face from the shelter of her bonnet brim. What unpleasant truth had he failed to face up to in the past? Prue wondered.

'Let me take Jon for a little,' she suggested. The questions buzzing in her brain were not the kind of thing one asked a man one hardly knew. Not in the middle of a London park, at least.

'He is heavy.'

'And he is set upon eating your hat. Let me distract him for a while.'

They accomplished the transfer with much wriggling and excited squeals from Jon and a muffled curse from Ross as his hat went spinning across the grass.

'See Papa run,' Prue said as she adjusted her slippery armful of wriggling baby. 'Oh, dear, the wind has caught his hat and it really is not funny, Jon,' she added as they both laughed.

'Excuse me.' She stepped aside to allow a fashionably dressed woman and her female companion to pass, but the other woman stopped.

'You must be the new Lady Cranford.'

'I am. You have the advantage of me.' She also had a dislike of her, Prue thought. The smile on the full lips did not reach the cool blue eyes that were assessing her with frank curiosity.

'Lady Heathly.'

I know who you are, the Earl of Heathly's wife, and I outrank you, Prue thought.

'Oh, yes, I have heard of you,' she said with a smile as false as the other woman's. She had heard her father speak of Heathly with disdain for his womanising and his position in the Prince Regent's circle of cronies—which probably explained his wife's sourness, she supposed.

Lady Heathly stiffened, presumably only too well aware of what Prue might have heard. 'I suppose I should congratulate a new bride, although I have to say I was quite taken aback—why, we all were—to think that Cranford should marry again so very soon after the death of his poor wife. Before he was even out of mourning.' Her smile thinned. 'It must be quite the romance.'

'Here he comes now,' Prue said, fixing the smile on her lips with an effort. 'Ross dear, Lady Heathly was remarking that we must be very much in love to have married while you were still in mourning.'

The other woman reddened and her companion made a sound that somehow combined embarrassment and reproof. Clearly they had thought to amuse themselves by sniping at Prue while her husband was out of earshot and had not expected her to fight back, let alone involve Ross.

'It is extraordinary the things people find to speculate about, is it not, my dear?' Ross lifted his hat in exaggerated greeting, then reached to take Jon from Prue's arms. 'No doubt, as you are not a friend of mine, Lady Heathly, you are not aware of my feelings on the hypocrisy of such conventions and the quite ridiculous rules they embody. Mourning—the true feelings and emotions—affects all of us differently. The artificial constraints society puts upon it reflect a desire to cover up distress, not to acknowledge it. As for myself, why, I had only to meet Prudence to know that she was meant for me.'

Chapter Seven

Lady Heathly and her companion swept off, cheeks red and backs stiff. Ross turned to Prudence and was surprised to read real distress in her expression. He had thought she had turned the tables neatly by repeating Lady Heathly's comments and she had come out with *Ross dear*, quite pat, but the two gossips had clearly upset her. In which case, he concluded, she had courage to stand up to the older woman—and one who would have greatly outranked her before her marriage—and fight back.

'You should not allow her to distress you.'

'It was sheer spite,' Prudence said, chin up. 'Bullying. I should not allow it to hurt. I suppose she has a daughter of marriageable age.'

'She has two, I believe. Or three, possibly. Why?'

'Because they have lost the chance to marry a marquis, of course,' she said with a flicker of a smile and tucked her hand into the crook of his elbow as they began to stroll again. 'If she had any idea that I do not give a farthing for your rank, she would be even angrier.'

Ross controlled the instinctive movement, the urge to pull his arm away. A lady walking with a gentleman had every right to expect to take his arm, especially if she was his wife. Honoria would cling at every opportunity, making certain everyone knew that she had married a marquis, even if he was the East End Aristocrat. It was the title that mattered to her, never the man.

With Prudence, as he was only too well aware, it was the wedding ring that she wanted, but he found he did not resent it as he had half expected to after making that impulsive decision. Prudence had been open about her motives. She was honest and seemed determined to uphold her part of the bargain—and that was refreshing. And the feel of her on his arm was unexpectedly pleasant.

He would have to take care or he would be lulled into thinking this was more than it was—into wishing for that. 'My rank means nothing to you?'

'Mama and Papa are beyond delighted, of course. But for myself, to be plain Mrs Ross Vincent would have been just as acceptable, believe me.'

Jon had fallen asleep, heavy and relaxed in the crook of his arm. Ross dipped his head so his chin brushed the lacy cap over his son's hair and realised that Prudence was looking at them.

'You love him very much and yet you made a very rapid decision to entrust him to me. It was hardly the love at first sight that Lady Heathly was sneering about.'

'Instinct.' Ross did not even have to think about it. As for love, that was nonsense, romantic twaddle. Even if it existed, it was short-lived, would not last out adversity. His parents' marriage had proved that.

'I have become used to sizing people up and I have learned to trust my gut.' Prudence made a soft sound, suspiciously like a snort, and he broke off. 'I suppose I should apologise for my language.'

'Not at all. Please, go on. You have to take care selecting a crew, no doubt.'

'That, of course, but growing up where I did, I learned fast that misjudging someone's character can lead to far more than disillusion. Make a mistake about who you trust and you lose your money—or your life.'

'And your internal—*compass*, shall we say?—your internal compass told you to trust me?'

'Exactly. Always watch the eyes, you see. Are the eyes in tune with everything else? Someone might not meet your gaze, might seem shifty. But you can probably tell if that is shyness or fear of you. If they meet your gaze and yet everything else shows unease, then something is amiss.'

'I understand.' She nodded vigorously, setting the little feather in her bonnet bobbing. 'You are looking for incongruity, of course. That is what one does with a text. What does not fit, what jars?'

'You were unused to small children, nervous, but you did not pretend to be anything else. You made a visible effort to be calm and cheerful with Jon, to respond to him.'

And she had not been interested in his title; he had

seen that almost at once. Prudence had been assessing him as a man she would have to spend a lifetime with and her recent experience had driven away any rose-coloured clouds about romance, leaving her clear-eyed and careful.

'You made a rapid decision also.'

'Men are not the only creatures with guts,' she said primly, then spoiled the effect with a gurgle of laughter.

A sense of humour. His wife had a sense of humour. She was going to find him poor company in that case if she wanted laughter and jokes and witty remarks. But she had friends and she could laugh with them, he supposed. And with Jon. His son would grow up knowing laughter as well as love with Prudence as his mother. Yes, he had made the right decision and in return he must learn how to give her the freedom she needed, the independence, not keep her caged in her role of marchioness and mother.

With a mental shrug he told himself that would require little effort. His ships needed his attention, his friends—the real friends that he would never introduce Prudence to—were there for him. He could trust Prudence to look after his home and his son when he was absent and not to trouble him when he was not.

'Time for luncheon and for Jon to take a nap,' Ross said as they approached the seat where Maud was chatting to another nursemaid. 'You will want to attack my library this afternoon, I imagine.' He thought she looked a little pale as they stopped and waited for Maud to disentangle herself from the other girl's charge, a boisterous toddler. 'Our library,' he corrected himself, thinking that perhaps she had felt snubbed.

'Yes, I look forward to that,' Prudence said.

That morning she had been almost unable to keep her hands from seizing books, making piles, reordering and bringing some logic to the library. Now she felt tired and curiously flat. Prue sank down on the nearest chair and looked around, wondering at her own lack of energy. It was not as though she had not eaten a pleasant luncheon of clear soup and cold ham followed by fruit and little cakes. It must be reaction, relief that she was safely married, that Ross did not appear to be Bluebeard and that Jon did not scream at the sight of her.

She certainly did not feel like translating and definitely not inclined to start moving books. What she needed was a plan, then she could enlist the help of two footmen and start organising. Prue found four sheets of paper, a pencil and a ruler and made a drawing of each wall with the bookcases, windows and doors marked in. She shaded out Ross's bay of shelves and studied the result. Theology should go at the beginning, she decided, and if the arrangement was clockwise, then the bay on the right of the door was the place for it.

Theology, philosophy—or philosophy before theology? This was more complicated than she had expected. Papa's library was not in a particularly logical order, but books were together by subject. This collection was much larger and cried out for proper organisation. Prue took more paper and went to curl up in the big chair by the cold fireplace. A list of subjects first, that was the logical way to go about it. A list and then she could organise that and then she would have a plan. She yawned. Perhaps if she just rested her eyes for a moment...

Prue woke, stiff and cold and feeling no better than she had before she sat down. And she had not made a single note either.

When she had dragged herself upstairs, forced smiles and chatter for Jon for half an hour and then changed for dinner, she wanted nothing more than a long soak in a hot bath followed by bed. What she was faced with was a husband making polite and dutiful conversation throughout four courses of a magnificent dinner.

The staff had exerted themselves, she realised. This was their way of marking the start of the marriage. They would know only too well that their master and mistress had slept apart last night and would doubtless have attributed that to Ross's consideration for her after a long and exhausting day.

They were all trying so hard. The footmen, whose names she still had to learn, were in immaculate livery and Finedon was directing them as though the Regent himself was sitting at the head of the table.

Prue smiled and nibbled and sipped and made appreciative noises to the staff and meaningless conversation with her husband and would have cheered, if she'd had the energy, when she was able to hide the remains of her dessert under the spoon and could stand up.

'I will retire now,' she said. 'Please thank Cook for an excellent meal, Finedon.'

Ross rose, Finedon opened the door for her and she escaped.

Too tired for a bath now, she thought as she trudged upstairs. *Tomorrow.*

She waved away the frivolous piece of lace and satin Tansy had laid out. 'Something comfortable. Something warm.'

And finally was left in peace to curl up and sleep.

Prue knew almost as soon as she woke what had been wrong with her the night before. Her courses had begun. How had she not realised? she wondered as she got up and dealt with matters. She knew when she was due; she was normally very regular. She must have pushed the possibility that she was carrying Charles's child so far down in her thoughts that she had blanked it out entirely.

So how do *I feel?* Prue wondered as she climbed back into bed. *Other than pasty and bloated and thoroughly uncomfortable. I do not know. I just do not know.*

Tansy came in at half past seven and made sympathetic noises and sent for hot bath water and found an even warmer and older nightgown and tucked an unprotesting Prue back into bed.

'You need to rest,' she said. 'I'll bring hot chocolate for your breakfast and then you can be comfortable, my lady. Such a pity when you're so tired after the wedding and so forth.'

Normally Prue would have got up, taken some willow bark tea, gone for a walk and then got through the uncomfortable first day by burying herself in some work. She had never taken to her bed before and she felt guilty now. Just until after luncheon, she promised herself, then she must spend time with Jon and perhaps, by then, she would know how she felt about… about everything.

There was no sign of Prudence at breakfast, but then, he did not know her routine yet. Strange that after one full day of marriage to her he should notice her absence now. Ross demolished his own breakfast, gutted the trade and naval information out of three newssheets and scanned the political and foreign columns for anything that looked like reliable news about the French situation. He found little to trust and nothing that looked new.

Prudence had still not appeared so he went to see his son. She had not been to the nursery either and, when asked, Maud looked uncharacteristically shifty. No, he decided, she was embarrassed. 'No, my lord. We haven't seen my lady yet today.'

She wasn't in the library either, although he found four pages showing the arrangement of the library shelves lying on a side table. When he asked Finedon if Prudence had gone out the butler, too, looked uncomfortable.

'I believe Her Ladyship is still in her suite, my lord.'

Sick? he wondered as he climbed the stairs again. She had certainly seemed subdued last night. If Prudence was ill and no one had told him there would be hell to pay.

When he tapped and opened the door, Hedges appeared like a diminutive guard dog and stood in his way. 'Her Ladyship's resting, my lord.'

'She is sick?'

'Er...no, my lord.' The abigail was positively pink now.

Ross simply sidestepped around her and strode towards the bedchamber door. On shipboard or in his own home, nobody kept secrets from him.

Prudence pushed herself up against the pillows as he came in. She was drained of colour so that her eyes looked huge, her hair was loose on her shoulders, and she looked utterly miserable in the second before she got her expression under control and some kind of smile on her lips.

'You are sick. What is wrong?'

'I am not sick.'

'Of course you are. You look frightful.' He snatched up the hand mirror from the dressing table as he passed and held it up to her.

Prudence winced and pushed it away. 'Thank you, my lord. That makes me feel *so* much better.'

'So you admit you are ill. Hedges, tell Finedon to send for the doctor immediately.'

'Tansy, please do no such thing. If you could just leave us.'

'My lady.' He could feel Hedges's glare burning a hole of disapproval in his back, but the door shut.

'It is simply the time of the month,' Prudence said with a snap. Annoyance, or perhaps embarrassment, put two red dots of colour on her cheeks. 'And for some reason it is making me feel very uncomfortable this time. I will get up this afternoon and go to Jon. I have no intention of neglecting him.'

Wonderful. Now he felt a complete brute, as, presumably, he was meant to. 'Of course you would not and his nurse can always bring him in here later for a few minutes to save you any discomfort.'

For a moment he thought she was simply going to nod and dismiss him, then her lower lip trembled, just a little, and she bit down hard to stop it.

'For pity's sake!' Weeping women he was used to and could disregard, largely by ignoring the storm and removing himself until it had blown over. Honoria would resort to tears when all other methods of persuasion failed, largely, Ross suspected, because she was wary of making her eyes and nose unbecomingly red. Prudence was perfectly all right, she had her woman, she was warm and safe, he told himself.

What he was not used to was the sight of his wife fighting back the tears and it stopped him in mid-turn towards the door. Ross sat down on the edge of the bed and took a long, hard look at Prudence's face, her eyes. 'It is not only the discomfort, is it? What is wrong? Are you distressed because you are not with child?'

The struggle between denial and confession was obvious and Ross thought her stubbornness was going to win, then that betraying lip trembled again.

'I don't know,' Prudence blurted out. 'I do not know whether I am relieved or sad, happy or mourning. If I wasn't feeling so…' She flapped her hand in the direction of her stomach. 'It isn't *that*. I always feel a bit uncomfortable, a bit emotional, for a day, then everything is fine. It never keeps me in bed—it just makes me sore and grumpy for a while. But this time I feel overwhelmed.'

'You wondered whether you would feel different about a child because of who its father was, how it was conceived. But now you know there is no child you still feel confused, but perhaps relieved. And guilty because you *are* relieved?'

'Yes. Oh, you understand, don't you? I didn't think you would. Yes, I am sad and thankful at the same time and guilty because I feel like that.' Her teeth closed hard on her lip again and something in Ross snapped.

'Come here.' He pulled her into his arms, probably too roughly, he realised as she gave a startled gasp. 'And stop biting your lip.' He loosened his hold a little and felt her shoulders shake. 'And cry if you want to. This is an old coat.'

She said something that muffled against his chest.

'What was that?' he asked.

'I do not cry. I never cry. I just get on with things. There is never any point in crying.'

'No, of course there is not. You just stay there not crying for a bit,' Ross said, as the front of his shirt became distinctly damp.

He became very aware that Prudence was warm and soft and that she was wearing nothing between his hands and her skin but cotton. Those wonderful curves, the ones he had been very careful to put out of his mind, were pressed against him and his body was informing him about the matter in no uncertain terms.

But she was clinging to him because she was distressed and trusted him and her very unselfconsciousness made it crystal clear that she was quite unaware of the effect she might be having on him. He might be a hard man, a cynic, an opportunistic scoundrel—he'd been called all those and worse in his time—but he did not take advantage of women. And he had promised. It was not her fault he was regretting that now.

Possibly she would come to regret it, too. Wishful thinking? Perhaps, but the problem was, how did they tell if that happened? He brooded on it while he sat silently holding her and gradually his arousal turned into something like very calm. If he told her he had changed his mind—that his appetite, as he had put it, had returned—she might feel threatened or she might feel obligated. Or both. And if she changed her mind then she was far too much of a lady to make that plain, he was sure. Or she would not want to risk a snub.

'Sorry.' Prudence wriggled free.

'That is quite all right.' He found a clean handkerchief in his pocket and passed it to her.

'Thank you.' She blew her nose with an unladylike vigour which was surprisingly endearing. 'You sighed and I do not blame you. An over-emotional wife is *not* what you agreed to.'

'I do not think you are over-emotional,' Ross said as he stood up. 'Your emotions seem more than appropriate to the situation. I sighed because of something else altogether, the recollection of an inconvenient undertaking I made. Rest now.'

So he was not to have a stepchild. He was not certain how he felt about that either and digging into his feelings was not a useful exercise, in his experience. Jon might have liked a brother or sister, though. If he and Prudence ever...

He needed to stay out of her company until he had himself under control, that was certain. Ross jogged rapidly down the stairs to the hall, startling Finedon.

'I am going down to the warehouse. I will be gone all day.'

'Dinner, my lord?'

'I will eat out. I have business to transact.'

'My lord, the hall is in some state of anxiety about the Corsican Monster and the threat of war. I promised to ask if you had any news on the subject, the newspapers being so inaccurate of late.'

If Finedon could not keep the servants' hall in order, then they must be working themselves into a state indeed. 'The word is that Bonaparte is having domestic troubles with his new constitution—I hardly think he is about to set forth to pillage Hanover Square.' Finedon produced a thin smile. 'And our allies the Russians and Prussians are advancing towards his borders in some force.'

'We may be spared war, my lord?'

'I very much doubt it. But you may reassure the staff

that I do not anticipate French troops to be marching down Whitehall.'

Ross took his hat and gloves from Giles, the footman, and hailed a hackney as he came down the steps. 'The Admiralty.' There was no reason to tell his household what his business was.

Chapter Eight

⁂

Prue slid out of bed and went to wash her face in cold water. She had told Ross the truth about rarely weeping, although to be honest she had not much cause to do so before. Charles had left her too frightened and angry for tears.

She certainly felt better now, whatever had caused that outburst, and Ross had been unexpectedly kind. Not that she thought he would ever be unkind, exactly, but she had not thought he would have much patience with a weeping wife. Not one who looked like she did, she thought after a despairing glance in the mirror at her red eyes and pasty skin.

If she got dressed, spent some time with Jon, which was sure to be soothing, and then spent the afternoon in the library that would make certain she was not burdening Ross with her megrims—or the sight of her looking plain enough to turn the milk.

Jon was adorable and they held a lengthy, and entirely incomprehensible, conversation, then played *This*

Little Piggy with his very pink toes before Mrs Goodnight came to give him a feed.

Yes, Prue decided, *he is quite enough for me at the
present*. But later? Would she feel the same next year?
The year after? What would Ross say if she told him
she wanted a child?

'Has the Marquis fled in the face of such a dangerous crowd of females?' Melissa asked.

A week after the wedding Prue's four best friends
had come to luncheon and to spend the afternoon and
were gathered round the luncheon table like, Prue
thought with affectionate amusement, an illustration
of female variety.

There was Verity, the picture of a fashionable young
matron with her exquisitely cut gown disguising her
rounding figure. There was Jane, the eccentric Countess with a paint smudge among the freckles on her
cheek and charcoal traces on her expensive lace cuffs,
chattering about the series of oils she was executing
of her father-in-law's entire domestic staff. And then
there was Lucy, the quietest of them all, who sat smiling gently, her mind doubtless lost in music.

And finally there was Melissa, forthright as always,
with ink stains on her fingers and her gaze darting
with unabashed curiosity around the room. Prue was
resigned to the house appearing in whatever Gothic
novel her friend was working on now.

'Ross has business to attend to,' Prue said, passing
Jane the butter. 'He is away from home a great deal.'

In fact, she had hardly seen him since the morning she had wept in his arms.

'But he is a privateer and we are not at war with anyone at the moment, so he cannot be doing whatever it is privateers do,' Melissa objected. 'Not legally,' she added, looking interested.

Oh, no, not a pirate hero next...

'He has a number of ships and, when we are at peace, they are ordinary merchantmen carrying cargo. Managing them seems to take quite a lot of work, but I have not had the opportunity to ask him about it.'

'Do you mind about the trade?' Jane, usually tactful, asked.

'No. It is not as though we want to mingle with the kind of people who would be unpleasant about it. Besides, Ross is a marquis and outranks most of them. It was what he grew up doing, how he made his living. I do not think he would be very happy turning his back on that simply because some people would sneer at wealth that was not inherited.'

'But if we do go to war with Bonaparte then he will go back to being a privateer?' Verity asked. 'I have to say, I did not consider that when I introduced you.'

She looked concerned and that made Prue, who had not considered that likelihood before, anxious, too.

'Surely Lord Cranford will not go to sea himself?' Lucy said in her soft voice. 'It would be dangerous and he is a married man now.'

'He was married before while we were still at war,' Prue said, trying to ignore a chilly feeling in her stomach that was warring with the cold salmon. 'But I do not know whether he actually sailed and took command after the wedding.' She would have a small wager with herself that he had. She could not imagine Ross sitting safely on shore while his men fought for his profit, or while he could strike a personal blow against the French. She had no doubts at all about his patriotism or his courage.

She would have to ask him. It might seem as though she was fussing, but a wife was entitled to know if her husband was about to put himself in deadly peril, wasn't she?

'You say he would not be happy to give up his ships and his trade.' Melissa attacked an apple with a sharp knife as though it was trying to fight back. 'But he does not appear to be very happy now.' She ignored her friends making shushing noises and glaring at her. 'He never smiles. At least, I did not see him smile on his wedding day which, I admit, is the only time I have set eyes on the Marquis.'

'He is still in mourning,' Prue said.

'So he is in love with his first wife?' Melissa let the ribbon of peel slide to her plate.

'Melissa,' Jane hissed. 'For goodness sake!'

'I have no idea,' Prue said with what dignity she could muster. 'He has done me a very considerable favour by marrying me and I have no intention of be-having as though I have any claim on his affections. It is hardly as though this is a love match, now, is it?'

'Of course not.' Lucy was always anxious to smooth over ruffled feelings. 'And I expect he is not really dour. That scar must make it difficult, if not painful, for him to smile.'

Prue could almost hear the others taking a sharp intake of breath. She would have had another wager that they had agreed beforehand not to mention the scar.

'No doubt it does,' she agreed, sounding, to her ears at least, just like her mother. 'You look as though you are keeping well, Verity.'

The others all smiled brightly at this abrupt change of subject, but did not seem any less tense.

Of course, Prue realised. *Verity has told them that I am not carrying Charles's child and so they are tactfully not mentioning pregnancies either.*

She set herself to discuss babies with every appearance of ease and gradually saw her friends begin to relax.

'Jon is such a pet,' she said, without having to pretend in the slightest. 'Would you like me to have him brought down now we have finished eating?'

'Can we go up?' Verity asked. 'I am comparing nurseries with all my friends to make certain I miss nothing out for this one.' She ran one hand tenderly over the swell of her stomach.

Prue led them upstairs, confident that Jon would amuse and charm them in equal measure and that no one would even think of asking her awkward questions about her marriage in the nursery. Or if they did, Maud's presence would surely be enough to keep even Melissa quiet on the subject.

Jon proved an excellent host and had everyone entertained by making interesting sounds, waving his

---

well-chewed toy dog, laughing when tickled and even being so obliging as to open his mouth so that Jane could peer in and look for teeth.

'I think the first one is about to come through, my lady,' Maud said. 'At the front. Do you see the gum is a little red and he rubs at it?' She smiled ruefully. 'He won't be such a happy little boy when it becomes sore, will you, my little lordling?'

When Jon began to fret for his feed the party broke up. Verity had promised the Duke that she would go home and rest. Lucy and Jane were intent on shopping for music scores and art supplies and Melissa was bound for the library in Albemarle Street.

Prue saw them out, then went to her room to change her gown which had suffered a little from Jon's attentions. She felt much better for the visit, she thought as Tansy made repairs to her hairstyle. She had been assertive about her relationship with Ross; she had defended her husband against speculation—really, she had been the ideal wife, she decided. And now she would reward herself with a few hours organising the library.

She ran downstairs, her mind busy with tactics. She had decided on how she would order the books—now it was a case of finding everything on each subject and putting it in the right position. If she went along all the shelves and pulled all the philosophy books out by several inches, then the footmen could clear the first bay of shelves on to the library tables and move all the philosophy books into it. Then she would do the same for religion and so on until everything was all in its rightful place.

There were steps on wheels in the library so she pulled them into position, climbed to the top and set to work. It was a dusty business because, however good the housekeeping, climbing up to dust behind books that nobody had touched for years was clearly not a priority.

But it was fascinating because she kept finding treasures—very old books, titles she had never read and some with lovely bindings. Prue gave herself a severe talking-to about distractions, finished the first bay and, leaving it bristling with books half-pulled-out, moved on to the next.

The top shelf was all mathematics. Very dull, in Prue's opinion. Very dusty and somewhat nibbled along the top edges. She made a mental note to ask for mouse traps to be set. The second shelf down was equally dirty, and the books were jam-packed into the bargain, but she could see one gorgeous blue leather binding with ornate gilding down the spine and the magic name Homer.

Prue tugged, it resisted. She shifted her grasp, worried about damaging the spine, then pulled again. The books on either side flew out like corks from a shaken bottle of ginger beer. One hit her on the side of the head as the Homer came free and she toppled backwards, the heavy book clutched to her as she fell.

Even though it happened so fast, she was braced for the hard library floor. Landing on something that was not solid boards, but which gave as she hit it, cush-

ioned her and held her tight, was such a surprise that
she gave a startled yelp and dropped the book which
landed painfully on her foot.

'What the blazes did you think you were doing?'

Prue blinked, trying to work out why she was upright and not sprawled on the floor with a broken leg,
and realised that she was held very firmly in her husband's embrace. No, that was the wrong word. *Grasp*,
that was it, she thought dizzily. His hard grasp that was
certainly no longer yielding. Implacable was probably
the correct description.

'Organising,' she managed to say.

My goodness, Ross is strong.

'You could have broken your neck or your back.'

It dawned on Prue that she was being held by a
very angry man and that being angry made the scar
on her husband's face turn white. His teeth, bared in
what could only be described as a snarl, looked sharp.

'Thank you for catching me,' she said, with a gulp.
There was no point in being defensive—she could have
hurt herself very badly and she knew it. No wonder
Ross was angry with her. But that was not why she
was feeling so very disorientated. He was very close,
very large and he smelt exotic, of timber and oil and
spices. Her head was spinning.

'I apologise.' She found her forehead was resting
on his chest, that, somehow, she had stepped forward,
close against him and not away as she had intended.
'I realise this is not within the spirit of our agreement.
I am not going to be of much use to you if I break my
neck.'

She could feel his heart beat, hear his breathing, feel the tension rippling through that hard chest and strong arms. *Oh, my heaven. That is what is wrong with me. Not shock. I want him.*

'No use?' It was almost growled out. 'Look at me, Prudence.'

She tipped her head back and swallowed hard.

'Have you any idea what *use* you could be to me right now?' The heat in his gaze was no longer anger.

'Yes,' she confessed. Then, 'Yes?' She was not certain she knew how to be any more encouraging, but she leaned in a little more. 'Please.'

'My understanding was that marital relations were repugnant to you.' Ross did not sound like a man attempting to seduce a woman, far from it. But when she tipped back her head she could see the pulse beating hard in his throat, sense that this was not anger she could hear, harsh in his voice. Nor was she such an innocent that she did not understand what was happening to his body, now so tight against hers.

'And mine was that you had lost your appetite for them.' Prue swallowed. What was the worst that could happen? That he let go of her and she landed in a humiliated heap at his feet? 'It seems that we were both wrong.'

'Go to your bedchamber,' he said abruptly.

What? She was to be dismissed like a naughty child? Prue opened her mouth to protest as Ross released her, stepped away.

'Your bedchamber. Or mine. Or any bedchamber in the house. Unless you want me to take you here and now on the carpet. Or carry you through the house for the amusement of the servants?' When she still stood there he added, 'I will be with you directly.'

Oh. Prue left the room, her legs unsteady, and prayed she did not meet one of the staff. Her cheeks were flushed, she was certain of it. Her hair was coming down at the back, she was dusty… She probably looked as though they had been rolling about on the carpet, in truth.

Tansy emerged from the dressing room when Prue closed the bedchamber door behind her. 'I was just sorting through your linen, ma'am. Is there anything I can do for you? Your hair—'

'Nothing, thank you, Tansy. I am just going to lie down—to…to take a rest for a while. I will not need you until it is time to dress for dinner.'

'Ma'am.' Tansy bobbed a curtsy and left so speedily that Prue felt her cheeks heating again. Had she realised why Prue had suddenly developed a desire for a mid-afternoon nap?

Now what should she do? Lie down or—

The door opened and Ross came in, closed it, turned the key, then leaned back against the door. 'Unless you have changed your mind?'

'No.' It came out as a squeak, not the seductive murmur that she had hoped for. Something in his face softened as though she had amused him. 'Do you ever smile?' she blurted out before she could catch her own tongue. 'I mean…can you, or does the scar— Does it hurt?'

Silence. The resonating silence that followed a

woman making a crashing faux pas. *Not one, but two feet in it, Prue*, she thought. Apologise? Or not? Perhaps simply sinking through the floor or spontaneously igniting with sheer embarrassment would help.

And then Ross smiled. It wasn't the best smile she had ever seen, definitely lopsided with the scar dragging at the corner and he was hardly laughing, but it was a smile and one that reached his eyes.

'No, it does not hurt, Prudence. It is stiff, it feels awkward, that is all. You really are the most extraordinary woman.'

'The most tactless, certainly. I am sorry.'

'Why? Everyone else flinches at the sight of my face, pointedly looks away, seems frightened or disgusted. Or pitying. You, since the first shock of seeing it, have never shown anything but mild curiosity.'

'Why should I? It is not as though it is a raw wound or some horrible skin disease. I do not like to think about how painful it must have been, or how nearly you lost one eye, but there is no reason for disgust or pity. Certainly not for fear. But that might be the result of you never smiling, don't you think? Or the tattoo, perhaps.' She tried a smile of her own. 'That is a trifle sinister. Does it go further up your arm?'

'You could find out now, unless you have changed your mind,' he said again.

'No.' She found her hands had somehow knotted themselves together and carefully relaxed them. 'I had better say this, I think. I went with Charles willingly. He did not force me or hurt me, more than I believe it is always uncomfortable the first time. It *was* uncomfortable and it was not pleasurable, I imagine because he did not care to trouble to make it so. But I only look back on it badly because of him and what he was and what a fool I was to be deceived.'

She took a deep breath. It was easier to say this now she had begun. Now Ross had smiled. 'And you very kindly agreed to marry me and I thought that if that meant you never wanted me in your bed, then I would understand… No, I would not,' she corrected herself, determined to be honest at all costs. 'I would not understand because men usually do want that, don't you? But I would accept it because that was our contract. But as I have come to know you I have begun to think that perhaps it was a pity,' she finished saying in a rush, her gaze fixed on the faint smile that still lingered on Ross's lips.

'In that case, we will continue where we left off in the library and afterwards, if you wish, I will tell you why I said what I did when we met.' He moved a step nearer. 'Would you like me to draw the curtains?'

'No.' Prue shook her head. She wanted to look at him, see him. The result was that he would be looking at her, but men seemed to like her body, her breasts at least, so perhaps he would not find her unattractive, just not pretty like her friends. She gave a mental shrug; there was too much else to worry about, just at the moment.

'There is something a gentleman should always do first.' Ross sat on the end of the bed and reached down. 'Take off his boots.'

Prue kicked off her own shoes as he peeled off his

stockings. Should she undress? But she did not think she could reach the hooks at the back of this gown.

But it seemed that Ross knew all about tricky hooks. And tapes and, quite rapidly, how to unfasten stays.

But of course he does. He has been married and there must have been women before that.

Whatever he had been feeling when they had agreed to marry, she could not imagine him ever living like a monk.

She was down to her shift and her stockings when he stepped back and said, 'I am wearing too much.' Coat, waistcoat, neckcloth, shirt were gone and now she could see the whole tattoo. The eagle's leg, feathered above the skin of the claw, extended up his forearm where it stopped just before his elbow.

She touched the feathers with her fingertip. 'So beautifully drawn.' Under her hand his muscles tensed and she flattened her palm over the design, ran it up his arm. Sleek, hard muscles, the roughness of hair, another, neater, scar near his shoulder.

'Don't stop. I want your hands on me.' His voice was harsh and she found that arousing. *He desires me.*

She wanted—needed—to touch him, but it was puzzling. Men did not need caresses; they wanted something else entirely, didn't they? Why was Ross not in a hurry to be inside her as Charles had been?

But it seemed Ross spoke the truth. He stood there, naked to the waist, and let her run her hands up and down his arms, over his shoulders, down over his chest. The hair there was dark, curling. Not very thick. She could see his nipples, watch them harden as her finger-tips skimmed over them, hear his breath catch.

Prue let her hand follow the hair down, felt his stomach tighten under the caress as though bracing against a threatened, tickling, touch. She found his navel, dipped one finger in and was rewarded by a gasp.

'Unfasten my breeches.'

She had to look down to do that, shift her gaze from the middle of his chest to the evidence, very visible, that he wanted this. Wanted her. She was not usually clumsy, but her fingers felt like thumbs as she fought the buttons on either side of the flap at the front of his breeches. She got them open, held her breath as he pushed the breeches down and kicked them away.

There had not been time to look at Charles. Everything had happened fast and, besides, he hadn't undressed more than was absolutely necessary. Ross was the first real man she had ever encountered naked. In the Classical sculptures she had seen there were fig leaves, or the men were politely unaroused. There were the grotesques, of course, and the erotic art, but those had been grossly exaggerated. This was… *Impressive*, she settled on in her own mind. Then, *Goodness, I caused that?*

It was a startlingly arousing thought. Instinct made her touch, just a light skim of her fingers upwards, and surprise made her gasp. So soft and yet so hard. One she had expected, been braced for, the other…no, not at all. She snatched her hand away as though she had been caught touching something forbidden, but frighteningly tempting.

'Prudence.'

She looked up and found the smile had gone.

'Have you changed your mind?'

'No. Why would you think—'

He scooped her up before she could finish the question. She thought she heard him say, 'Thank God for that', between clenched teeth, then she was on the bed caged by his arms, imprisoned by his body.

Now was the time to be afraid. She expected it, braced herself for it and found that all she felt was need and eagerness and a vast ache of curiosity. This was nothing like it had been with Charles. This was so much more intimate, intense—and yet Ross had not touched her except to lift her.

Then he kissed her and every part of her curiosity, her reasoning, her intellect, shut down in the face of pure sensation, pure feeling. Charles had never kissed her on the mouth, never *tasted* her like this man was, as though she was a banquet he was devouring.

Ross's hand slid over her bare skin lightly, trailing shivers and quivers as it went, slid between their bodies, stroked her breasts…

Prue tensed. They were too big, she had always been sure of it. Men stared at them, Mama and dressmakers fought to cover and contain them, but Ross seemed enthralled by their curves, their weight. His thumb teased across one nipple and she cried out as he moved, took it between his teeth as she arched up into his hardness and heat and struggled to pull him closer, closer.

His hand moved again and, shameless now, she parted her legs as he stroked into the secret folds, into her and out, caressing and playing, teasing while she writhed beneath him. 'Yes. Now, Prudence, come for me.'

She did not understand him, but her body did. Overcome by sensation, blinded by light, her scream taken in by his kiss, she surfaced again to find herself clinging, panting to Ross's shoulders.

There were no words for it, no time to find them, to understand what had just happened before Ross was within her. Tightness, implacable maleness filled her, but no pain, not that sharp struggle she had felt before, that resistance as her body—so much wiser than her mind—had fought against Charles. She wanted this, wanted Ross, and opened her eyes so she could see him as well as feel him.

His eyes were open, too, but she did not know if he saw her. His face was taut as though in pain, its dark power and raw masculinity beautiful to her in a way it had never seemed before. Ross possessed her, but she knew, deep down in some essential female consciousness, that she had captured him. She held him within her as the waves overwhelmed her again and she cried out and shuddered against him.

Chapter Nine

A shaft of light, golden from the setting sun, cut across the ceiling. What time was it? Ross found he did not care and was too relaxed to do much about it in any case. The house was not on fire; there was no gunfire; no one was screaming… No need to move.

Beside him Prudence stirred and he tensed before she gave a little sigh and curled up more comfortably, her head tucked under his right arm, her nose against his ribs, her breath a soft tickle.

He should feel guilty. He had told her he did not require her to come to his bed and had not lasted even three weeks since that promise. But she had wanted him, too; he had not justified his actions by pretending that. Prudence had desired him and had reached for him again as they lay entwined after that shattering first climax.

She had seemed happy, he thought, turning his head to look down on the top of hers. All he could see was tangled mousy blonde hair, pale skin. He could feel her breath against his ribs, the swell of one breast just touching him. She had seemed so shy of those breasts, he thought with a smile that tugged uncomfortably at the scar. Entirely shy and yet so entirely frank about desire. Her honesty terrified him—he was not used to it and he doubted he could match it. Sooner or later he was going to disappoint her, as he had disappointed Honoria.

Or he would discover soon enough that she was not all she seemed now. It was pathetic, he told himself, this need to be wanted, to be...to be liked, to imagine his wife was an ideal that would, soon enough, be shown to be unobtainable.

Ross pushed away thoughts of his own scarcely acknowledged needs. Disappointing Honoria had taken less than three weeks. All she had seen at first was his title—somehow that had managed to eclipse the scar—and then she had found herself married to a man whose origins were the slum streets of the docks, who despised the title, despised the *haut ton* she aspired to even more, and who refused point-blank to stop trading, stop fighting, start being a marquis.

But ambition was a powerful thing and the first Lady Cranford had understood one thing clearly—if her husband was reckless enough to get himself killed before she gave him an heir, then she would be nothing, just the widow of a man whose title and possessions would go to a distant cousin. But if she was mother of his son, then she would have it all—the title, the money, the position and the status, all until the boy reached his maturity.

Ross eased up against the pillows. Uncomfortable thoughts were better when one was not flat on one's back, vulnerably naked. Discovering that one's wife firstly wanted you merely for stud purposes and secondly was looking forward to your demise with complacency, if not pleasure, was enough to kill desire in any man.

Fool that he was, it had taken him a while to realise why a woman who showed every sign of thoroughly disliking him still wanted him in her bed. Her triumph when she announced that she was with child, the eagerness with which she made it quite clear that she was now going to sleep alone, might simply be what any expectant mother might show—he had no experience there. But her smug relief when she presented him with a son cleared away the last of his illusions.

What his wife desired was to be left alone—and, if he could manage it, to be a widow. He was prepared to oblige her with the first—he found no more pleasure in her company now than she did in his—but he was damned if he was going to give her the second. They were wed and she would have to put up with it because he was not so sick of his life as to be careless of it.

But a man was less of a man if he forced himself on a woman. Or if he broke his promises. Holding those beliefs, he found it surprisingly easy to ignore the desire, to wall it up behind a barrier of honour and anger.

Honoria would have curled her lips at the thought that the East End boy might have grown up with any concept of honour. In her mind what she read into his scrupulous avoidance of her bed was weakness and that went some way towards lessening the fear she felt for him. Because fear there was, for his big, tough body, the slashing disfigurement of the scar, the terrifying world he came from.

Beside him Prudence stirred again, as though disturbed by his bitter thoughts. He could feel her waking, the moment when she took a long breath, smelt his skin, discovered that he was beside her. The instinctive tensing when she realised they were both naked, the deliberate way she made herself relax before she acknowledged that she was conscious. No coward, Lady Cranford.

'Awake?' Ross asked as he flipped the edge of the cover over his lower body. This was new for Prudence: she did not need to be reminded of the raw realities just yet.

'*Mmm.*' She pushed away from him a little, sat up, blushed and took hold of her side of the covers with a gesture that almost succeeded in being casual as she tugged it up over her breasts.

'Are you well?' he enquired gravely.

'Yes, thank you.' She was still blushing, but her voice was steady. 'Verity and Jane said it was good with the right person and they were correct.'

'I might not be the right person, merely your husband,' Ross offered, playing devil's advocate for some reason he could not fathom.

'You knew who I was,' Prudence said. 'You saw *me*, not just a female body in your bed. You did not forget who was with you. I think that matters.' She fiddled with the edge of the sheet. 'And you know what you are doing.' The colour flooded back into her cheeks.

'I should hope so,' he said, then caught the unspoken message. 'And the other man—he did not?'

'I am sure he did. I imagine that he has been with many women. But he did not care about me. He just wanted to do it, quickly, like someone who was hungry and greedy so gulps their food down.'

'Then let us hope he had indigestion,' Ross said as he got out of bed and found his clothes.

He dressed without looking at her, wanting to give her the privacy to collect her thoughts, compose herself. They were almost strangers and she had been, essentially, a virgin. It would take a while for her to become used to him. To this. He must be careful, give her the space and time to adjust, not see him as just another greedy man.

He went to the mirror, straightened his neckcloth and experimented with a smile. Was she right and he never smiled? Probably. He had found little to laugh about recently and he must have got out of the habit when the wound was still fresh and hurt like hell. He would try to remember to at least smile at his son.

'Shall I send your woman to you? No? Then I will see you at dinner.'

Prue twisted round to plump up the pillows, curled her arms around her knees, and then sat and stared at the gloomy landscape on the wall opposite. She had been intending to have it exchanged for something cheerful ever since she had moved into this room.

She pulled her thoughts back, made herself deal with what had just happened and not find a distraction.

That had been revelatory. Not painful, although it had felt uncomfortable for a little while: her husband was not a small man in any direction. *Melissa is right about feet.* But he had cared that she had found pleasure and it had been an unspoken dialogue, a conversation between their bodies, even though she could hardly speak the language yet. Prue gave a little wriggle and lay back, savouring the way her limbs felt heavy, her body felt sleek and relaxed.

How strange that it could be so good when there was no love between them. They had nothing in common except Jon; they had no conversation, no shared friends or acquaintance. And yet… She had persuaded a smile out of Ross and that must count as a wifely achievement. Or perhaps a friendly one. They were not in love, of course, but they could be friends if they both wanted it. Friends and lovers.

June 8th, 1815

Almost a month had passed since they had married, but little had changed. Some things, like Ross's regular visits to her bedchamber, she certainly did not want to alter.

Regular, she thought, but not frequent. Once or twice a week, enough for her to become more confident, to learn to touch and to reciprocate, to discover how to murmur encouragement for what she particularly liked, to read in Ross's reactions when she most pleased him. He had a particular weakness for having his back massaged, for her kissing her way down his spine...

From Verity's and Jane's little asides, the way their husbands were with them, it was clear that their love-making was far more frequent than that. Jane, laughing about something Verity had whispered to her, had let slip that Ivo was aiming to make love in every room in their home—in daylight.

But they were in love, Prue reminded herself. She and Ross had quite a different kind of marriage, one she should be grateful for.

The library was organised, her work was going well and she felt quite pleased with it. Ross always enquired politely over dinner—on the occasions when he ate at home—how it was progressing, but he never asked to read any of her translations. She had been on the point of asking him why, then realised that, unlike any other aristocrat, he had not been schooled by a tutor in Latin and Greek. His father had taught him a great deal, but surely there had been no room for Classics in a slum.

Matters were...*easier* with Jon, who held out his arms and gurgled with pleasure when he saw her. His grin was toothy now and more baby teeth were coming through, which made him a cross little boy sometimes, but still adorable.

Really, there was nothing to feel at all flat about now she had swallowed her bitter willow bark tea and settled herself in the comfortable library chair for some light reading from the small hoard of novels she had unearthed.

'Am I disturbing you?' Ross strolled in, leaning against the end of the nearest bookshelf.

The honest answer was, *yes*. Now she knew that tall, muscled body intimately, had grown used to the scar, the tattoo and even the rare smiles, Prue had to admit to herself that she found her husband very disturbing indeed.

She did not love him, she told herself—how could she; she hardly knew the man? But when she saw him there was this little flutter, low in her stomach. When he smiled, so very infrequently, something warmed inside her. It was not easy, remembering not to reach out and touch him as they passed unexpectedly about the house, or to kiss him good morning or goodnight. He never kissed her except when they were in bed, so he clearly did not expect it of her, she had decided. It would be pathetic to initiate a caress, as though she was desperate for him.

'Not at all,' she said now and put down her book. Then she saw *The Times* folded in his hand. 'Is it news about the war? Has there been a battle?'

The government had finally ended weeks of speculation and debate and had declared war on France on the twenty-fifth of May, although not a great deal appeared to have happened since. Certainly there had been no fighting reported.

'No, do not have false hopes that this will end peacefully.' Ross shook his head when she let out a sigh of relief. 'The fight will come, it is inevitable and it has been ever since Bonaparte reached Paris. I am picking up rumours down at the docks that he is beginning to move troops towards the frontier.'

He tossed the paper on to the table and sat down in the armchair opposite her, long legs sprawled out until his booted feet almost touched her own slippers. Almost, not quite. He was always so careful of her space. Or perhaps it was his own that he was defending against a casual, over-intimate touch. 'The army has been buying up horses—they say over six thousand. The armaments trains are on the move to the ports. The Channel coast defences have been reinforced by the militias. It must come.'

'You are right, of course. I have been reading the newspapers, too, but I suppose I keep hoping that Napoleon will see sense, realise how large the forces that are gathering against him are and negotiate.'

'The man sees this as his manifest destiny— he will not yield without a sword at his windpipe and perhaps not even then.' He sat up, pushing back the hair that had flopped over his forehead.

He needs a haircut, Prue thought, amused at her own wifeliness.

'What I came to ask was whether you would care to spend some time at the coast.'

'With war looming? Would we have to leave Jon here?'

'The coast is perfectly safe. Napoleon does not have a fleet capable of landing troops—besides, the navy has command of the Channel. The defences are being strengthened to reassure the public, not because anyone expects an invasion. I must go down in any case because I have business there, but this incessant rain has ceased at last and the weather looks likely to hold for a day or so. I thought the sea air and the change might suit you both.'

'I have never been to the seaside.' Naturally, if one's husband decided, then a wife was supposed to agree, whatever her opinions, but Prue rather thought that if she shook her head Ross would simply shrug. Duty done—he had taken the trouble to ask her. 'I would love to come and I am sure it will be good for Jon. Whereabouts do you wish to go? To Brighton?'

'No, Ramsgate. I have several ships there. Ships that I have been negotiating to put at the disposal of the army. The government has discovered that now they have, finally, found the steel to push through a declaration of war, they have a vast amount of supplies to transport.'

'You will sail with them? To France?'

Ross did not answer her for a moment, then he smiled, just a little. 'No, not to France. But I intend to sail to Ramsgate and I hope you will enjoy the little voyage along the coast. If you have never been to the seaside, then I imagine you have never been on a ship.'

'Sail there? Not go by road?' That was quite another matter. Prue had no idea whether she would be seasick, terrified or actually enjoy the experience.

'Why should we spend hours bumping over the roads and having to eat poor fare at wayside inns, when we can sail in comfort? You will find it a novelty, Prudence, and I will send the carriages down ahead of us to use when we are settled.'

When she hesitated he sat up as though to stand and said, abruptly, 'But I will be taking you away from your friends.'

Prue made up her mind. 'Not at all. Lucy and Melissa went home to their families days ago. Jane and Lord Kendall are visiting his grandfather near Bath. Verity and I had a vague plan to visit an exhibition at the Spring Gardens next week, but it was merely a suggestion.'

The truth was, with the others away she was reluctant to impose herself too much on Verity. The Duchess had a very full social life as well as her antiquarian interests and the plans she was making for the arrival of the new baby. Prue felt uncomfortable about monopolising her time and knew she should try to make her own friends, new friends. And that was easier thought than done when one was shy and married to a man who raised eyebrows simply by existing, one who made no secret of despising the very social circles that it would be acceptable for his wife to frequent.

Prue had decided that she must endeavour to find some charitable work to involve herself in. That, surely, would be an easier environment in which to make friends. And learned societies often allowed ladies to attend lectures—she might find others there to talk to if she went regularly. It did not appear to occur to Ross that she might need squiring about or that, if they did not entertain, then they would not receive invitations in return.

She had asked Tansy, who had been a housemaid

when the first Lady Cranford had been alive, if she had gone about much in society.

'Oh, yes, ma'am. She and Lord Cranford hardly ever went out together, so it seemed to me. She would say it was terribly middle class for husbands and wives to be in each other's pockets. She used to laugh about it. She had— What do you call them? *Cissie* somethings.'

'Cicisbeo,' Prue had said. 'A lady's trusted gentleman companion. Not a lover, someone her husband is content to allow to squire her about.'

'That's it, ma'am.' Tansy had hesitated, her hands still on the pile of fine linens she had been folding. 'I think she wanted to make His Lordship jealous, but he wasn't and that made her cross. I'm sorry, ma'am, I shouldn't listen to gossip in the servants' hall, let alone repeat it.'

Prue had thought it sounded rather sophisticated and very sad. At least the possibility of her attracting a string of faithful *gallants* was so improbable that she didn't even consider it.

'So you are at liberty to accompany me?' Ross asked and she realised that he had been waiting for her to make a decision.

'Yes, of course, I would be delighted at the adventure. And I will try not to be seasick,' she added, in an attempt at a joke.

'I doubt you will be,' Ross said. 'Fresh air is the answer for that.'

'Nelson was always seasick, so they say,' Prue murmured, but Ross was already standing up, so she did, too.

'When do you wish to leave?' she asked, as he turned away.

Ross swung back, their hands brushed and she froze, catching her breath at the unexpected touch.

If I reach out to him, curl my fingers into his...

They had both gone very still. Then Ross said, 'Tomorrow, after breakfast, if that would be convenient.' He sounded perfectly polite and, when she nodded, left Prue with the strong impression that he expected her to make it convenient. And that casual caresses outside the bedchamber were not welcome.

She pushed away the hurt of that and focused on being mildly irritated instead. Did the man have any notion of what was involved in packing for a small child for an unspecified length of time? Or for a lady, if it came to that. How long, what would they be doing—and what did one wear on a ship?

She rang for Finedon, informed him of what was happening. 'It occurs to me I should have asked Lord Cranford where we will be staying, for how long and how many of the staff he requires,' she said.

Finedon greeted the information with a murmured, 'Very good, my lady. His Lordship has a house very close to the harbour. There is a skeleton staff and I will send the rest with the carriages tomorrow with the required additional personnel.'

'Carriages?' How many did they own? she wondered.

'The town coach, the curricle and the travelling carriage,' he clarified as though she had asked. 'Shall I send Hedges to your chamber now, my lady?'

'Yes, thank you. I will go up now and inform Maud as well.'

And Jon would need his wet nurse, she realised. Maud had begun weaning him, but she had explained to Prue that it would be months yet before he no longer needed Mrs Goodnight. Perhaps they should all go by road, but instinct told her that for Ross introducing his son to his ships, to the sea, would be important.

Maud, thankfully, was quite calm about the prospect of a journey by sea and assured Prue that Mrs Goodnight would expect to accompany Jon wherever he went, either taking her own baby with her or leaving her with a relative. 'But I will start packing right away,' Maud said with a rueful smile. 'You would not believe how much luggage a baby needs, ma'am.'

Tansy showed rather more alarm when her mistress told her she had no idea how long they were going for or what she would be doing. 'I will pack for a month and for everything except Court appearances,' she said after puzzling for a while over the likelihood of full dress balls at Ramsgate. 'At least the royal family doesn't go to there, not that I've heard, anyway.'

Thank heavens for competent staff, Prue thought as she went down to pack up what she needed for her work. Then she paused, her hands full of dictionaries. Ramsgate, the seaside, the journey, would all be new experiences, new environments to be with Ross. What if she showed that she expected to be with him most of the time when he was not working? Showed that she would like him to squire her to concerts or to assemblies?

She sat down, chin cupped in her palm, and stared at a volume of Sappho's verse as though a Greek woman two thousand years dead might offer clues to a relationship with a nineteenth-century husband.

No, there was no help there, but perhaps she might improve things between them, make Ross her friend as well as her occasional lover, if she put her mind to it.

You have been too passive, she told herself. *You have a brain, Prudence. Use it. If you can untangle ancient Greek you can translate the modern male, surely?*

Chapter Ten

'All of this?' Ross stood on the pavement outside the house, fists on hips and no hint of a smile on his face, as footmen heaped baggage on to the coach that was to take them to the docks. 'The longest we might possibly be at sea is about seventy hours and the weather and tides are too favourable for that. This much luggage would take us to the Indies.'

'We have a baby,' Prue said. *Seventy hours?* She had thought it might be twelve at the worst. 'You clearly have no concept of how much luggage an infant requires,' she added with all the authority of someone who had only just discovered this for herself. 'And a nursemaid and a wet nurse. We have his food—'

'Yes, you mentioned the wet nurse.'

'Solid food as well. He is weaning, you see. Then he will need changing and washing, entertaining, keeping warm, somewhere to sleep, familiar toys so he does not become agitated—' The list that Maud had recited tripped off her tongue most convincingly, she thought.

'Enough.' Ross held up his hands in surrender, apparently unimpressed by this display of maternal expertise. But he did not say that Jon and his entourage must go by road, Prue noted. Her instincts about that had been correct.

Tansy, with a speaking glance at Prue, climbed up beside the coachman, leaving Maud, Mrs Goodnight, Jon and Prue to squeeze into the coach with Ross and the bag that Maud deemed necessary for the first part of the journey. Jon woke up as they moved off, opened his mouth and Maud promptly popped in his coral and silver teething ring. They were all going to be very glad of the contents of that bag before they reached Ramsgate, Prue thought.

Piccadilly, Haymarket, the Strand, Fleet Street and St Paul's were all familiar to her from sightseeing or shopping excursions, but beyond the cathedral she was in unfamiliar territory.

'This is the heart of the City,' Ross said. 'There's the Mansion House, the Bank of England, the Royal Exchange.'

She craned to see what he was pointing at, staring at the bustling streets full of soberly dressed men and far fewer ladies than she was used to seeing in the West End. Ladies did not generally come into the City unless escorted to their men of business or law or to attend the Cathedral: Mama had been very clear about that.

The streets narrowed, the crowds became more mixed, the shouts and calls of street traders louder. 'There is the Tower and the Royal Mint beyond it,' Ross said.

Suddenly, it seemed, the streets narrowed further, the dwellings became smaller, dirtier, shabbier.

Mrs Goodnight was asleep with the air of a woman who had learned to snatch it where she could, neatly and unobtrusively. Maud was absorbed with Jon.

'Is this where you grew up?' Prue asked Ross quietly.

'Close. It was a little further east of here, along the Ratcliff Highway. Less salubrious than this.' He glanced out of the window as a group of drunken men began to shout insults at each other, egged on by a slatternly looking woman holding a bottle. 'In the lodgings along here, you might get two rooms for a family if you were lucky.'

This was better than where he had grown up? Prue struggled with the urge to protest that he must be exaggerating. But this was not something anyone would jest about, let alone Ross. 'It must have been hard for your parents,' she said.

'It was easier when my mother was alive. She knew the area, was used to hardship, knew all the tricks and strategies to make life a little better. Even when they were not—' He broke off, glanced away. 'When she died my father had to manage without that almost instinctive knowledge. He did his best.'

Prue glanced at Maud, who was crooning a lullaby, engrossed in the fretful child. 'He must have loved her very much.'

'To give up his comfortable life, his status?' Ross's voice was flat. 'He did love her, I am sure, but I am not sure he anticipated just how thoroughly he would be cut off by the family, estranged from his world. There is much romantic talk about love between men and women as though it is something solid, enduring, when in fact— There are the dockyard gates.'

What had he been going to say? she wondered. There had been a bitter note to his voice, a question. How long would his father's love have lasted if his shocking wife had not died when she did? Surely he could have tried for a reconciliation with his family when that happened, if only for his son's sake. It was chilling to think that help, that forgiveness of the prodigal, might not have been forthcoming or that the love that had brought them together had withered like a starved plant in the brutal conditions.

Then she glanced at Ross's profile, that bleak, harsh face, and wondered. What if love had died even earlier and sheer pride had kept his father estranged from his family, had condemned the boy to a life in the slums?

She looked away, out of the window, so he would not see the pity in her eyes. 'My goodness, it is like entering a fortress. Or a prison, perhaps.'

'It is walled, it is gated and it is protected. There are goods worth thousands of pounds in the warehouses here,' Ross said as he dropped the glass down to speak to the man in a dark uniform who stood alongside. 'Good morning, Smithson. I'm taking out the *Dawn Ghost*.'

'Aye, my lord. I saw they'd brought her up to the East Wharf earlier. Smooth passage and good winds to you.' He touched his hat brim as he signalled to someone out of sight and Prue saw the gates swing open.

The carriage moved slowly along narrow alleyways between towering warehouses with, between them, occasional glimpses of water crowded with shipping. Carts pulled by horses, barrows pushed by sweating men, moved through the site like organised ants.

'It looks new. Clean and orderly,' she said, surprised.

'It is new and not finished yet. They are still building and I suspect this is only the first. London's port is thriving.' He sounded more relaxed now as he studied the scene.

Familiar ground, home territory, Prue thought as the carriage emerged on to the dock and drew up alongside a sailing ship. Ross got out, helped her down, then turned to assist the other two women while Prue studied the ship with a curiosity not unmixed with apprehension. It did not look very big.

She could see one row of wooden flaps above the line of the dock, then the height of the wooden side, whatever that was called, where there was a gap and the gangplank ended. The length from front to back—stem to stern?—seemed reassuring, but the height of the two masts made the little ship look worryingly top-heavy.

'What do you think of her?' Ross asked as sailors ran down the gangplank and began to gather up the luggage.

'Um… It's, um…tall,' she managed to say. Ross had worked hard for his ships, must be proud of them. She should show appreciation, but surely this could not be one of his privateering vessels—how would it fight?

'Yes,' he agreed. 'A good height and she carries a fine spread of sail.'

'And she is big enough to capture another ship?'

'*Dawn Ghost* is a brig. She's fast, manoeuvrable and the navy use a lot of them. The navy's brigs have thirty-two-pounders, but I use fewer and lighter guns—she only carries enough to deal with merchantmen. You do not seem very convinced, Prudence.'

'Oh, no. I am simply not used to ships at all and had no idea what to expect. She looks very smart.'

'She had better be,' Ross said ominously as he took her arm and guided her towards the gangplank. 'Up you go.'

There were no handrails or ropes, so she took a deep breath, walked up as fast as the steep slope allowed and found herself on deck being saluted by a grizzled man in a blue coat with brass buttons. 'Welcome on board, my lady. I'm Jonas Thwaite, the Master. Would you care to see your cabin, ma'am?'

'Yes, thank you. I had best see that the baby is settled.'

Thwaite summoned a sailor who opened a hatch. 'Just down the companionway, ma'am.'

That turned out to be a ladder. She really had to work out what everything was called on a ship.

'Through here, my lady. Main cabin's at the stern. Mind your head now.'

It was a miracle that Ross did not suffer from permanent concussion, she thought, because even she had to take care to duck under the beams. But the cabin was a pleasant surprise, with two portholes, a bunk, a table and chairs and chests of drawers roped down to the floor. No, the deck, Prue reminded herself.

Mrs Goodnight was perched on the bunk, feeding Jon, while Maud sorted through the baggage. 'They've put us in the cabin next door, ma'am. There's three bunks and a chest they've taken the lid off and tied down to be a crib. I'll just sort all this out so we can leave your things and we will be out from under your feet.'

'Bunks? Do they expect us to be *sleeping* on board?' Somehow she had not imagined that. Or sailing in darkness either.

'Well, we might, ma'am. And you might want to lie down and take a rest. Or you might be seasick.' Prue's expression must have been betraying because Maud added hastily, 'Not that I expect you will be, ma'am. But just in case.'

'But I have just realised—what about your own daughter, Mrs Goodnight? Where is she? How thoughtless of me not to have considered her.'

'No need to fret, my lady,' the wet nurse said comfortably, shifting Jon from one side to the other and setting her bodice in order. 'I left her with my sister, Jane. She has a daughter just a bit younger. She loves being with her aunty.'

'Oh. Good.' Prue blinked a bit at this cheerful swapping around of infants, but Mrs Goodnight seemed quite happy about it, so she supposed it was not an imposition. 'I am going outside,' she said as Tansy came in with two seamen carrying the rest of the luggage. 'You all rest or come out as it suits you. The sea air will be safe for Jon, will it not, Maud?'

'Oh, yes, my lady. He'll enjoy it and seeing the sea, I'll be bound.'

Which was more than she might, Prue thought, making her way out on deck. What if she was sick? She rather thought that as the wife of the captain and owner she would be expected to be a fine sailor.

Once she was back on the deck she found a pile of crates lashed down under tarpaulins by the main mast and took refuge beside it, hopefully out of the way. There were at least a dozen sailors moving purposefully about the deck, hauling on ropes, climbing the rigging. The gangplank came in with a clatter, the gap in the side was closed and ropes were thrown on deck from the wharf. It seemed they were about to leave although how, with no sails hoisted—and no wind in any case—she had no idea.

Prue looked for Ross, then sat down with a bump on the nearest crate when she saw him. He was wearing loose trousers like the sailors, a shirt open at the neck with a neckcloth and a blue coat like the Master. And his feet were bare.

They all had bare feet, she realised. It must be to help grip on wet planking or when they were climbing. Then she saw his face and realised that Ross looked almost happy. He was taking command and had shed the uncomfortable trappings of being the Marquis of Cranford. Now he was simply the captain of the *Dawn Ghost* and was clearly very much at home.

The ship began to move and she saw that there were ropes over the side, men were hauling from the wharf and, when she got up and looked down at the water, two boats with rowers were towing them towards an improbably small opening in the side of the dock.

Ross was at the great wheel, the Master was peering over the pointed bit at the front and shouting incomprehensible things, then the rowing boats dropped the tow lines and the *Dawn Ghost* slid into the narrow gap as though she had been greased.

Prue stayed where she was as they emerged into the Thames, the sails were hoisted and the ship began to move, although she stayed standing up, uncertain whether she should be sitting there. Then she realised that Ross was at her side.

'I am not in the way here?' she asked.

'Not at all.' He leaned against the stack of crates, his gaze on the passing banks. 'We caught the turn of the tide perfectly. See how fast she's moving, even though there is hardly any wind.'

Prue glanced up, saw that only two sails were hoisted and they were almost flapping, not tightly filled. 'Goodness.' She clutched her hat and steadied herself by grasping Ross's arm. 'That is a long way up.'

He stiffened and for a moment she thought he would free himself. 'Dizzy? I almost jumped overboard the first time I was told to get aloft. Just looking at it made me feel ill. You soon get used to it.' He settled himself with his feet apart and then, to her amazement, put one arm around her, holding her close. 'Warm enough? The breeze on the water is always cooler than you expect.'

'I am all right at the moment.' Prue let herself relax against his side, shaken by the unexpected gesture. It was rare for him to touch her outside the bedchamber, let alone offer a gesture which might be taken for affection. Yes, he was happy, in his element, in command of his world, that was what was different.

'Do you still climb the mast?' she asked.

'Of course.'

Before she could protest he had released her, walked to the side, jumped up and was climbing the mesh of ropes that slanted upwards.

Prue clamped her lips tight on a yelp of protest. One or two of the crew looked up, grinned, then went back to their work as their captain passed the first horizontal pole, or whatever it was called, that held the biggest sail, then the second, then, impossibly high to her eyes, the third.

He came down fast, hand over hand, and landed back on deck with a solid thump. He looked windblown, tough, excitingly dangerous and a jolt of desire hit her.

'What a pirate you look,' she said severely, to cover her reaction.

'Privateer,' he corrected, then grinned at her. 'Did I frighten you? You are quite flushed, breathless.'

No wonder! That casual, crooked grin, those muscles, the bare feet...

'Goodness, no. I was just holding my breath. I suppose I was a little bit apprehensive.'

There was a look in Ross's eyes that suggested he recognised more than nervousness in her expression. Recognised it and responded. Prue was not certain she was capable of dealing with that, not here on deck in front of a crowd of sailors. 'Oh, what a beautiful building! What is it?' She pointed over his shoulder and Ross turned.

'The Royal Naval College and the Queen's House beyond it. Greenwich Observatory at the top of the hill.' When he looked back at her that flash of heat had gone.

Prue was not sure whether to be relieved or annoyed at her own cowardice. She had wanted to become close to Ross, but at the first sign of it she had backed away. But it had been desire she had seen, not any change in the way he felt about her as a person. Desire would not last, she told herself.

For a moment there he had thought he saw something in Prudence's face, something he had not realised he wanted to find in his wife. When he had touched her it had been simply to steady her. He had felt her stiffen, as she always did when he touched her outside the bed-chamber, but this time, instead of respecting that, he had gone with his instincts and pulled her close, felt her soften against him. And then he had succumbed to a juvenile urge to show off and had climbed the rigging.

When he had come down he thought she had been excited, aroused even, but of course, that was not the case. The next moment she was asking about the Naval College, finding an excuse to move away from him.

'I must check some details,' Ross said and walked towards the wheel. There were no details to check, everything was under control, except, it seemed, his imagination. Or his feelings.

When one of the crew shot out of his path like a scalded cat he realised he was frowning. Scowling, probably—the scar had a tendency to exaggerate expression.

He stopped by the leadsman who was checking the depth of the channel and stared out at the widening river. The West India docks were coming up ahead, just before the turn at the Blackwell Reach, and the river traffic was denser again here.

Plenty to concentrate on, plenty to think about besides his wife. He desired her and that desire was returned in bed with more than simply dutiful submission. Prudence was sensual, responsive and showed every sign of enjoying that part of their marriage. That was excellent, more than he had hoped for.

But he did not want more, he told himself, and he was sure she did not either. Perhaps, like him, she knew instinctively that she did not want to risk any emotional involvement.

Prudence did not touch or cling, did not appear to want kisses or caresses when they were not in bed. Her responses to his questions about her translation were polite, but hardly gushing—she clearly did not wish to confide in him or discuss her work. And that was perfectly all right with him—he had no desire to bring his business concerns home to her. The doubts and questions that were beginning to plague him about his life were things he could deal with himself, alone, just as he always had.

So what was he looking for just then, when she had turned those speaking eyes on him? Not friendship, surely? A man did not make friends with his wife, for goodness sake.

But then he had never known a woman like Prudence. She did not seem to need him at all. Yes, she deferred to his opinion when she asked about a domestic matter. Yes, she welcomed him to her bed. But she appeared to be quite self-contained, quite content to go her own way, live her own quiet, busy life without him.

He had wondered if she would be lonely, but Prudence showed no signs of moping. He was used to loneliness. She, he thought, was not, but clearly she was self-sufficient.

All of that was satisfactory, Ross thought. He could dismiss his wife from his mind again, concentrate on navigating the *Ghost* down towards Tilbury. Instead, he found himself looking for her, felt a flash of something like panic when she was not where he had left her and then he found her again, standing with Hedges and Maud. As he watched she took Jon from the nursemaid, hands confidently under his arms, kissed him on his laughing face, then tucked him in against her breast.

He had been right to marry again so quickly. Jon would never know he had been without a mother. One who loved him. Because there was no mistaking that look when Prudence saw the boy, reached for him. His son was hers now and he realised with another jolt—today was providing them with uncomfortable regularity—that she might be carrying his child soon. He was taking no care to prevent it.

She had been sad when she discovered she was not with child before, even though it would have been fathered by the swine who had betrayed her. And there was the next jolt, the anger he had not felt before. He had been disgusted when he had heard Prudence's story, of course he had. The man was a disgrace. But it had not been personal. Now it was. He needed to know who that man was and to punish him, make the sorry excuse for a human wish he had never been born. But Prudence did not want him to know.

So which took precedence? *My wishes or hers?* Ross pondered as he found himself crossing the deck to his wife's side. Hers, he decided, unless he stumbled across the truth anyway, in which case it would be a pleasure…

'Come up to the bows,' he said, putting one arm around both his wife and his child. 'Hedges, fetch a warm cloak for your mistress. Smith, put one of these crates up for'ard as a seat.'

Prudence let him lead her, settled herself with her back to the foremast with Jon on her lap and smiled up at him. 'I think I like your world,' she said with a chuckle that made Jon laugh, too. 'At least, I do with the sun shining and no big waves.'

Yes, it was a day for receiving jolts. That one had been right over the heart.

Chapter Eleven

It was magical, slipping down the widening river in the sunshine, her husband by her side, Jon asleep in her arms, warm under the cloak Ross had enveloped them in.

Greenhithe, Northfleet and Gravesend went past, then Tilbury Fort that was standing when Queen Elizabeth had ridden here to rally her troops in the face of the Armada, then the final bends before Ross said, 'This is the estuary now.'

Prue asked questions now and again. When would he have all the sails hoisted? Why did he need that man measuring the depth if this was such a well-used river? Was this where the English navy fought the Dutch and, when the wind whipped up and she pulled the cloak tighter, didn't his feet get cold?

That made Ross laugh. He wore boots when necessary, he explained. Then Maud came and took Jon and still Ross stayed beside her.

'Should you not be steering it?' she asked as the

wind became stronger and proper waves appeared. Spray flew through the air, the sails snapped tight.

'*Her*, not *it*. Ships are always female. And Thwaite can sail her perfectly well without my interference.' His hand was warm where it rested on her shoulder.

'Why are ships female?'

'Because they are beautiful and strong and occasionally very contrary.'

One finger began to stroke up and down her neck. Prue suspected that Ross was unaware that he was doing it and leaned into the touch a little. She gave a snort of displeasure as she was certain she was expected to. 'Contrary? Hah!'

Ross did not rise to it. 'Canvey Island.' He pointed to the north shore. 'The Isle of Grain coming up ahead to the south. Then we will pass between Sheerness and Shoeburyness and we'll be at sea.'

'*Ness* means nose. I think it's a Viking word,' Prue said, pleased to be able to apply some of her learning to this new world. 'Imagine the Vikings sailing up here in those long boats with dragons on the front. And the Romans. And now us.' She shivered. 'Just as long as it is not the French.'

'No chance of that. Are you cold?' When she shook her head he pulled her to her feet. 'Walk up and down, begin to get your sea legs. We will have something to eat soon.'

Finding some sea legs was as difficult as it sounded, although they all tried to master the knack of walking without lurching into a run, or tripping over their own feet. Mrs Goodnight announced that she was staying down below out of sight of that 'nasty wet stuff', but she was munching happily through the basket of provisions she had brought, 'just to keep my strength up', so Prue did not try to persuade her on deck.

She felt much better out in the air, the smell and the motion down below making her feel peculiar after a minute or so, and both Tansy and Maud agreed with her. They settled into a nest of cloaks and rugs among the stacked crates, Jon secure in the middle, and there they stayed.

Prue ate a bread roll filled with cold meat, then an apple, and drank some cold tea, wondered for a moment whether that had been wise, then fixed her gaze on the horizon while her insides decided to co-operate.

'Come and try the wheel,' Ross said when he found her clutching the foremast with one hand and trying to control her bonnet with the other. 'I'd take that off, if I were you. It catches the wind like a sail.'

It felt decidedly daring to be out in public without a hat, but on the other hand, Prue reasoned as she eyed the distance she had to navigate to reach the wheel, a ship was hardly *public*.

She managed it with a rush and a stagger; the man at the wheel touched his forelock and stood aside and Ross made her stand in his place.

'One hand here, one here. I've got you.'

And now she was sandwiched between him and the wheel, the spokes warm and hard in her hands with Ross's curled over them, his body a sheltering bulwark behind her.

'Ross! I don't know what to do.'

'Look at the compass. See? That is the course we're steering now. Now watch the sails. They are full, pushing us along because the wind is just right. If it starts to push us off course we correct, like this.' She felt the pull, the resistance as he moved the wheel. 'But if the sails start to flap then we have to decide whether to tack or to alter sail somewhat.'

He talked as they went, moving the wheel, explaining all the time why he was doing what he was doing.

'You are a good teacher.' She indulged herself a little, leaning back against him. 'I like your world. I like this.'

'Fair-weather sailor,' Ross said, his breath warm on the chilled skin of her neck.

Prue twisted round to look up at him and he bent his head and kissed her, hard and fast, then he was looking forward again and she was panting, just a little.

'You are prejudicial to good discipline, Lady Cranford, flirting with the helmsman like that,' he said. 'You will have us running aground at this rate.'

'I think someone would notice before it became that serious.' She gave a teasing jab back with her elbow and heard his quick gasp of a laugh. 'I can see why you love this. It is wild and free and yet it is a constant puzzle, problems to be solved, calculations to make. Very satisfying.'

'It is,' Ross agreed. 'As a boy I ran away and went to work on the Thames barges and the lighters. I never wanted to come back to land. I am still not a landsman and crops and flocks and estates are as much a mystery to me as sailing this ship would be to the average member of White's Club. Go and sit for a while, Prudence, you will have aching muscles if you work this wheel much longer.'

'You are doing all the work.'

'Just guiding you.'

'Come and sit with me—talk,' Prue said. 'Please? Cannot someone else steer?'

'Then come up to the bows again.' Ross signalled to one of the sailors who came and took the wheel, exchanged a few words that might as well have been in ancient Egyptian to Prue's ears except for *red sands* and took her hand to steady her along the deck.

They passed Maud, dozing among the crates with Jon in her arms, and Tansy, who was knitting something blue and complicated.

'What do you wish to talk about?' Ross asked once they were settled.

'Tell me about running away to the ships.'

'That was an exaggeration. I found work on one of the Thames lighters—they are the flat-bottomed boats that take cargo from ships moored out in the Pool of London to the wharves.'

'I thought ships went into the docks now?'

'Not all, not yet. You couldn't get anything much bigger than the *Ghost* into the London Dock, although the new ones downstream will take larger ships. But not every master wants to pay dock fees—some feel safer from theft in mid-river, others do not want the authorities taking too close a look at their cargoes. It is hard work, but it taught me a lot about the river, the tides—and the business. My father died. I moved on to the sailing wherries, then hoys, then ships, small ones at first, then coastal traders. I saved every penny I could, went into partnership on a battered old skiff with a friend. Built it from there.'

He made it sound straightforward; Prue suspected it had been anything but easy. 'How did you become a privateer?'

'We came across a French trading brig aground on a sandbank. We, with perfectly good intentions, came in to help. They fired at us—we took that somewhat amiss and retaliated. As we were smaller, shallower and handier and their captain was dead drunk—hence the grounding—we took them. Got her afloat again, brought her in and didn't look back.'

'And your partner?'

For a moment she did not think he would answer, then Ross said, 'Dead, three years later. The same fight that gave me this.' He touched his scarred cheek. 'He had no family. We had agreed whichever of us went first, the other took the business.'

'And then you inherited the title. I should tell you that the Duke told me the background to that.'

'I imagine he did. Your friends would not have introduced us without investigating my background.' He said it without, she thought, any resentment. He would expect her friends to take care for her.

Ross lent back against the mast and closed his eyes, listening to the water against the hull, the snap of sails, the song of the wind in the rigging. All as familiar as the beat of his own heart, but with it, Prudence's breathing, the rustle of her skirts beneath the cloak. She was a restful companion. He considered the word. Yes, *companion* was fitting. She was good company, questioning but sensitive and easy to talk to. He had never found it easy to talk to anyone except the men who shared his world of the sea.

'Can you tell me about your wife?' Prudence asked and his eyes opened abruptly.

'Why?' It came out as a snap. 'I told you I did not love her. There is no cause to—'

'To be jealous? Of course I am not.' There was the echo of the snap in her own response. 'But it is like living with a ghost in the house. I would find it much easier if I knew a little about her, that is all.'

'She was Lady Honoria Gracewell, elder daughter of the Earl of Falhaven.'

'How did you meet?'

'I knew I had a responsibility to marry *suitably*. To father an heir. Just as I had to learn to manage the estates. I went to all the right places to meet eligible young ladies, spent a great deal of money at the fashionable tailors and I received a very ambiguous welcome.'

Prudence gave a little huff of amusement. 'I imagine you did. A marquis should always be acceptable. But one with your background and that dramatic scar, which I imagine was more obvious then—that must have agitated the hen coops!'

At least she did not pretend not to understand. 'I scared the young ladies. I shocked most of the matrons when they realised just where I had grown up. But there are some in the Marriage Mart who are not so…nice in their requirements. The title and the money is enough.'

'Especially if they have not taken in a Season or so?' Prudence enquired innocently.

'Quite.' Ross closed his eyes again, went back in his mind to those hot, crowded ballrooms, those gay, noisy soirées where smiles and flirtation hid a desperate need to make a good match, land the right catch.

'Her father was dubious about me, but her mother was avid for the match. Honoria seemed attractive enough, intelligent enough. Then I began to believe, after we were married, that Honoria had ice water in her veins, not blood. It became quite clear that she would have married just about anyone if he had the title, the money.'

'And when you were married to her you found that living with her was more difficult than you imagined?'

'Not at first,' Ross admitted. 'At first she was—' He glanced around to make certain they were not overheard. 'She was passionate, surprisingly so. She conceived within four months of the wedding day and clung to me, most flatteringly. She was not well, she needed me, she was frightened when I went to sea.

'It was not until Jon was born that I realised just what was in her mind. She stopped clinging, she positively encouraged me to go to sea again—it was my patriotic duty. At first I thought her coldness in bed was because her experience during the birth meant she recoiled from risking becoming pregnant again. Then I heard her talking with her mother and it became clear just why she was so triumphant about giving birth to a boy. The heir. Why she wanted me at sea again and in the way of all that French shot.'

'The mother of an underage, fatherless heir has a great deal of power,' Prudence said slowly, working it out. Then she sat up straight, hands clenched into fists. 'The...*witch*. You can go and get yourself patriotically killed so she doesn't have to live with her East End Aristocrat any longer and she has the title, the use of the money, the freedom. Oh, I could box her ears.'

She swivelled round on her perch so she could look at him. 'How horrible for you.' She was fierce now. 'It is one thing making a convenient marriage if you are both open and honest about your motives, but this? Horrid creature. What happened to her?'

Prudence's immediate support, the way she leapt to his defence, shook him. Why he should have supposed that she would think him simply a suspicious husband ready to blame his wife for their unsatisfactory marriage, he did not know.

'It was foolishness, ill luck. She insisted on going with a party of pleasure to Vauxhall, by boat. It rained, she became thoroughly chilled, the infection settled on her lungs... It happened so quickly I do not think anyone realised just how ill she was, not even her. I should have realised—her parents certainly thought so.'

Prudence was silent, then she surprised him. 'Poor woman. She never lived to see her son grow, never lived to have the chance to see that she was married to a good man...' She sighed. 'What will you tell Jon as he grows up?'

'When he is old enough, simply that his mother became ill and died, nothing more.'

'Yes, it would be unkind to let him suspect for a moment that he was not the product of a happy marriage,' she said thoughtfully. 'When he is a little older we can begin taking him to place flowers on her grave, then he will grow up hearing her name even before he understands he has lost her.'

'That is kind of you.'

She gave him a frank, almost reproving, look. 'It is easy for me to do and I am happy to share him with a memory we can create for him.'

'I should have said *generous* as well as kind.'

'You think I should be jealous of her? You never loved her—and we do not have a love match anyway, you and I.' She shrugged. 'So what is there to be jealous of?'

There was no answer to that, Ross realised. Right from the beginning he had valued Prudence's forthrightness, her lack of wiles. He had not been looking for a love match—so why did it feel like a slap to have it pointed out that, whatever this marriage was founded on, it was not love? He was suffering from hurt pride, presumably. What a coxcomb he must be to be surprised that a woman was not falling in love with him when he had no intention of reciprocating the emotion!

Then his focus sharpened on his bare feet, on the tattered canvas trousers flapping around his ankles, on the savage tattoo on his hand. He was forgetting who he was, where he had come from and the fact that what he looked like meant his wife could never forget it.

'Where are we?' Prudence asked. She sounded sleepy.

Ross stood up, shielded his eyes to study the shore. 'Whitstable just ahead. The wind is holding up for us. We should be in Ramsgate not long after dark. Why not go and sleep, join the others in their nest?'

Prudence nodded, so he held out his hand, pulled her to her feet and steered her to the main mast. He waited, watched as she spoke to the other woman, kissed Jon who blinked sleepily at her, then curled up without fuss in the shelter of the crates.

'That's a lovely lady you have there, Cap'n, if you don't mind me saying so.' Thwaite joined him when he moved to the stern. 'Nice word and a smile for everyone, makes no fuss about making camp on deck—and she's a pleasure to see with the little lad.'

'Yes, I was more fortunate than I deserve, Jonas.' Ross took the telescope out of the Master's hand and studied the coastline. 'A fair bit of shipping about.'

'And all of it ours and most of it taking cargo to our troops.' Thwaite scowled. 'They should have shot that murderous scum Bonaparte when they had him instead of leaving him loose to slaughter more of our lads.'

Thwaite had lost his two sons, one in the Peninsula at Vittoria, the other in the last days of fighting as the Allied forces struggled over the Pyrenees into France. His wife had pined away with grief and died only a few months ago.

'Aye, the Allies should never have trusted his honour to stay put,' Ross agreed. 'But we will hammer the nails into his coffin this time.'

'I've a mind to go and volunteer,' Thwaite muttered. 'Some of the lads are saying the same thing. Give them Frenchies a taste of our cutlasses, see how they like that.'

'You are doing more good here, keeping supplies moving,' Ross said as mildly as he could. He didn't want to fire up the old hothead, give him an argument and have him plunging into God knew what, getting himself killed out of sheer pig-headedness. 'That is why I am going to Ramsgate. I've an agreement with the army to carry troops or armaments over to Ostend. Horses, even, if we can build the stalls. If we do that, then I am going to need to have someone at the helm who knows what he's doing and that is you.' When Thwaite simply grunted, Ross thrust the telescope back at him. 'I'm relying on you, Jonas, just like I always have.'

'Aye aye, Cap'n.'

The old devil would sulk now, as only a surly old sea dog could, but it wouldn't stop Thwaite doing his job, he hoped. If he thought Ross would risk him, or any of the younger men, getting blown to smithereens in some Belgian turnip field, then he had another think coming.

Chapter Twelve

Prue woke to find the sun setting and *Dawn Ghost* battling into a confused and choppy sea.

'Is it a storm coming?' she asked the ship's boy who brought them tea strong enough to take the glaze off the mugs.

'Oh, no, ma'am. This is nothing to worry about. We're just meeting the Channel here, so it gets a bit rougher, you see, what with the North Sea hitting the Channel head-on, as it were. That's Margate over there—you can see the lights. We're going to round the North Foreland, then things will calm down, don't you fear. Then we slip down to Ramsgate harbour, all safe and sound.'

'I will take Jon down for his feed,' Maud said, getting to her feet while Prue held the baby. 'There we are, nice and steady now. It's all very well, my lady, now and again for a novelty, but I wouldn't want to be doing this with a baby every day of the week.'

'It has rocked him to sleep, though,' Prue said. 'He hasn't been fretting over his teeth so much.'

'That's the sea air, I expect, my lady. We'll all sleep well tonight.'

Prue wriggled into a comfortable position to watch Ross, who was standing near the foremast, spyglass in hand, as rock-steady on the pitching deck as he was on the terrace at home.

Home? she thought. *I suppose it is now. My home, our home.* That brought a warm glow to her insides which were, she realised, quite happy now, even on the rougher water.

Ross looked content, easy in his skin. This was the real man, not the captive inside the smart clothes, tied to his desk with endless decisions to make about leases and crop rotations. Perhaps she could encourage him to employ a really efficient secretary, someone with a good understanding of land management, then he could spend his time doing what he so clearly loved.

She was glad he had asked her to come on this journey and to make it by sea. She was beginning to come to know him now, perhaps to understand him better. She could not have imagined him opening up, confiding the story of his first marriage, before now.

Perhaps it was not that he was coming to trust her more, she thought, with a sudden dip in her confidence. Perhaps it was simply that he was happy and relaxed at the wheel of his ship so he found it easier to tolerate her.

Poor little Jon, she thought. The child of that unhappy marriage, of that calculating, selfish woman.

And I should not judge, she reproved herself. *I do not know what might have made her like that.*

* * *

It had been dark when they reached Ramsgate, although the harbour was bright with illumination—the lighthouse by the entrance, the lanterns on the mass of ships and boats crowded inside, the twinkling stars that must be the houses of the town climbing away from the sea. Prue was too tired and too concerned about getting Jon safely off the *Dawn Ghost* and on to dry land to pay much attention to her surroundings. The house was just a short distance away, Ross said. There would be supper waiting.

As far as Prue had been concerned, if it contained a bed, and Maud, Tansy, Mrs Goodnight and Jon were all comfortable, that was all that mattered. Without as much as a glance for her surroundings she had refused supper and tumbled into bed.

Now, waking in a bedchamber already full of light through the thin window blind, she sat up and looked around. Not a large room, but modern and comfortable. A big, soft bed that did *not* contain a husband—where was Ross?—and a window, she found when she released the blind, that gave her a sweeping view over the harbour.

Thank goodness it had been dark and she had been too preoccupied with Jon to notice the narrowness of the harbour entrance or how crowded the enclosed basin was with ships. Even with Ross at the wheel, entering at night must be fraught with dangers.

Now all was a picture of organised chaos. She might know next to nothing about the sea, but she could recognise warships when she saw them in among a mass of vessels very like *Dawn Ghost*. Beyond the harbour arms the sea was dotted with more ships, some at anchor, others with sails set, looking as though someone had tipped up a basket of clean white handkerchiefs, scattering them across the ocean as far as the eye could see. People bustled along the quaysides, small boats rowed between the anchored ships and, as she watched, a file of soldiers marched into sight and formed up, packs at their feet, muskets at the slope.

Ross had told her that the Royal Navy had control of the seas, but she had not imagined so much power, so much activity. Napoleon would never get across the Channel, she was certain. But that still meant he had to be confronted on land. How many thousands of lives would be lost for one man's belief in his own destiny?

That thought had her pulling on her robe and looking for Jon. Even as she did so she recognised the impulse for what it was: an irrational reaction to danger. Jon, thank goodness, would never have to fight Napoleon Bonaparte. But Ross? She pushed away that nagging thought.

The room immediately opposite hers was the same size with the identical panoramic view of the harbour and a very masculine look to it. The bed was empty, the covers tossed back. This was Ross's room and, she realised, he must own this house; it was not a lodgings.

In the room behind hers she found Maud and Mrs Goodnight who were already dressed. So was Jon, laughing and kicking on a blanket in the middle of the floor. He reached out his arms when he saw her and she went to scoop him up. 'Goodness, you are growing heavy, young man. And, no, my hair is very firmly attached to my head, thank you. Is everything all right?' she asked the other women.

'Perfect, thank you, my lady. Tansy went down to the kitchen a moment ago when we heard you moving about. She'll be sending up your hot water and ordering breakfast.'

'Have you seen His Lordship?'

'He went out at dawn, they told me downstairs.' The wet nurse came to take Jon, who was clearly determined to see just how well fixed Prue's hair was. 'Down to his ship, I'll be bound. Now then, my little lord, don't you be grizzling at me. We can't have all what we want.'

That was very true, Prue thought as she went back to her room, encountering Tansy as she did so. You could not have everything you wished for, but she thought she had more than she had ever expected, just weeks before. Far more. So it was ungrateful to have a little ache for what she did not have. Ungrateful and pointless.

Ross came in as she was sitting down to breakfast and joined her to take a second one himself. This morning he looked smart but practical—crisp white linen, blue coat, buckskins and boots. Sharp and powerful, Prue thought with an unexpected glow of pride in her husband. The scar would not seem out of place here where soldiers, naval men and tough local sailors thronged the streets.

'I have been talking to the quartermasters and the

harbour master to see what they need from my ships,'
he said as he stole a slice of toast from the rack in
front of her.

'Ships?'

'I have three here already now and one coming in
today or tomorrow from Ostend. They do not want us
converting for horses, which is a relief, but we'll be
carrying small arms and ammunition, which doesn't
need any work on the vessels, and some troops, which
will. Bulkheads moving, extra water casks loading,
that sort of thing,' Ross added when she raised an in-
terrogative eyebrow.

'Jonas is working on that,' he added. 'Which means
I have a day to show you the sights of Ramsgate if you
would like that.'

Prue dropped the butter knife into the marmalade.
Ross wanted to show her the sights? Ross wanted to
take a day away from his beloved ships and his business for what she was fairly certain he thought of as
frivolity? She had already decided that her idea of asking him to squire her around would be selfish under the
circumstances, so the offer took her aback.

'I would enjoy that,' she said mildly, retrieving the
knife. 'What is there to see in Ramsgate besides the
harbour?'

'The pier, which forms the east arm of the harbour,
makes a good promenade. We might be able to see
France, so you can wave to Boney if you are so inclined. Then there are shops—not as good as Margate,
but I can show you where they are. The main library is

just around the corner from here and I know you will want to locate that. Then there are the baths—or do you want to try bathing from a machine?'

'I had not thought of it,' she said, not very sure she liked the idea now she was contemplating it. 'Will the sea be cold?'

'Very. I wouldn't try it until at least August, myself, but perhaps you are made of sterner stuff.'

'Most definitely not, then. I think I will confine myself to admiring the sea from the shore.'

'Wise woman. The Assembly Rooms are up the hill, if you would not consider this evening's ball too provincial an entertainment.'

'You are offering to take me to a *ball*?'

'You endured a long day at sea for my convenience. It is the least I can do.'

'Well, fortunately for you I told Hedges not to pack a ball gown as we did not have time to properly consider all the other things one needs to go with it.' She smiled at him. 'So you are saved.'

'Yes,' Ross said, giving her a heavy-lidded, considering look that made her toes curl. 'Yes, I believe I am.' Then, before she could be so foolish as to ask him what he meant by that, he finished the toast, tossed his napkin on the table and stood up. 'I will go up and spend some time with Jon. Let me know when you are ready to go out.'

It felt very *wifely*, somehow, to be promenading along the East Pier, her arm tucked firmly against

Ross's side, her nicest bonnet tied securely against the breeze and in company with a multitude of complete strangers who, despite that, still bowed, smiled or raised their hats as they passed.

'It does not seem very like a pier,' she said after the first few yards. 'I thought piers went straight out to sea. I have seen pictures.'

'You are right. Piers have metal or wooden legs to carry them over the water. Someone had a cunning idea with this one and combined the harbour wall with a promenade and that gives us a much longer walk.'

'And a chance to observe the ships more closely. I can see *Dawn Ghost*. Which are the other two that you own?'

'Those two brigs over there just before the frigate. *Evening Shadow* and *Dark Phantom. Night Spectre*, the other brig, is on her way back from Ostend. There's a ketch as well, *Will o' the Wisp*. She is much smaller. I use her for coastal work, running messages, that kind of thing. She's over there behind *Phantom*—you won't be able to see her from here.'

'Such names! Why are they all named for ghosts?'

'My ships need to be as elusive as spirits, as frightening as spectres,' he told her.

She could hear the amusement in his voice, but also the seriousness and that gave her a sudden qualm. '*Needed* to be, surely?' she asked, hoping for reassurance. 'They are purely trading vessels now, surely? Once the need to carry troops and supplies is over, that is.'

'I suppose so.' He half turned and looked across the Channel at the heavy clouds that obscured the distant coast. 'If we beat him.'

'We will. And then you will not be doing anything dangerous any more, will you? Not more dangerous than sailing already is,' Prue added, eyeing the grey sea with the choppy white horses doubtfully.

'You do not wish to be a wealthy, titled widow, then?'

He was teasing her. Or she hoped he was. Even so, she felt a spurt of anger, sudden and hot. 'No, I do not. It is not amusing to say that. I would hate for Jon to lose his father and I... I would miss you. Leaving aside the fact that I would wish no one dead,' she added hastily when he looked down at her with that sudden intensity she had glimpsed at the breakfast table.

'You would miss me?'

'Of course I would. You are my husband.' She remembered what he had told her about his first wife and realised that might not be a very convincing argument. 'And I like you. We are lovers.' Prue could feel the heat in her cheeks despite the breeze and hurried on. 'And we are friends, are we not?'

'Perhaps we are. Perhaps that is what this is,' Ross added so quietly that the words were almost lost on the wind. He cleared his throat, added more strongly, 'I do not envisage taking up privateering again unless the British Navy loses control of the seas.'

'So you will not risk your life again?'

'So fierce.' The twisted smile was wry. 'No, I will not, leaving aside the normal hazards of the sea.'

'You promise?' She gripped his forearm, suddenly full of dread.

'Such intensity! Yes, I promise.'

She breathed out, wondering why that flash of fear had hit her like that. Not a premonition, surely? She did not believe in such things.

'Now, tell me,' Ross said, oblivious to her turmoil, 'why has that female in front of us come out here wearing a bonnet the size and shape of a coal scuttle and expressly designed to catch every zephyr of air? She will take off like a kite in a moment and, as I have promised you to do nothing dangerous, I will not be able to save her as she flies towards France.'

'She has just purchased it,' Prue said, determined to ignore her foolish fancies. 'She considers it to be the latest crack and, as it cost her a great deal of money, she is determined to wear it whenever possible. Or impossible,' Prue added as a particularly strong gust caught the brim and sent the woman staggering backwards.

Ross ran forward and caught her before she landed on the cobbled surface and she twisted round in his arms, laughing up at him.

'Oh, my goodness! Why, thank you, sir. How gallant you are. So *strong*.'

She was very pretty, Prue saw. She also noticed with some amusement that the stranger did not appear to be disconcerted by Ross's scar and was fluttering her eyelashes at him with great aplomb.

Ross set her on her feet, expression stony. 'Do not mention it, ma'am.'

Prue was half inclined not to rescue him, just for the fun of seeing him extract himself. But it was not really fair to abandon her husband to the wiles of a young woman who she strongly suspected was one of the muslin company.

She moved just as another couple came up to them from the seaward end of the pier. They were in their early fifties, she thought, noticing them simply because of the lady's very smart walking dress and the expression on both their faces. How odd to come to the seaside if it made you feel so sour, she thought.

No, not sour, Prue realised almost immediately. That was real dislike and it was directed squarely at Ross.

He had seen them, too. He bowed slightly, then raised his tall hat—and they cut him dead, ignoring him as though he was invisible and they had a very bad smell under their noses.

Prue took three hasty steps forward, linked her arm through Ross's and stared back at them with furious hauteur. When they had swept past she turned to Ross and gave the young woman with the impractical hat a frosty glare.

The damsel giggled, simpered at Ross and tripped off towards the end of the pier.

'Who the blazes was that?' she demanded, too angry to watch her language.

'A female of the class ladies are not supposed to notice,' Ross said with a smile that was clearly forced.

'I do not mean her and you know it. Who were those unpleasant people who just cut us?'

'They cut me. I doubt they noticed you. They were Jon's grandparents. I would not have suggested that you come here if I had realised they were staying. They normally spend a few weeks at Brighton.'

'Ross, I saw the way they looked at you—it was almost as though they hate you.'

'I have the very poor taste to be alive while their daughter is dead,' he said. 'And they are doubtless still fuming over the fact that I have remarried before a year was out. It must seem to them that I am not honouring her memory.'

'Even giving them every allowance for their grief over Honoria, it is still a horrible way to behave.' Prue felt quite queasy. The world was full of unpleasant people, she was not so naive as to think otherwise, but it was still a shock to encounter such malevolence at close quarters, directed at someone she—

'Prudence?' Ross looked down at her. 'What is it? You must not allow them to upset you. After all, we are unlikely to encounter them again.'

'I—I'm not upset, exactly.' She struggled to find an explanation for her sudden gasp, her stumble. 'Not about… I mean, I am more shocked, that is all.' She tried to articulate a coherent sentence despite her rioting thoughts. 'That is, I mean they should have more self-respect and dignity than to behave is such a way.' She managed to find a smile. 'Now, had we better hurry in case your fair admirer is carried off from the point of the pier and needs rescuing again?'

'She will not be my admirer now that she has seen I have my wife on my arm. And it was I who needed rescuing—do not think I did not notice that you found it amusing and were in half a mind to leave me to my fate.'

'She is a very highly finished piece of work, is she not? Do you think those brazen curls could possibly be natural? Look, she has found another Galahad and a retired admiral, at the very least, by the look of him. Oh, dear, she appears to have turned her ankle on the cobbles, how clever of her.'

Ross followed her lead and appeared ready to ignore the unpleasant encounter as they both admired the young woman's technique with the white-haired gentleman who was giving her his arm back towards Prue and Ross. The girl dimpled prettily at Ross as she passed him.

Despite everything, Prue burst out laughing. 'She winked at me, the little hussy! I do hope he is a nice man.'

They had reached the far end where the pier widened out into a circular bulwark with a lantern on a tall pole at its centre. It was not as attractive to look at as the little stone lighthouse on the opposite side of the harbour entrance, but it made a focal point to gather around for those promenading to rest and admire the view over the harbour or out to sea.

'There are benches against the wall. Shall we sit a while?' she suggested, wanting to be still and close for a little.

'If you will not be too cold.' Ross dusted a bench

with his handkerchief for her and they sat gazing at the bustling harbour and the town beyond.

Ross appeared to be engrossed in the shipping. Prue was just grateful for the silence to try to come to terms with the fact that she seemed to have fallen in love with her husband.

Chapter Thirteen

'You are very thoughtful.' Ross thought he had kept his reaction at the unexpected encounter with his in-laws well under control, but it seemed it had distressed Prudence. She was staring rather blankly at the harbour scene as though she had received an unpleasant surprise.

'It is the novelty of the seaside, I think.' She was immediately responsive, giving him a quick, almost uncertain smile. He felt the urge to smile back, then the cynic in him noted how quickly she could mask her own feelings, how easily she moulded herself to be what he wanted.

'And this amount of fresh air after London is positively soporific,' Prudence added. 'I cannot decide whether I want to walk for miles or curl up and go to sleep.'

'We could compromise. We will stroll back along the pier, then I will show you the best shopping streets and the circulating library and you can explore with

A Marquis in Want of a Wife

Hedges, or a footman, when you have rested. Or whenever you want.' The investment in time was worth-
while: she would know her way around and would not
need him for the rest of the stay.

He would not walk too far, or too briskly, though.
For all her efforts to pretend otherwise Prudence was
definitely subdued. He was feeling unsettled himself.
It was not the confounded Gracewells—and there was
a misnamed couple—he was used to the attempts by
Lord and Lady Falhaven to snub and slight him.

Of course, Jonas was decidedly out of sorts and an
unhappy master on board ship was always a concern.
Probably, Ross told himself, it was being left to oversee
the alterations to three ships that had put his nose out
of joint and when Ross checked later he'd find Jonas
grumbling about not being *some damned carpenter.* It
was foolish to worry too much about Thwaite's mut-
terings against Bonaparte.

Or it could be Prudence and her talk about friendship. He had not married again for *friendship.* How
did one become friends with a woman, anyway? They
were virtually a different species. Bed sport was one
thing... Quite a good thing with Prudence, now he
came to think about it. Ross did his best to ignore the
wave of arousal that thought provoked.

Yes, making love to his wife was normal. It was not
what he had married her for and he was trying not to
bother her too much with his presence in the bedchamber, but still, he was not complaining. At all.

But was this friendship? He worried about Prudence, thought about her at odd moments when he

found himself forgetting what he was supposed to be thinking about and ended up smiling like an idiot. At least the tug of the scar alerted him to it or the crew would think he was running a fever.

It was not as though she was particularly pretty. Or sophisticated. Or showed any signs of doting on him, thank heavens. She was intelligent, self-reliant, composed and Jon already loved her. That was quite enough. And he had to remember that everything had seemed good when he was first married to Honoria.

Even so, none of this explained why he felt different now that Prudence was with him or why he had volunteered to take her out that morning, because it was only just now that he had rationalised it by deciding it would leave him free for the rest of the time. It was not as though he was unused to sharing the house with a wife— 'I am sorry, did you say something?'

'Only that the beach does look inviting and if this was August I would enjoy taking Jon down there to paddle and build castles out of sand. But not until the sea is warmer. Are you distracted worrying about your ships? If you want to go down to the harbour I can walk back to the house from here—I can even see it. There is no need to worry about me, Ross.'

'I am not worried.' *Disturbed, but not worried.* 'I will show you the circulating library before we go back. It is just up this hill.'

'I had a most enjoyable walk, Tansy,' Prue shed her bonnet and gloves as the maid helped her out of her pelisse. 'I thought after luncheon that you and I could go to the library and then I must do some work. My translation has been sadly neglected lately.'

She ate alone because Ross had gone down to the harbour again. She almost thought the word was *escaped*. It was strange to wonder that because he had seemed to enjoy their walk. Perhaps the encounter with Lord and Lady Falhaven had upset him more than he showed. He would see it as a weakness, she supposed.

Horrible people. No wonder his wife had been such an unpleasant woman with parents like that. Ross had grown into a decent man from very humble beginnings which were no fault of his. Why was that something to be sneered at? She fumed for a while on his behalf, then faced the fact that she was doing so partly so that she did not have to think about falling in love with the man.

But had she? Wasn't love supposed to make you dreamy and dizzy, happily infatuated? She was definitely not infatuated with Ross, who was far from perfect—secretive, grumpy, antisocial and not handsome. Although he was most attractively masculine and in the bedchamber… She jerked her thoughts back from that and stuck a knife in the cheese with some force.

Perhaps it was the fact that they were lovers that was making her imagine emotions that, surely, she could not be feeling. Ladies were not supposed to actively enjoy sexual congress, so was she making excuses to herself? Poetry was another symptom, she remembered. Was it not the case that people in love were always writing poetry or reading it? But her translations from the Greek were showing no signs of turning into odes to Ross's deep brown eyes.

But, indisputably, she enjoyed being with him, missed him when she was not, felt a desire to hold tight to his arm, press close to his side, breathe in that masculine scent of plain soap and leather—and now, salt and a trace of tar.

But whatever this was she felt, Ross did not feel it, too. He was startled by the notion that they were friends, that was clear enough. Will, the Duke of Aylsham, brought Verity flowers and jewellery at every opportunity. Ivo, Jane's husband, had a perfume specially created for her and he was always bringing flowers home as well. That was proper lover-like behaviour as Prue understood it—and Ross was showing none of it.

He would probably be hideously embarrassed if she let him guess she might—*might*, that was all—have romantic feelings for him. It would ruin their friendship, their easiness together. So she would not allow *might* to become *definitely* and then everything would be comfortable and safe. It was all a matter of willpower.

The sun was still shining when Prue and Tansy set out for the circulating library which, as Ross had said, was just up the hill and around the corner from the house.

Withersden's Library was on two floors and boasted, so the sign in the window announced,

A most select collection of the latest works of literature, daily replenished from the Capital, in addition to guidebooks, newspapers and journals.

*Telescopes and musical instruments may be
hired by the week and on the upper floor is a
most commodious lounge with sea views, ideally
suited to the needs of the most discerning visitor.
Agent for select lodgings and boarding houses.
Tide tables, shipping news, et cetera, et cetera.*

'Shall we see if it lives up to its advertising?' Prue
led the way in, ready to enjoy herself. She loved everything about bookshops and circulating libraries—the
smell, the unexpected discoveries, the fun of brows-
ing, even the other customers were a source of interest and amusement.

The ground floor had two counters on either side
with assistants tending to customers and, beyond, well-
filled bookshelves. Stairs led upwards and the sound of
murmured conversation drifted down. 'Shall we see if
they have the latest fashion journals?' Prue suggested.
'I really should not borrow any more books. I brought
six with me, as well as my work. I will see if they have
a local guidebook I can buy as well.'

The young male assistant in his smart black suit of
clothes sold her a copy of the *New Margate, Ramsgate
and Broadstairs Guide* and assured her that Acker-
mann's *Repository*, *La Belle Assemblée* and the *Ladies'
Monthly Magazine* were all to be found on the upper
floor. 'And, naturally, we take several copies of each
issue, ma'am, so there is no danger that our patrons
might have to wait.'

'Very efficient,' Prue murmured as they climbed to
the next floor where racks of periodicals stood around

one open space divided up with tables and chairs. A window with three telescopes on tripods gave a view over the harbour and there were several inviting sofas and upholstered benches.

The telescopes appeared to be the preserve of a group of elderly gentlemen who were studying the shipping with great interest. Several others had the daily news-sheets spread out on the tables, but the more comfortable seating was in use by only three ladies, two of whom were deep in low-voiced gossip while the third appeared rapt in a novel.

Prue and Tansy found a magazine each and a sofa to share and began to leaf through the publications.

'Oh, what a peculiar hat! Do look, my lady—it makes her appear as though someone has upended a whole bucket of flowers over her head and she can hardly see out.'

'Apparently it was seen in Kensington Gardens,' Prue said, looking at the caption. 'The original wearer must count herself fortunate if she was not watered by a passing gardener in error. And see what the *Ladies' Monthly* says. "Our fair countrywomen are to be congratulated on the improvement made to the fashions this month. Those frightful French bonnets, etc., have given place to the more simple but elegant English taste." Oh.'

Standing not a yard away was the lady who had cut them so rudely on the pier, Ross's first mother-in-law.

Prue reminded herself that she outranked the other woman and also that she possessed considerably better manners. 'Good afternoon. Lady Falhaven, I believe.'

Beside her she could feel Tansy gathering herself to stand. She put her hand on her arm to keep her seated.

'You are married to Cranford.'

From that blunt beginning there was clearly going to be no attempt at friendship. 'I am Lady Cranford, yes.'

'Where is my grandson?'

'At home, with me. And with his father, of course. Jon is in the best of health, although fretful because of teething.'

She is a rude, unpleasant woman, but Jon is her grandson. Surely I can behave better than she does?

Prue found a smile. 'Would you care to visit him? The house is quite close, although I expect you know that.'

What will Ross say? Perhaps I should have asked him first, but Jon is my son now and it is my home, too.

For a moment she thought she saw hesitation, the beginning of a smile. Had she imagined that fleeting look of longing?

'Certainly not. Set foot over that man's threshold? My grandson should be with us, his grandparents,' the older woman said. Her voice was low, but the vehement tone had several people look up and glance in their direction. 'Not with that…that slum brat who pretends to be a marquis.'

'In which case it is a pity that your desire to have your daughter marry above her station overcame your irrational dislike of my husband,' Prue said coolly, even as instinct made her wonder if it was unhappiness that was making the woman lash out so. Unhappiness and guilt?

'How dare you!' Lady Falhaven drew herself up, recoiled, the picture of affronted pride. 'Who are you to talk about our station? Some obscure squire's daughter?'

All feelings of sympathy fled. Prue put up her chin, kept her voice low and her tone arctic. 'The daughter of parents who taught me to judge worth on character, not on birth or status, Lady Falhaven. And the wife of a patriotic gentleman of integrity and courage. Good day to you.'

She looked down at the journal on her lap and pointedly turned a page.

There was a sharp intake of breath and the swish of skirts.

'She has gone,' Tansy whispered. 'You were wonderful, my lady. I was quaking in my shoes, but you made her show herself up like a Billingsgate fishwife.'

'She certainly looked as though she would like to take a gutting knife to me,' Prue said with a shudder. 'We will give her a few minutes. I have no desire to encounter her on the street.' There was no triumph, she found, in routing someone so very unhappy and disturbed.

Prue wondered, when Ross came home for dinner, whether she should say something about the confrontation. One look at his face made her decide to keep it to herself.

'A tiring afternoon?' she asked as a tureen of crab bisque was set in front of them.

'Does it show?' he asked ruefully.

'You seem a little weary, that is all.' Prue ladled out two bowls and decided that, despite everything, she had an appetite.

There was no point in probing. Ross's face had set into those harsh, unsmiling lines she remembered from their first meeting and she did not expect him to be any more forthcoming about his feelings now than he had then.

'I am concerned about Jonas Thwaite,' he said, surprising her.

'The Master? I remember. A nice man, I thought. I hope he is not unwell.'

'Only in his head—he is all fired up to go and fight Boney himself, take revenge. Both his sons were killed in the Peninsula, his sister's boy, too, and his wife just faded away with grief. He has half the crews stirred up with this nonsense about volunteering, marching off to war. I had to waste time going from ship to ship, convincing them they are doing a far more valuable job supplying the army with the weapons and men it needs than acting as cannon fodder on some Belgian field.' He drank some soup and tore a bread roll into pieces. 'At least, I hope I have convinced them. Not Jonas though, the pig-headed old fool. He was still muttering when I left. I will have to keep an eye on him.'

'Will you relieve him of his duties?'

'I am tempted, but he knows far more than I do about what is needed to convert the brigs to carry men and that is what is most important right now. We have to get the troops across. Besides, if I keep him on I know where he is. If I stand him down, he'll just get on the next ship crossing to Ostend.'

Ross reached for the decanter, poured red wine and took a long swallow. '*Night Spectre* came in from Ostend just before I left. And that's another thing—we've got the army swarming all over her getting in the way while we load the armaments and I have had to take men off the refit to relieve her crew. They deserve a night ashore.'

'Cannot the troops manage the loading by themselves?'

'Let the army loose on a ship?' Ross looked almost comically alarmed at the thought. 'Goodness knows what damage they'd do—probably drop a heavy weight straight through the bottom—and they've certainly got no idea about loading and trimming. She'd probably sink mid-Channel. I will have to go down again tonight when I've eaten. Besides *Spectre*, we're loading water casks and provisions for the troops on *Phantom*. She will be ready to sail in the morning, too.'

He glanced across at Prue as though seeing her properly for the first time since he had come in. 'I am sorry, this is a poor holiday for you.'

'Nonsense. I am thoroughly enjoying myself. I have all manner of plans for tomorrow if it stays fine. Shall I bring Jon down to the harbour to wave the two ships off?'

'If you do, take one of the footmen with you, as well as Hedges. The dockside is crowded and the company is not the most refined, to put it mildly.'

Prue waited until he went upstairs to change again,

then, paying heed to her instincts, followed him up. 'Will you not rest a while, Ross? Just for an hour?'

Ross gave her that twisted smile that made something inside her glow in response. 'This is nothing. At sea you keep going around the clock if that is what is needed. A little hard work and lack of sleep has never done me any harm.'

'Even so, stay a little with me?' Prue suggested. There was so much to worry him and she could not believe it would all ease up after that night. This could go on for days. She moved in close, lifted a hand to his cheek, smooth from his rapid before-dinner shave. 'Just an hour…'

'Are you attempting to seduce me, my lady?'

'Perhaps I am,' she said, discovering a wicked desire to behave very shockingly and not simply because it might relax Ross. 'But I suppose I had best just help you to undress. So you can put on your other clothes immediately afterwards, of course.'

She widened her eyes in mock innocence, then squeaked when Ross caught her around the waist and pulled her close for a kiss.

'You are developing wifely wiles,' he said when he released her. 'You think to lure me into bed and then hope I will fall asleep for an hour or so.'

'Well…' *I am hoping you will kiss me again, certainly.*

'I suppose you will help me change as readily as my valet does,' Ross conceded as her hands went to his neckcloth. 'And rather more pleasurably, too.'

And somehow, as his coat slid from his shoulders

and she began to unbutton his waistcoat, his fingers were working on the fastenings of her gown.

'Just an hour,' Ross murmured as they fell on to the bed, he still in his shirt, she in chemise and stockings.

Was it because she knew now that she was falling in love with her husband that made this different? Prue wondered as Ross's hands drifted over her body. Or was he really more tender, more intense than he had ever been before?

It was all the more arousing because they were still half-clothed and the unexpected brush of bare skin on naked flesh had an intensity that was shockingly new.

'Yes,' she murmured. 'Yes,' as he came over her and she curled her legs around him. 'Oh, yes…'

For a moment Prue could not work out what had woken her, then the strike of the big hall clock came again. One, two…

'Hell's teeth!' Ross sat up next to her, throwing off the blanket that one of them must have tugged over their drowsing bodies. 'Is that midnight?'

He did not wait for her reply, but got out of bed and reached for his clothes. 'I knew this was a bad idea.'

Prue tried not to take it personally, swallowing something that might have been a protest, or possibly a sob. To hide her face she rolled over and checked the little clock that stood on the table on the far side of the bed. 'Yes, midnight.'

She began to get up, too, but Ross was already pulling on his boots. 'Stay there, go back to sleep, Prudence. Don't fuss.' That was definitely a snap.

A minute later the front door banged closed behind him. Prue pulled on her robe and went to the window and there he was, striding down to the harbour, a powerful, dark, angry shadow making for the lights and the ships and the ordered chaos of working men.

He would be too kind to actually say he blamed her for distracting him, she supposed. But she had, even if for the best of intentions.

Prue examined her conscience. *And because I wanted to make love with him, now that I understand how I feel*, it prompted her.

They were at war and Ross had his duty to do, she reminded herself as she let the curtain drop and went back to bed to try to sleep.

She fell into an uneasy doze almost immediately, a half sleep full of dreams and faces. Lady Falhaven, her fingers curled like the talon on Ross's hand, leaning over her. *'I want my grandson. Give me my grandson, you nobody.'* Ross, his face a mask of anger, shouting at her, *'I have my duty to do. I do not want your pathetic love.'* And somewhere in the distance there were swirls of smoke, the sound of gunfire, the metallic tang of blood.

Prue woke again as the clock struck one and rose, lit the lamp, turned it low and went back to bed to lie, eyes open, wondering at the sense of dread that lurked in the shadows.

Chapter Fourteen

'Where is Thwaite?' Ross demanded of the Mate as he dropped on to the deck of the *Night Spectre*, dodging a sweating military gunner who was staggering under the weight of one end of an ammunition box.

'He's not on board here, sir. He was on *Phantom*, Cap'n, last I saw of him, but that was a couple of hours since.'

'Carry on, Gregg.'

At the *Dark Phantom*'s berth Ross found the Sergeant of Marines who, with Harry Tovey, the bo'sun, was directing the labouring soldiers and crewmen as they loaded up crates of arms and ammunition. 'How is it going, Harry?'

'Well enough, but we could do with the rest of the crew, Cap'n.'

'Where are they?' Now he had been watching for a few minutes Ross could see that there were fewer of his own men visible than he would have expected.

'Gone with Mr Thwaite, sir. He was here just after

eight and took a dozen of the hands with him. Needed more on the fitting-out, I suppose. Hey, you there! Mind how you go with that, you lubberly lump!' He swung down on to the deck and began to berate a confused soldier who had tripped on a coil of rope.

Ross went back on to the quayside and followed it around to where *Dawn Ghost* and her sister, *Evening Shadow*, lay. Carpenters were at work on the dock cutting planks into lengths for boarding up partitions and the sound of hammering rose from the open hatches of both brigs.

Johnny Peters, the Mate of the *Shadow*, stood watching, hands on hips. He looked, Ross thought, considerably more fraught that he had earlier in the day.

'Not going well, Peters?'

'Would be if I'd got the men, Cap'n. I want to get the rigging checked over and the water on board, never mind the provisions, but most of the crew are tied up helping the chippies.' He saw Ross glance over at the other brig. 'Not quite as bad on *Ghost*, sir. He didn't take as many from her.'

'What do you mean? Who has taken men?'

'Why, Mr Thwaite, sir. Came past with a dozen of the men, took six from here. Said you'd changed your mind about letting those who wanted to fight go over to Ostend.'

'He said *what*? Where the hell is he?' As he asked he realised what was missing. *Will o' the Wisp* was no longer to be seen. 'Did Thwaite take the ketch?'

'Aye, Cap'n. In a right hurry they were. I suppose they was frightened that you'd change your mind when you came back. All the *Wisp*'s crew wanted to stay here and I've got 'em down below with mine which is some help. Four extra men are better than none.' Peters gave him a gap-toothed grin, then turned back to demand of the carpenters how much more sawing they were going to do.

Ross took a moment to count to ten, backwards, then made up his mind what he was going to do about this. 'Peters.'

'Cap'n?'

'I did not give permission for them to take the *Wisp*. Thwaite must have misunderstood me.' He had done no such thing, the bull-headed old devil, but for the sake of discipline Ross could hardly say so. 'I will go after them on the *Spectre* just as soon as she is loaded. I am leaving you and Tovey to finish the work here and I'll alert Dodgson to finalise the discussions with the military and supervise the loading. Make sailing decisions with him.'

'Aye, aye, Cap'n.' Peters shifted uneasily. 'You going to bring them back?'

'It is their decision.' He was going to do his utmost to persuade them, but he could hardly use force, however much he felt like it. 'I want my ketch back.'

He strode off to speak to the bo'sun, then went to disturb the evening of Dodgson, his agent in the port, who had retired to the comfort of his own fireside.

That done and orders given, Ross climbed the steps back to his own house. He intended to have a word with whichever footman was around, put together his own pack in his dressing room and leave a note for Prudence. He was angry enough without a confrontation with his wife.

He should have known better, he realised, as the door of his bedchamber creaked open.

'Where are you going? What is wrong?' Prudence's hair was down and she clutched a thin robe around herself. He thought she looked sleepy and desirable. And succumbing to that earlier had kept him from stopping the suicidal mission that Jonas had set out on, dragging eighteen other hotheads with him, Ross reminded himself savagely.

He carried on rummaging in the cashbox he'd taken from his desk. He needed more money and there was a bag of sovereigns in there. Gold would grease more wheels than banknotes. 'That damn fool Thwaite has taken the ketch and eighteen of the crew and set off to fight Napoleon. Or, much more likely, be killed in the attempt. I'm taking *Spectre* over to Ostend, see if I can catch them and knock some sense into a few heads. And retrieve my ship.'

'At this hour, Ross? Could you not wait until daylight?'

He flung his shaving kit into the pack on top of the money and followed it with a couple of shirts. 'If I had done what I should have and gone straight back down after dinner, I would have been in time to stop them.' *Probably.*

'But—'

'I am quite capable of sailing at night, Prudence.'

'Yes. Yes, of course. But you cannot blame yourself, Ross. They are all adults.'

Ross jerked the strap closed around the pack and turned for the door. 'I am their captain. I am responsible for them. I trusted Thwaite, even though I knew he was becoming obsessed, and the men trust me to put a master in command who can be relied upon, who they should look up to and obey. The responsibility stops with me.'

'When will you be back?' Her spine was straight now, her chin was up.

He felt as though he had slapped her. He probably had, verbally. It would be a lesson to them both to treat this marriage as what it was, a matter of mutual convenience. Not, damn it, a love match.

'I meant well,' Prue whispered as the sound of Ross's boot heels striking the pavement faded away. And much good that was. She had wanted him to rest and now he was going to have to sail at night into a confrontation with his own crew. If he got them all back safely, he would still be tired and angry. If any of them insisted on going on, heading into the bloodbath of the coming battles, then he would never forgive himself. Or her.

Which was unfair on both of them, she decided. Ross was being stubborn and pig-headed: his crewmen were adults who should be able to work out for themselves what their responsibilities were. But she could understand all too well why he could not be cold-blooded about it. He had failed to fully recognise the danger and he had a strong sense of responsibility.

She probably could not love a man who shirked responsibility. And she did love Ross, she was sure of that now.

How long would it take him to get to Ostend and return? She should have asked, but perhaps if she went down to the harbour in the morning someone on the remaining two ships could tell her.

It was foolish to worry. Ross was an experienced sailor; the French fleet was not at sea; no one was going to be firing cannon at him. Even so, she eased open the nursery door and stood for a while looking at Jon, fast asleep with his thumb in his mouth, until she felt calmer, a little comforted. Ross had promised her that he would not deliberately go into danger again. He had promised.

When she arrived at the foot of the gangplank of *Dark Phantom* the next morning the man who introduced himself as Harry Tovey, bo'sun, looked uneasy. 'Best allow five days, my lady.'

He was clearly not used to ladies intruding into his masculine world and was wincing at the colourful language that was drifting up from the open hatches.

'Should be less, but he's got to get there, get the cargo unloaded, find Mr Thwaite, sail back.' He scratched his head, considering. 'You have to allow for the tide not being right, the docks being crowded and having to wait for a berth. And the weather could change, that kind of thing, ma'am.'

'Yes, of course. So foolish of me not to have asked my husband before he left. I am not used to being a sailor's wife yet, you see, and I'm afraid I fret more than I should do.'

He blushed and grinned and she caught the look of relief on his face when she thanked him and turned away.

She was upset and half angry, half guilty, and the fact that her courses had arrived that morning to make her feel even more miserable was no help. She had not expected to feel so disappointed not to be with child.

At least she had the address to find Ross's agent, Mr Dodgson. She would make certain he understood that he must send her any news he had just as soon as he received it. She did not care if he thought her fussy or nervous, she told herself, taking a firm hold on the shiny brass knocker of the smart little house a stone's throw from the quayside: Ross need never know.

It was ten in the morning. Ross could hear the clocks striking in the church towers as the coast approached. Ostend was so low-lying that they could almost hear it before they saw any of it, the only landmark the stub of the lighthouse rising up on the horizon. They had made good time, but this was a foul harbour to enter at the best of times and the sea was littered with vessels waiting for the flag to be hoisted at the end of the wooden pier to signal that the tide was finally right.

He paced as the angles of the stone fortifications became clearer, the tiled roofs of the houses showing sharper and redder. Someone seemed to have been building little pyramids on the quayside, but when he focused the telescope he could make out that they were piles of cannon balls.

He could see red coats in plenty, British flags flapping at mastheads, but he could not see his ketch and for the first time began to worry that Thwaite had guessed he would pursue and had landed somewhere else along the coast.

Then the flag on the pier was run up, the helmsman returned his nod and steered for the harbour mouth and he saw her. *Wisp* had her sail furled and the deck looked empty. He had missed them, the little ketch slipping in when the state of the tide had kept the larger ships out at sea. As he watched he saw little Jem, the cabin boy, uncurl himself from the foot of the mast, rub his eyes and stare around him. Even at that distance Ross could tell the lad was anxious. And alone. There was no way you could hide nineteen men on a ketch.

Ross took Gregg, the Mate, on one side. 'When we dock, find the quartermaster in charge of the military supplies and start unloading on his orders. If I am not back by the time you are empty and the tide's right, sail without me. Put a couple of steady men on *Wisp* to wait until I get back. Here's some cash for them, that should last until the other ships come across.' He dug into his pack for paper and a pencil. 'And take this for my wife.'

He scribbled a hasty note.

Following them inland.
Will return as soon as possible.
R.

With any luck he would find them with some of the troops assembling in the town. If not, he'd just have to hope that someone had noticed nineteen English sailors heading away from the port.

With the pack on his shoulder he went down the gangplank and headed for the nearest group of redcoats. No use asking officers—the sergeants always knew what was going on. There was tension in the air, excitement, sweat and gunpowder. It quickened his pulse, gave him the kick of excitement that had been missing from his life for months. There was no danger, of course, he wasn't going near the fighting, but there was reassurance in knowing that Prudence had Jon and would look after him for a few days.

Prue stood in the hallway and unfolded the crumpled, unsealed, scribbled note. 'And this was all he gave you?'

'Yes, missus. My lady, I mean,' said the Mate, who had introduced himself as Gregg. 'Cap'n said to sail without him once we'd unloaded and could catch the tide.'

'And how long after he left were you able to sail?' She was surprised to find that her voice was steady when what she wanted to do was rant about idiot men who went haring off towards battlefields in pursuit of other idiot men who ought to be able to look after themselves. Which was not fair, she knew. Prue found a smile for the sailor, who was regarding her warily, and saw him relax.

'Took a day to unload, ma'am. Then we'd missed

the tide. It's a right bu— I mean it's a tricky harbour, that one, so we didn't sail until evening and took twelve hours to get across. Saw *Ghost* and *Shadow* just leaving the harbour here as we came in. The Captain will be back on one of them soon enough, ma'am, mark my words.'

'Yes, of course he will. Here.' She gave him a coin and he grinned, touched his forelock and let himself out.

On the sixteenth of June, both brigs were back in harbour, but there was still no sign of Ross, nor any message. Prue's supply of wifely understanding was running very low, her level of anxiety high. It was not helped by a distant rumble that she thought was thunder, far away in France, until someone at the library, an elderly retired general, remarked to the room at large that it was cannon fire.

'Where?' she asked as excited chatter broke out around them.

'Hard to say, ma'am. If the weather and the wind are right, the sound can carry very great distances and that's extremely faint. They say Boney's heading for the frontier—Wellington may have caught him there.' He shrugged. 'We will have to wait for some fresh news to come in.'

Then, on the Saturday, the seventeenth, there was finally a letter from Ross, sent on the fourteenth. 'Brussels!' Prue waved it at Tansy. 'He had just arrived in Brussels and he managed to get this letter sent early

with some official despatches. He has located the men
at last—some of them, at least—but they have volunteered and he is having to argue with the military on
the grounds that they are his crew and should be ex-
empt from military duty. But the army is saying because they volunteered that alters the legal position.'

She studied the letter again, searching for reassurance and failing to find it. 'It sounds quite dreadful,
although some of them have changed their minds and
want to return with him, but others do not. He says
there is no sign of the French, although they are known
to be advancing on the frontier and the Prussians and
Wellington expect to catch them in a pincer movement.'

'And we heard distant gunfire on the sixteenth, two
days after that letter,' Tansy said. 'They must have
caught Boncy. We will hear soon, my lady. The master will be back with the lads safe and sound in a few
days, don't you fear.'

Ten of them. That was the best he could do, but at
least he had most of the married men and Sam, who
was only sixteen. It was the seventeenth of June and
it had taken him six days. Now they had to get back
home.

The sound of gunfire, of cannon, from the south
filled the air, adding to the sense of urgency, the air of
near-panic, that was not helped by the pealing of church
bells. Wellington was fighting Marshal Ney, they said.
The troops had streamed out to a place called Quatre
Bras, a crossroads to the south of Brussels, but word
was that the outlying camps might be too late getting

there. As for Napoleon himself, he was somewhere to the south-east, perhaps confronting Blücher. It was hard to tell truth from rumour, but it sounded horribly as though the wily Corsican had succeeded in separating the two Allied armies.

Already, wounded men were coming back into the city, adding to the sense of alarm. Civilians were finally fleeing in any way they could and horses, mules and carriages, carts even, were selling for sky-high prices.

'How are we going to get back, Captain? It's a long march and I've still got the blisters from getting here,' Sam asked.

He was not really grumbling, Ross knew. Like all of the men he had a touching—and worrying—faith in their captain's ability to get them all home safely.

'There's no horses or carts—they've all been requisitioned by the army or bought at some ludicrous price by civilians evacuating.' Ross led his little band across what had once been the fashionable Parc, its elegant formality now reduced to a ruined mess of a marshalling ground. He had finally managed to extricate the last of them from an army unit there. Now they needed to find their way down to the canal.

'We will go by barge. They'll be glad of some experienced hands, I imagine.' And if not, then he'd buy something, anything, that would float and get the men out that way. He broke off as a stack of wooden boxes slid off a wagon in front of them, sides bursting open, scattering rifles in the mud.

'Oh, for— That's not the way to load it, you idiots.'
Two soldiers, neither of them looking either competent
or old enough to be out without their mothers, flapped
about trying to pick up the guns. 'Give them a hand,
men, get those rifles out of the mud and shift the cases
so the load balances.'

A harassed corporal, clearly attracted by the sound
of command in Ross's voice, jogged over, looked at the
men. 'Sailors? Thank God, I'm almost out of men to
shift this lot. We need to keep the train moving, Wellington needs all the supplies he can get.'

'Where to?' Ross heard himself asking. It hadn't
been what he was about to say. But this was clearly
urgent. He turned to the men. 'What do you say, lads?
No fighting, we agreed on that. But we can help shift
these arms down to the men who need them. We probably shipped them over.'

'Aye, we'll finish the job,' said Billy Watson, one
of the oldest of his crew. 'Rifles do no good here and
the bullets need to be in them Frenchies, not in the
mud. Yes, lads?'

On a chorus of agreement Ross turned back to the
corporal. 'Where to?'

The man pointed. 'Through the Namur Gate to the
south, follow the road straight on, through the forest,
on to a village called Waterloo. You can't miss the way,
just follow the rest of the wagons. Wellington's fighting south of that at the crossroads, Quatre Bras, but
they might be pulling back by now. Can you take four
wagons between you?'

* * *

The next day in Ramsgate, Sunday the eighteenth, as the household was walking up the hill to church, one of the footmen stopped. 'Listen! There's no sound of that cannon fire now, is there? Perhaps the battle's won!'

During the service there were prayers for the Allied armies, prayers that Prue joined in fervently. Surely Ross was on his way home by now? Surely the fighting would be a long way from Brussels, somewhere near the border.

On the way out of church Prue stopped at the door to shake hands with the minister and found Lady Falhaven at her side.

'Good morning.' It was Sunday; they were just out of church, she reminded herself, managing a social smile as she turned down the path through the churchyard.

'What is this I hear about Cranford joining the army?' Lady Falhaven demanded, falling into step beside her as her husband followed behind.

'The *army*? Wherever did you hear that?'

'I have my sources.'

'Thoroughly inaccurate ones,' Prue retorted, Sunday charity forgotten. 'Ross is in Brussels on business.'

'Business? The civilians are fleeing Brussels because it will be overrun by the French. It may already be so. Have you not seen them getting off the ships in the harbour here? Even the ones who had gone to Brussels for the sake of economy have left, I hear. And a friend of mine saw Cranford in Brussels on the fourteenth, talking to senior army officers.'

Prue did her best to ignore the cold clutch in her stomach. 'As I said, Ross was there on business. He has been shipping men and supplies for the army.' If some of Ross's men had deserted their duty, she saw no reason to confide that. 'If the authorities have instructed civilians to leave, then I am sure Ross will co-operate fully. If not, he will finish his business. He is experienced in matters of conflict—he will make the right decisions.'

I can only hope and pray.

'It is quite extraordinarily careless of him,' the older woman said with a sniff. 'He has responsibilities, a son.'

'Jon is safe in my care.'

Sunday, Prue reminded herself. *Charitable thoughts...*

'A stepmother? A bluestocking?'

'I am sure I cannot imagine why either of these things, although perfectly true, are a handicap to rearing a child. Good day, Lady Falhaven. Lord Falhaven. I see someone over there with whom I have to speak.'

Which was perfectly true. Mr Dodgson, Ross's port agent, was just ahead of them, his wife on his arm. Prue hurried down the path. 'Mr Dodgson!'

'My lady. Good day. How may I assist you?'

'Good morning, Mrs Dodgson. Mr Dodgson, I apologise for interrupting you, but I wondered if you had any news of my husband. Or any news at all from Brussels, for that matter.'

'None I can place absolute reliance upon, my lady.' He offered her his left arm as his wife returned Prue's greeting from his other side. 'English families are returning now, having left Brussels in a panic, as are Belgian refugees, but as for the news and rumours that led to their flight—we cannot tell at present what is the truth and what is alarmist talk.'

'I thought I heard cannon fire again yesterday, but nothing today.'

'Yes, so did I. We know Napoleon has crossed the frontier—it can only be a matter of time before battle is joined. Perhaps today will be the day.'

They were walking downhill with a view of the Channel spread out before them, thick black clouds in the sky, the far coast invisible. Faintly there came the sound of cannon fire again. Somewhere battle had been joined.

Oh, Ross. Come home safely. I love you.

But he had promised her, that day on the pier, that he would take no more risks, that he would not go to war again. He was a man of his word; she could take comfort in that.

Chapter Fifteen

Ramsgate—June 21st, 1815

By Wednesday there was still no word from Ross and, hoping for some distraction, Prue visited the library to find it in turmoil. The first mail coach to arrive had brought a pile of copies of the *Morning Post* and a crowd surged around the steps as a gentleman read from it.

'There has been a battle to the south of Brussels,' a lady whispered to Prue as she squeezed into the crush. 'Poor, gallant General Picton has been killed.'

'It says that, "an Officer was on the road to London with the official accounts, and in the meantime the report brought by Mr Sutton, the Packet Agent, is sufficiently circumstantial to prove its authenticity",' the gentleman announced over the gabble of excited comment. 'Wellington has brought Napoleon into what is described as a *"sanguinary contest"* on the seventeenth,' he continued.

Four days ago and still no word from Ross. Prue told herself that perhaps the army had prevented all movement of civilians, had impounded the ships in Ostend, and fought to present a tranquil countenance to the household when she returned, Tansy subdued at her side.

The next day, when there was still no news by noon, she went down to speak to Mr Dodgson. The harbour was busy, ships were sailing in, others tying up, the wharf sides were crowded with civilians. Puzzled, Prue walked into a crowd gathered round a wall where someone was pasting up pages from that day's *Morning Post*.

Tansy wriggled into the throng and out again. 'It's a casualty list, my lady. The killed and wounded. It's ever so long—and they say that's just the officers. It must have been a dreadful battle.'

Prue took her hand and together they forced their way through to the agent's house. He opened the door when she hammered on it, and showed them into the front parlour. 'A great battle, my lady. And the French defeated. Look what it says here.' He pointed to the column in the newspaper he held. '"We have this day the supreme happiness of announcing one of the most complete and comprehensive victories ever attained, even by British valour..." Bonaparte's escaped, but it seems his army is in tatters.'

He beamed at her, but under that relief and pride she could see something else.

'Mr Dodgson, what is wrong? What have you heard? Is it Ross?'

'I hadn't liked to worry you with it, ma'am,' he said, plunging her into immediate alarm. 'It might just be rumour, but one of my fellow agents was in Brussels and he fled as Wellington was falling back on a place called Mont St Jean, south of the city. He got back last night. He said he saw the Captain—His Lordship, I should say. He was with some of his crew and they were helping the army with wagonloads of arms. Wagons heading towards the fighting, my lady.'

'I see.' But she did not see. Not at all. Prue sat down on the nearest chair. If Ross was unharmed, why had he not returned? But he had *promised*. Promises, she thought bitterly, clearly meant nothing if the person you were making them to was not important 'None of the missing men are back?'

'No, my lady.' The paper was scrunched up in the agent's hand now and he tried to smooth it out as though that would help matters.

'Very well. Please let me know immediately if there is any news. I will go home and try to decide what to do for the best.'

As she made her way along the dockside Prue saw more ships were tying up and passengers disembarking. They were English refugees from Belgium, she realised, fraught and tired and trailing exhausted-looking servants struggling with mounds of luggage. Then she heard snatches of French and a language she did not know and realised that Belgians were with them.

'If the news is right, my lady, and Wellington's

thrashed Boney, they are going to wish they'd held firm and stayed where they were, not run away,' Tansy said, glaring at the back of one party who'd elbowed past them.

'Hmm,' Prue agreed absently. What should she do? What could she do? Then she saw the front door was open and a strange footman stood on the steps. 'We have visitors, Tansy.'

Inside the hallway was a hubbub of noise and, over it, the wail of a frightened child. 'Jon!' Prue forced her way in, past the unfamiliar footman. 'What on earth is going on?'

Then she saw Lord and Lady Falhaven and beside them, another burly footman with Jon, red-faced and bawling, in his arms. Maud was confronting Lady Falhaven, with Mrs Goodnight behind her.

'You give him back this minute. I don't care who you are! He belongs with my lord and my lady and— Oh, my lady, they took him before I realised what was happening.'

'Be quiet, all of you,' Prue said sharply. 'You are frightening Jon. Lady Falhaven, whatever do you think you are doing?'

'Taking custody of our grandson,' the older woman said. She was white-faced. Beside her, her husband regarded Prue with hostility. 'His father is dead and you are certainly no fit guardian for him.'

It took Prue a second to realise exactly what Lady Falhaven had said. 'Dead? No. No, that is arrant nonsense. You have no grounds for saying that.' Somehow she managed to keep the panic at bay, keep steady on legs that threatened to buckle under her even as she heard the staff gasp.

'Lady Brandon and her husband have just heard news of their son who was in the battle. His friend Lieutenant Smithers accompanied Major Percy, who's taken the news to the Prince Regent. He brought a note from his friend Reginald Brandon, reassuring his mother that he was but lightly wounded and mentioning seeing the body of our late son-in-law as he knew she would be as amazed as he was to find him on the battlefield.'

It was a lie, Prue told herself as the sounds in the hallway ebbed away and her vison darkened. Then Jon gave another wail and she snapped back, sick, but coldly calm.

One thing at a time; that is all I can cope with.

'Give me Jon,' she said, reaching for him as Maud, Tansy and Finedon all surged forward beside her.

The footman held firm and she realised that even if the entire household attacked the interlopers it would terrify the baby and they might hurt him if they tried to drag him free.

'Stop. Stop, everyone. Hush, Jon, it is all right. Where do you intend taking him?' Somehow she managed to speak calmly. Jon's cries subsided into hiccups at the sound of her voice.

'To our home in Norfolk.'

'I see. He needs his nanny and he needs his wet nurse,' Prue said, the words coming more easily now she was making decisions.

'The child is not weaned?' Lord Falhaven asked, regarding Mrs Goodnight with some alarm.

'No, he is not. And unless you wish him to scream constantly, you need his nursemaid as well. Maud, Mrs Goodnight, are you prepared to go with Jon until we can resolve this?'

'Yes, my lady,' they said in chorus.

'Thank you, I knew I could rely on you. Then go and pack up his things, please. Lady Falhaven, I say before these witnesses that you remove Lord St James from this house against my express wishes and I only allow him to go because I do not wish him hurt or frightened. You will be hearing from our lawyers.'

Until Maud and Mrs Goodnight came hurrying down, laden with baggage, Prue talked to Jon, smiling at him, trying to calm him down. It gave her time to fight through the mass of emotions—the fear, the anger, the blind panic—and when the door closed behind what she could only think of as the kidnapping party, she knew what she had to do.

'Finedon.'

'Yes, my lady.' He was not quite wringing his hands, but he had gone pale and Prue realised that he was probably older than she had realised.

'You will go to London immediately and find the Duke and Duchess of Aylsham. They may be at their country estate, in which case, please travel there. I will write to them, asking the Duke to immediately set in motion whatever means he can think of to retrieve Jon from those people. If you cannot find the Duke, then you will locate Lord and Lady Kendall. They may be in Bath.'

'Yes, my lady. May I ask what action you propose to take yourself?'

'I am going to Brussels, Finedon. I do not believe my husband is dead, but something is very wrong. I can do nothing here—Lord and Lady Falhaven are quite correct, I have no power and no influence. But we need Lord Cranford—or he needs us.'

'I'll come with you, my lady, of course. I will go and pack immediately.' Tansy ran upstairs before Prue could thank her.

'I suggest you take Jacob.' Finedon beckoned one of the footmen forward from where he loomed at the back of the hall. 'You will be safe with him.'

Jacob was well over six feet in height and broad in the shoulders, with large brown eyes and curly brown hair that had been cropped so he looked like nothing more than an amiable young bull. 'I'll look after you, my lady, never you fear,' he assured her, then relapsed into blushing silence.

'I am sure you will, Jacob. You had best go and pack a bag. Finedon, I need money.'

'Indeed, my lady. Gold is always acceptable abroad. I will open the strong box.'

'And, Finedon, please send a message to Mr Dodgson. We will need passage to Ostend as soon as possible.'

I will find Ross, Prue promised herself as she followed Tansy upstairs.

She stopped on the top step, gripped by fear for

Ross, for poor Jon, so frightened and confused, and dug her nails into her palms until she conquered the desire to simply sit down where she was and weep.

I will find him and then I will shake him until his teeth rattle for frightening me so. As for breaking his promise, I do not know whether I can ever forgive him.

Pain… Ross tried to separate out what hurt through the fog of misery. His head throbbed… His leg. His chest. The pain came in waves. There was light behind his closed lids, so he was not in his grave, not in a coffin. Yet. The way he felt, that might not be far off. He was badly hurt, he knew that.

Jon…should have thought…

He could hear voices a long, long way away. Smell… blood. And, strangely, onions and tobacco. *Thirsty…* Too difficult to speak, too painful to open his eyes. He croaked something and, after a moment, something wet touched his lips, water trickled into his mouth.

Prudence. Thank God. Prudence, I'm sorry, Lo—

'Ah. *C'est bien*,' said a strange voice. A man's voice. In French.

Oh, hell, Ross thought and drifted back into an uneasy stupor.

She had expected Brussels to be in confusion and at first, as Prue led her little band up the hill from the canal port, she thought it was. Then she began to see pattern, control, an over-arching discipline. Yes, there were crowds of people, but the bustle was purposeful. Soldiers marched in small groups, muskets on their shoulders. Nuns, veils fluttering, hurried from place to place amid housewives clutching vast baskets who queued patiently besides carts, clearly straight in from the countryside, loaded with vegetables and indignant, squawking, chickens. Through it all officials in uniform and in ordinary clothes strode about making notes, issuing orders.

And everywhere there were the wounded. They groaned on carts. They sat propped up against walls under the shelter of overhanging eaves, eyes shut, faces turned to the sun, or they were carried or helped into virtually every building they passed.

Four days after she had left Ramsgate, eight days after the battle, and they were still bringing in the wounded. Was Ross here, or still lying out there? Or dead? She was not ready to believe that yet.

'Gawd. Where do we start, ma'am?' Gregg, the *Spectre*'s Mate asked, staring round.

The entire crew had announced they were coming with her from Ostend to Brussels, leaving only Old Ramage, with his wooden leg, behind to mind the brig. Eight sailors, Jacob, Tansy and herself to get to Brussels had seemed impossible until the men found a canal barge whose owner they knew and they all packed on board alongside bales and barrels, medical supplies and harassed army officers.

Prue's mind had felt frozen. She was afraid to think about Jon, afraid to think about Ross in case the fear stopped her moving. All she knew was that she had to get to Brussels and she could only be thankful for Tansy and the men who were helping her get there.

Now she had arrived and it was time to think, to make decisions, to stop being a passenger and take control. 'I am going to find the military headquarters, see what they know. There cannot have been too many groups of sailors, surely? Tansy, you and Jacob go and see if you can find us lodgings. It might be difficult—there are so many of us. Here, this should help.' She handed Tansy a fat purse.

'We just need something over our heads, ma'am,' Gregg said. 'A barn, stables, that'll do us.'

'Thank you, Gregg. Do your best, Tansy. We will meet here…' she gestured at the great porch of the church they stood beside '…in two hours, I think. Now, Gregg, can you come with me and have the other men search and ask around? Some of the men the Captain had with him must have got back here, surely. Again, back here in two hours.' The clock struck nine as she spoke. 'Eleven o'clock.'

They split up, set off. Gregg put his hand on her arm. 'Won't you stop and rest first, ma'am? Have a bite to eat, a cup of coffee in one of these places.' He gestured to where appetising smells were wafting out. 'They call them *bistrots*. Quite respectable for a lady, ma'am.'

'Later,' she said, although weariness was making her light-headed and she could not recall when she had last eaten. 'Can you ask that sergeant there where military HQ is?'

Gregg wove his way among the carts and hailed the harassed-looking sergeant, who was consulting a vast list and snapping at an equally harassed clerk. 'Hey, Sarge!'

He stopped dead in the middle of the street, causing a man pushing a handcart to swerve and swear, as a skinny youth yelled and waved, 'Gregg! Gregg!'

'Hell. *Sam.*' Gregg pushed through to the opposite kerb, grabbed the boy by the arm and dragged him across to Prue. 'It's Sam, ma'am. One of the idiots the Captain went to fetch back.'

'Where is he?' Prue demanded 'Just tell me, quickly. Is he dead?'

'No, ma'am. No, the Cap'n's not dead, he's...'

The world went quiet, then the darkness slid over it all, taking her down into velvety depths. She felt hands holding her, then nothing.

Prue woke to find herself inside a house. She blinked at the ceiling, lumpy with beams, then at a blue-painted wall, then struggled to sit up and found she was on a chaise longue.

'Madame, vous êtes réveillée,' a man said.

'Yes. I mean *oui.*' She gave herself a little shake and managed, *'Vous êtes français?'*

The man was short and thin with a straggling beard and a pair of wire-rimmed spectacles on the end of his nose.

'Non. I speak English bad, now. Many years since I use it. I am Walloon, speak French good. I am Professor Guy Damseur of the university.'

'I understand.' Prue, her brain working now, spoke in French. 'What am I doing here?'

Without speaking the man moved aside and she saw a bed and on it, still and white, Ross.

'Ross!' Prue stood, even as the room swayed around her, and fell on her knees beside the bed. 'What is wrong with him?'

'He and his men were taking ammunition supply wagons to the front at Mont St Jean. A shell landed on a wagon ahead of them. It blew up. He was hit on the head. There were wood splinters in his legs. His ribs may be broken—I am not certain. I think he may live, *madame*. He is a stubborn man and now you are arrived and he can hear your voice, it will help. Once, long ago, I study a little medicine. I use it now for him and the other ones in this house.'

Ross stirred against her hand as she touched it to his cheek. His skin was hot and dry, but she did not think he was feverish.

'Ross, wake up. Look at me—it is Prudence. Oh, I am so angry with you. So angry.'

It seemed the Professor's English was good enough to understand that because he gave a little snort. 'He needs water. Try to get him to drink, *madame*. I must look to the others.'

Prue looked up. 'You have the rest of his men here?'

'All but the one who died there on the road. Only four are injured.'

'They chose to come,' she said bitterly. 'He came to bring them home.' But the professor had gone.

Prue took a sip of water, then a gulp and felt a little steadier. 'You are going to drink,' she informed Ross. 'Wake up and drink and get better because Jon needs you. I need you.' His features seemed blurred, then she realised she was crying. 'I will not cry,' she told his unresponsive figure as she scrubbed at her eyes. 'You do not deserve it. You broke your promise. You cannot love me, I know that, but we both love Jon. Wake up for Jon. Please.' There were strips of clean cloth on the table by the water jug and she guessed they must be to moisten his lips, drip water into his mouth, because if his ribs were broken it might be dangerous to force him to sit up.

Prue reached for them and began to patiently squeeze water between the cracked lips. 'You will get well, Ross,' she ordered him. 'I am going to stay here and nag you until you do.'

Home. He was home? That was Prudence he could hear. She sounded irritable, which was unusual. Ross willed himself to stay conscious, to listen. Yes, she was angry with someone, someone who had let her down. He supposed, wearily, that he must open his eyes, lend her his support in dealing with whatever this was.

Her face swam into focus above his as he blinked against the sudden light. She was pale and there were the snail tracks of tears down her cheeks. Whoever had made her cry was going to be very sorry indeed, just as soon as he managed to get on to his feet.

'About time,' she said crossly and scrubbed one hand over her face. 'You have been lying there for over a week.'

'Where…?' He realised he recognised this room as though it was somewhere he had seen in dreams. He must have been slipping in and out of consciousness. But Prudence had not been there before. 'Where are we?'

'In Brussels.' She stood up, moved out of his line of sight and he shifted his head painfully on the pillow to keep her in view. He found he did not want to lose sight of her again.

'Brussels.' Then it came back in a flurry of images, as though someone had ripped up a child's coloured book of prints and thrown it up in the air to fly around his head. His crew, the wagons, the mud, the gunfire. One vast flash of an explosion. 'The men.' He tried to sit up and was knocked back by the stabbing pain in his chest.

'Paul Jones was killed by the blast,' Prudence said. Then added, fast, 'The others have minor injuries—some wood splinters, bad bruises. They are living downstairs here. Just now most of them are helping the nuns with the wounded in the convent next door.'

As he absorbed the news about Jones she moved back so he could see her. There was the flicker of a smile on her lips and a knot deep in his chest eased. 'They are on their best behaviour,' she said.

'Why are you here? How did you get here? When?'

'Yesterday. The battle was nine days ago. I came across on the *Night Spectre*. They left one man with her and the rest came with us—Tansy and Jacob the footman. We were about to begin searching and young Sam saw us in the street.'

So Sam, the youngest, was well enough to be out and about, Ross realised with relief. Then, his thoughts beginning to order themselves, he asked, 'But how did you know to come, Prudence? Who told you I was here?'

'Word reached Ramsgate that you were dead,' Prudence said, her voice hard. 'I felt it might be…convenient to discover the truth, although I found it hard to believe, as you had given me your word you would no longer be fighting or going into danger.'

Then he saw the anger in her eyes, the set of her mouth, and realised that he had forgotten that promise and that he had let Prudence down.

Chapter Sixteen

'I forgot,' Ross admitted. 'I am sorry.'

'Forgot you had a son? Forgot you had a wife?' Prudence was furious and he could understand why. If she was told he was dead she would have every reason to believe it when the last she had heard from him was from this city, virtually on the front line of the battle.

'I—' He had broken his word, now honour demanded that he at least spoke the truth. 'I acted as I would have done before Jon was born. It was one step after another, deeper and deeper into the thing. If I had turned back at Ostend… But I did not. Then I found them all, persuaded most of them to come back with me.'

'And walked straight into a battle,' Prudence said flatly.

'They needed help with the supply train. The troops needed ammunition.'

'And there was no one else, of course.' She turned away and began folding something.

Keeping her hands busy, he thought, because otherwise she would want to slap him. He tried again, managing to drag himself up against the pillows a little. 'At that precise moment? No. I should have turned back at Ostend. I am sorry,' he repeated.

'Yes. I am sure.' Prudence carried on tidying, then, as though she could not contain it, she burst out, 'You have a son. You were so anxious about him growing up motherless that you married me. He was within a hair's breadth of losing his father.'

'I knew he would be safe with you.' Ross felt his own anger rising. He had responsibilities to his crew as well as to his family. He had responsibilities to serve his nation, if he could. He was an able-bodied man, used to fighting. Of course he had to do what he could, for his men, to support the army. 'The soldiers out on the battlefield left wives and children, too.'

Prudence came and stood at the end of the bed, looked at him. 'I did not know what had happened. All I knew was that you had given me your word. I understand that you felt responsible for the men. I understand that you wanted to support the troops. I feel guilty that I am angry and hurt and that I did not understand you enough to have expected this. I suppose you would say it is my fault for, f—for feeling too much.'

She turned on her heel and walked out. The door closed behind her gently and he heard her walking down the stairs and stop for a moment as though she would come back. Then the click of her heels continued down.

* * *

Five minutes later young Sam and Gregg came in with a tray with a bowl of broth on it.

'Her Ladyship said as how we're in charge of nursing you now, Cap'n.'

'You can start by telling me what's wrong with me. And help me sit up, damn it. I feel like a beached porpoise here.'

He had to get out of this bed, out of this room. He had to look after his men and get back to Jon. And, somehow, he had to find a way to heal the hurt in Prudence's eyes. He could have done things differently; there were always alternatives.

And I should not have made easy promises and then forgotten about them, he added in a bitter aside to himself.

But what had Prudence almost said, just before she left? Her fault for what? How could she feel too much? Perhaps she was chiding herself for being oversensitive, but somehow that did not seem right. That knot in his chest, the one that had loosened when he had realised she was with him, tightened again. She had courage, his wife. Courage to set out into the chaos of war to find him, even if it was simply because she felt it was her duty, or that she had to find him for Jon's sake.

Gregg stood next to the bed and eyed him dubiously. 'The professor says you might have broken your ribs and, if you have, then you might puncture a lung.'

Ross began to probe along his ribcage, swore, then swore more violently. It felt as though he had been kicked by a dray horse. But he kept going, teeth gritted, and nothing moved under the hardest pressure he could manage.

'Nothing is broken. Find more pillows.'

Gregg and Sam stuffed them down behind him until he was sitting, sweating but upright. 'You heard about Jones?' Gregg asked.

'Aye. Have any of the others turned up—the ones who volunteered?'

Gregg nodded. 'Three without a scratch, the rest not too bad and they'll be all right unless infection sets in. I managed to get to see them. They're in the big convent on the other side of the city. Thwaite's dead, they told me,' he added, shaking his head. 'He's with his sons now, at least. That's what he wanted.'

Ross pushed that away to deal with later: the living were more important now. He flipped back the covers over his lower body. 'What's wrong with my legs?' They were bandaged and, when he moved them, throbbed with pain.

'Wood splinters,' Gregg said. 'The professor got them out. I reckon you could build a chair with the wood. He says you'll be fine provided—'

'Provided no infection,' Ross said, replacing the covers. 'Give me that soup. Then some hot water, soap, towels and my clothes.'

'Can do all that and your pack's safe. Flew up in the air and knocked out Sim, so it's muddy and bloody, but it's all there.'

When Gregg came back with the water ten minutes later he put it down on the dresser and jerked his head at Sam. 'You watch the stairs, lad. Give us some warning if Her Ladyship's on her way up. She'll give us hell if you get up, Cap'n.'

'You are only obeying orders,' Ross said as he swung his legs off the bed, steadied himself and stood up. 'I will be the one in the line of fire, believe me.'

The room swayed, then steadied as he took a cautious breath. 'Give me your shoulder, Gregg, before I fall flat on my face. I'm not going anywhere without a shave.' He took a lurching step towards the washstand. 'Where's Bonaparte?'

'Paris, they say, Cap'n.' Gregg handed him his razor. 'Wellington's chasing him down.'

'Good.' He hissed as raising his arm sent stabbing pain through his chest. 'The man's a confounded— *bugger*—menace.'

Prue sat by the kitchen range with her mind only vaguely on the potatoes that were boiling in a vast vat and which she should be watching. Ross was conscious and not seriously injured, thank heavens, but she was still angry with him. Understanding why he had done what he had did not seem to help, nor did the fact that she knew her own feelings about him were making it all worse.

She had told him how she felt and he had apologised. Now she should be able to forgive him, but she could not find it in herself, despite realising that Ross was a fighter and a leader and his promise to her had probably been filed away in his brain as an agreement not to take to privateering again if the war went on.

Louise Allen   221

She was being unfair, she argued with the black cloud of misery inside her. She loved him, that should be enough, but it was not. He had left her, not unprotected exactly, but powerless. She was his wife, Jon's mother, but she had no weapons to fight with. Jon's grandparents had been able to carry the boy off and she had been unable to stop them.

I have failed as a wife because Ross does not take me seriously as a partner in this marriage. I have failed as a mother because I could not stop them taking Jon and now I do not even have the courage to tell the man that I love him because I fear rejection. Or his pity.

The potatoes boiled over with a loud hiss and clouds of steam and she jumped up to swing the pot off the fire, then sat down again to suck on a slightly scalded wrist, tears welling.

And I will not cry. I do not understand what the matter is with me. I've found Ross—he is alive and his wounds will heal. Will and Verity will be doing all they can to get Jon back. Almost all Ross's crew will be going home to their families. Napoleon is defeated and the world will be at peace very soon.

And yet she felt completely and utterly flat. Miserable.

And that would not do. She was giving up, wallowing in unhappiness. Prue sat up straight, put her shoulders back, wiped her eyes on her apron, and went to put her hand and wrist into cold water. She would make her peace with Ross, get him well. Meanwhile she would organise transport, get them all home and then she would tell him about Jon, because if she told him now he would set out immediately and make his wounds worse.

Jon was with Maud and Mrs Goodnight and even his wretched grandparents would recognise that their life would be infinitely more difficult if they dismissed the very people that could keep Jon calm and happy.

Yes, that was a plan. A week here for Ross to recuperate. That would be ideal. She would write to Verity that evening and there should be a reply before they set out. All the men would be fit to travel as well and—

Halting steps on the stairs had her looking up, expecting Gregg or Sam with dirty dishes and an empty water ewer. Then she saw who it was. 'What are you *doing*? Ross, go back to bed, this instant.'

'I am sure that tone will work wonders with Jon in a few years, Prudence, but I can assure you it will not persuade me to be a good boy.' He arrived at the bottom of the stairs, white around the lips and, she could see, at the knuckles where he gripped the handrail.

'I have no hope of that,' she retorted. 'Oh, for goodness sake, Ross, come and sit down, at least.'

She went to his side, put her arm around his waist and after a moment Ross put his hand on her shoulder as he leaned in just a little. It was the first time he had touched her for days, she realised, choking back the treacherous lump in her throat. This was hardly an embrace, but it was something. Something precious.

'I was planning our return home,' she said when he had sat down in the chair on the other side of the fireplace. 'I had thought in a week's time.'

'Are the men fit to travel?'

'Yes, all of them here are. I do not know about the men in the military hospital, but we could send Gregg to find out.' She hesitated, then decided there was no point in trying to soften anything. 'The one who was killed with you, Paul Jones, they buried at the edge of the wood near where he fell. They said there was no hope of finding a decent burial in any of the church-yards and the looters were stripping bodies.'

'He's as well there as anywhere,' Ross said harshly. 'He has no family, thankfully.'

She got up to check on the potatoes again, decided they were cooked through and began to lift them out on a pierced spoon.

'Why are you cooking? Are there no servants here?'

'They are nursing the injured and shopping to feed this houseful of men. Brussels is crammed with peo-ple, most of them injured or exhausted.'

'Then the sooner we get out, the better. Why, if the men are well enough, are you talking about a week? Is there a problem with transport?'

'Horses are as rare as unicorns, but I had thought of using the canal, as we did when we came. It will be smoother for the injured and probably faster. As for why a week, I was estimating the time it will take you to heal.'

'Then we leave tomorrow.' He raised his voice to a shout. 'Gregg!'

'Sir?' The sailor came down the stairs two at a time.

'What state are the men in who joined up?'

'Pretty fair, Cap'n. They were a healthy lot to start

with, they heal well.' He shifted his feet. 'I reckon most of 'em regret joining up now.'

'I did my best to get them out of it,' Ross said. 'They'll have to wait until things settle down here. Then if they want to leave and the army won't release them, they'll have to write to me. I know a few of them can write. I'll see what I can do for them then.'

'Can't say better than that, Cap'n.'

'We leave tomorrow,' Ross said. 'Get down to the canal docks, find out what's available. You know how much room we will need. Haggle a bit, but I'll pay what it takes.'

'Aye, aye, Cap'n.' Gregg shot a furtive look at Prue's face and bolted.

'Are you mad? Do you want an infection? Gangrene?' she demanded, showering the kitchen with potato water as she waved the ladle in frustration.

'The wounds are clean, healing. We are going home, Prudence. I do not want you here. It isn't right or fitting for you. No, don't look like that.' He held out his hand to her and when she took it, tugged until she had no choice but to sit on his knee or the arm of the chair.

She perched on the narrow strip of wood and left her hand in his. 'I was worried about you. I am still worried.'

'I know,' he admitted. 'I have never had anyone to worry about me, I am not used to it.' He gave her hand another little tug until she was leaning against his shoulder.

He was solid and warm and, without thinking, she put her arms around him, hugging as close as she could in that awkward position, nuzzling her face against his neck, exposed without coat or neckcloth. The familiar scent of her husband's skin, the brush of his hair against her face… 'I missed you,' she admitted.

'Really? I did not think I had been so attentive a husband that you would notice my absence.'

'Well, I did. In bed and out of it,' she added defiantly and felt the muscles in his jaw shift as he smiled.

'Truly?'

'Truly.'

'I am still going to take us all back to England tomorrow.'

Prue wondered if he was being deliberately provocative. 'Very well. I did promise to obey.'

'And now you are wondering whatever possessed you.' Yes, he was definitely smiling now.

Prue felt some of the weariness begin to slide away. She must have been so tense, she realised, so braced to deal with the fear, the sheer hard work of getting this far.

Ross was injured and under no circumstances was she going to allow him to try to walk to the canal basin, even if she had to hit him over the head and have the men take him down in a wheelbarrow. If she could get him to the ship safely, if infection did not set in, then all she had to worry about then was Jon. *All!* Prue told herself to keep putting all her trust in Maud and in Will and Verity. Fretting would not help.

The worst of the exodus of panicking British visitors had left, Gregg reported when he returned from the docks. The army was restoring order to the transport system and a barge was available the next day—at a price. It would be cramped, he warned Ross, but it would get them to Ostend.

The next morning they waved goodbye to the Good Samaritan professor with heartfelt thanks and promises to write when they reached home, and set off down the hill, a ragamuffin collection of tattered, battered men, one smart London footman and two weary women.

Gregg had acquired a hand cart—Prue did not like to enquire just how he had managed that—and she bullied and nagged Ross into sitting on it along with two of the men, one with a broken ankle and one with similar leg wounds to himself.

The good-natured joshing as the men took turns wheeling the cart made Prue smile. Morale, it seemed, was good and Ross, surrounded by his cheerful crew had, imperceptibly, relaxed.

Tansy, who had by her own account spent an enjoyable time in Brussels flirting with a large number of wounded soldiers in between bringing them water and helping the nuns, was chattering to Jacob, who loomed over her like an anxious sheepdog with a very frisky lamb. Prue wondered whether there might be a romance brewing there.

When they reached the moorings they found themselves sharing a large barge with a number of soldiers sufficiently well to be moved, but still bad enough to be sent back to England with a prolonged recovery ahead of them. The members of the crew who were fit enough, along with Jacob, helped tend to them while sending scornful looks in the direction of the group of harassed army clerks—'pen pushers'—who were jammed in at one end of the barge and keeping to themselves away from what they clearly thought was a mob of rough sailors.

Prue and Tansy settled down with Ross and the two men with leg injuries and filled water bowls, rolled bandages and pretended not to hear the ripe military language.

Ross, to Prue's surprise, settled as comfortably as the hard boards and cramped position allowed and went to sleep, as did most of the men once they had done what they could for the wounded.

'Saving our energy, ma'am,' Gregg said when he came and wriggled into a space next to her. 'Nothing we can do, so best to sleep. At sea you learn how to do it almost anywhere, any time.' He glanced around her at Ross. 'The Captain will heal, ma'am, don't you fret. He's fit and he's tough, for all that he complains that he's a landlubber now.'

Prue decided to believe him. If Gregg was worried, he simply wouldn't have said anything to her, she realised. The hard knot of worry that had lodged in her chest since Ross had left for Ostend unravelled a little and with it some of the anger she felt. There was a touch at her waist and she looked down to find he had curled round in his sleep and put his arm around her waist. She shifted a little until his head was pillowed against her breasts, pulled her cloak over them both and let herself drift off, happier than she had been in well over two weeks.

She had forgiven Ross; he had turned to her with trust, with affection, if only in his sleep. She had one of her menfolk safe. Now, with Ross home, there could be no difficulty in retrieving Jon from his grandparents. Then they could work together at being a family, a real family, and not one by arrangement.

Chapter Seventeen

The next morning when they reached Ostend, Ross insisted on walking off the barge and along the wharf, past the lock gates to the harbour. It hurt like the devil—he couldn't help but limp—but something revolted in him at the thought of being carried on board his own ship. There was probably a refusal to show weakness in front of his own wife, too, he acknowledged to himself as he hobbled along, teeth gritted.

'If those wounds start bleeding because you are so pig-headed, I will be *very* annoyed,' Prudence said balefully. But she kept her voice down so his men did not hear him being nagged by his wife and, whenever he halted to get his breath, she stopped in just the right place for him to rest his hand on her shoulder.

Tactful woman, he thought on a wave of affection and let himself lean for a moment. Then Old Ramage came hurrying along the dockside, lurching on his wooden leg, waving his crutch in the air in greeting and the moment of closeness was lost as everyone was loaded on board, the injured taken down below, the able-bodied sorting themselves out at the ropes at Gregg's orders.

The man was doing well, both with the ship-handling and the way he dealt with the crew. He was a competent mate and he deserved promotion, Ross thought as he sent Prudence and Tansy to sit by the main mast and Jacob went below to take care of the injured. With a battered crew, three of them over on the *Will o' the Wisp*, no master and himself not precisely at his best, he needed every available skilled hand on deck.

The tide was right, by some miracle, and they were out to sea, with the wind set fair for England well before noon. Ross stood up from the barrel by the wheel where he had lodged himself to keep an eye on Gregg's handling of the *Spectre*. 'Are you all right here for a bit?'

'Aye, Cap'n. She's handling like a dream, reckon she's as glad as us to be heading home again—' He broke off to shout a warning at a sailor who had let slip a rope and Ross noted how the other man hurried to make it fast with a grin and a nod to Gregg.

'She's handling well for you, which is more to the point,' Ross said. 'I'm in need of a new master. Interested?'

'I am that, sir!'

They discussed it for a few minutes, then Ross limped off to tell all the hands the news. 'Gregg has the ship. I'm a passenger.'

'Aye, aye, sir.' They went back to work cheerfully and he saw he had made a popular choice.

'They like him,' Prudence said when he lowered himself to a crate next to where she was sitting.

'That isn't always a good thing, but he is no soft touch.' He looked round. 'Where is Hedges?'

'She's down helping Jacob. I suspect there may be a romance developing there.'

'If you say so. I don't notice that sort of thing.'

'Do you mind? I might be wrong, but if they want to marry, you wouldn't object, would you?'

'It is none of my business.' She had pulled her hair back into a simple braid and Ross found he was playing with the end of it, letting the silky curl run around his fingers, catching in the roughness of weathered skin. Pretty, that hint of brown running through the blonde. Like Prudence herself, it needed close attention before you noticed its charms.

He realised that he must have sounded dismissive. Prudence was taking an interest and he did not want to snub her, or neglect the welfare of his domestic staff, come to that. 'There is a big room up in the attic that could be done out if they need somewhere of their own. If they are married, that is,' he added firmly.

'Of course,' Prudence agreed. 'I do not think Tansy would stand for anything irregular.' She turned her head and felt the tug on the braid. 'Whatever are you doing with my hair?'

'Amusing myself,' he admitted. 'This is pretty, plaited like this. It makes you look like a girl.'

'And I look like an old hag normally, I suppose?' She

turned some more and he kept hold of her hair so his arm came around her until she was snug against him. They were quite private behind their little barricade of crates, the men busy around the wheel or in the bows.

'You look, as you always do, charming. But now you have roses in your cheeks and your eyes are bright and your hair is curling and I rather think, my lady, that you are beautiful.'

She blushed rosily and dimpled a smile at him, then put up her hand to feel his brow. 'Are you sure you are not running a fever, my lord?'

'Very sure.' But he did feel light-headed. Perhaps those blue-grey eyes gazing into his were mesmerising him. Light-headed and compelled to touch her face, he stroked his fingers down the curve of her cheek, along the graceful line of her upper lip. Her mouth was made for kissing and he leaned in, felt her rise to meet him.

As their lips met, clung, something inside him, that knot of feeling, of restlessness, seemed to unravel. He let go of her hair, put both arms around her and gathered her close and, finally, found a name for it.

'I love you,' Ross murmured against her mouth, wondering if he had said it out loud, or simply felt it, breathed it. He lifted his head and she opened her eyes, her expression a little questioning.

'Did you say something, Ross?'

No, he had not spoken aloud. *Thank heavens.* What had come over him? 'I was just about to say that…that I appreciate you coming for me. You did not expect to find yourself almost on a battlefield, not for a marriage that was, I suppose, a business proposition.'

He found he was working out what to say as he spoke because the last thing he wanted was to blurt out something so ill-considered again.

'You have no need to apologise,' Prue said. She was blushing a little, could not meet his eyes. 'I had to come—there was no way I could not.' She took a deep breath, her smile trembling a little as she turned her head to him. 'You see, I love you.'

When he just stared at her a glow of humour crept into her eyes. The smile was steadier. 'You have only just realised?'

'Yes. Just this minute. I had no idea,' he admitted. It was a disconcerting, unfamiliar feeling to have a woman express her love for him. Just now had been an aberration, a product of his injury and fever. He did not love Prudence, of course not.

He loved his son, knew he would die for him, knew his heart lifted when he saw him, felt deep anxiety when he was sick, hated it when he was distressed. He had loved his father, although he hadn't realised it until he died, and he must have loved his mother with an instinctive love that needed no conscious recognition.

But this was different. Parents, son—they were part of him, blood-tied. What he felt for Prudence was... No, not *love*. He struggled to find the word, then re-alised it was completion. She completed him. From now on, without her, he would be less. With her, the world was brighter, larger, happier.

'It is terrifying, to be loved,' he said, the first words that came into his head.

'Is it?' She laughed, pulled his head down for a

kiss, then released him just so far that they were nose to nose, cross-eyed when they tried to look into each other's eyes. 'I should not have said anything, I do not want you to feel… I mean, I know there was no expectation of that when we agreed to marry.' Her smile became brave, a little forced. 'And I do not expect you to feel the same now.'

He could not answer that, did not know how to and still be kind. 'When did you realise?' Ross sat back enough to watch her. It was as though he was seeing a different woman and yet the same one, the cheerful, intelligent, practical woman who had taken his son to her heart, who had asked nothing more of him than his protection and some space for her books. But now she was part of him in a way he hardly comprehended and, it seemed, he meant even more to her.

'On the pier, that first morning in Ramsgate,' Prudence said. 'Just after we encountered your in-laws.' All the amusement drained from her face and for a moment she looked older, anxious. Then she smiled again, the moment passed and he wondered if he had imagined it. 'Anyway, we walked along to the end, sat and rested and I realised, as though something opened inside me and let out all these feelings, all that love.'

'You said nothing.' He found he was stroking her hand, his fingertips running over the long, slender fingers, tracing the lines of the tendons, the little callous on the middle finger of her right hand from hours holding a pen, the faint, steady beat of her pulse under the fine skin of her wrist.

'It seems I do not have your courage,' she said, a little ruefully.

'Courage? Why does it need that?'

'What if you had laughed? Or felt pity for me because you did not return my feelings?' she said. 'What if you had been angry because you felt it laid an obligation on you to pretend?'

She shifted on the crate so that she could lean back against his chest. 'It seems wrong to be rewarded as I have been for making that terrible mistake with Charles. First I was given Jon to love and now you. And when I thought I had lost you I found you again. It is nothing like I felt for him, not in the slightest, you know.'

'How is it different?' he asked. Prudence seemed to have lost the inhibitions she had shown when she first told him she loved him.

'I do not think you are perfect, or the most handsome man I have ever seen. I know you are grumpy and antisocial and autocratic—'

'Hey!' Ross protested.

'But it doesn't matter because I love you for who you are, not for a fantasy about some ideal man who does not exist.'

'Hmm.' He decided he was prepared to accept that because it meant that Prudence accepted him for who he was. She saw him, he realised, just as she had said that she saw her, the first time they had made love.

That clear-eyed gaze studied him, read him like a book—parts of which she still had to decipher—and loved him anyway. What had he done to deserve her?

Because he might have his faults, a ship's hold full of them if he was honest, but Prudence was just about perfect.

'I wish Jon was here—asleep below decks just at the moment,' he added, dropping a kiss on the corner of her mouth. 'But here and awake in a while so that we can share this feeling with all three of us, our whole family.'

'Yes,' Prudence said and turned her face sharply against the front of his shirt, burrowing close. 'I wish he was here, too,' she added, the words muffled by cloth.

It struck him, as it had not before, what a strain this must have been for Prudence. He had vanished into a foreign country, heading into a war, an imminent battle. Most women would have sat at home, wringing their hands or stoically waiting. But his wife would not do that.

Not, he realised, if she loved him, any more than he could have done if the positions had been reversed. If he was dead, then she would want to know. If he was wounded, then she would want to help him, and that help might have saved his life if he had been so unfortunate not to have had his crew, all of them working together to get their tattered little company back to Brussels.

But Prudence was a gently reared young lady, a scholar who had never left England, only once been on a ship. She was not an adventurer by nature or experience, but she had set out none the less, had brought the right people with her, had found him. But she must have been fearful and anxious for every moment for him, for the child she had left safe at home, for herself.

'Have I said thank you for coming to find me?' he asked. The top of her head, all he could see, was not very expressive, but he thought she became even tenser.

'You do not need to. You would have come in search of me.'

'You would not have done anything so reckless and you would not have forgotten a promise once made either.'

'Perhaps not.' Prudence sat up straight and he suspected she took a surreptitious swipe at her eyes. She certainly kept her face averted. 'How long before we land?'

'The wind is in our favour, the sea is calm. Late tonight, I expect, unless the weather changes, but I do not sense that.'

They fell silent, both of them weary, as the little ship flew ahead of the wind for England. Ross kept an eye on the sails, on the crew, but Gregg changed the men at the wheel, saw the sails tended, sent the hands below for mugs of thick, dark tea and bowls of stew in rotation, and eventually Ross relaxed, dozed, uneasily aware that Prudence was awake, tense, in his arms. Something was wrong, but he would trust her to tell him when she was ready to confide.

Prue did not have to wake Ross as the lights began to appear, beacons in the dark guiding them home. Sailor's instinct, she supposed as he stirred, sat up straighter and then levered himself to his feet, the breath hissing between his teeth as his abused legs took his weight for the first time in hours.

'What woke you?' she asked as he stood above her, stretching.

'I can smell the land, the wind feels different and Gregg has all hands on deck. It will be a while yet, go back to sleep.' Ross stooped to run his hand lightly over her hair and Prue forced herself not to flinch away. Soon, very soon, he would discover that she had allowed Jon to be taken and had made the choice to leave him and go to Belgium. And, having found Ross, had told him nothing and let him think Jon was safe in his own home.

But telling Ross would not have helped, would only have added to his stress when he was recovering. She could argue that, but could she justify to him leaving England? She sat up, pulled the blankets and cloaks around her, and watched Ross limping across the deck, speaking to the crew, leaning far back to look up at the sails gleaming white in the reflected lamp light from below. There was no sleep to be had now.

As the ship bumped against the quayside and ropes were thrown to the waiting dock hands, Prue saw there were carts drawn up waiting for business, the horses with their heads in nosebags, the drivers dozing at the reins.

'You get your lady home, Cap'n. I'll sort this lot,' she heard Gregg say. 'They've all got somewhere to go and no one's bad enough to need the doctor at this hour.'

There was a murmur of agreement from the hands

and the able-bodied went ashore to negotiate with two of the cart drivers to take the injured to their homes.

Prue slipped down the gangplank and hailed the driver of the cleanest cart. 'Can you take us up to Sion Hill? My husband has leg wounds.'

'Aye, missus, I can do that.' He got down and took off the horse's nosebag, tightened a few straps, then waved aside the money Prue offered him. 'I'll not be taking coin from men who've been hurt fighting that confounded Frenchie. Besides, it's hardly a step up the hill.'

He helped her up into the cart then, when Ross limped across, kicked a box under the tail of the cart to tactfully give him a lift up. 'Is it true Wellington whopped the bastard, Captain?'

'Wellington and Blücher along with a hell of a lot of brave men who won't be coming home,' Ross said.

The horse, considerably less alert than his owner at that hour, plodded up the hill to their front door. The driver gave Ross a shoulder to lean on to get down, then lifted Prue on to the pavement.

'He wouldn't take any money,' she said as they climbed the steps to the front door.

'I'll find him later. Don't have my latch key,' Ross said, banging on the brass dolphin knocker. 'It's somewhere on the road to Waterloo, I think.'

'My lord! My lady!' Finedon had apparently just struggled into his coat. His hair was ruffled and his neckcloth slightly askew. 'Thank the good Lord you are both safe. My lord, shall I call the doctor?'

'No,' Ross said.

'Yes,' Prue countermanded. 'Please, Finedon. But not until we have bathed and changed and breakfasted.' She willed him to say nothing about Jon until she had at least got Ross up to the bedchamber and she could tell him in decent privacy.

'There's several letters for you from the Duke, my lady, I could tell by the franks. And Maud has written to you in a covering letter to me so I knew what was going on. And His Little Lordship is well, but—'

'Jon?' Ross said sharply, halfway to the foot of the stairs. 'What is this about Jon?'

'I—' The butler shot Prue an imploring look.

'Come into the drawing room, Ross.' She took his arm. 'We cannot talk out here.'

He went, but she could tell he was holding on to his temper by a thread.

'What is wrong with Jon?'

'Nothing.' Prue pushed the door closed behind her and leaned on it. She needed the support. 'Your in-laws came here, to the house, on the twenty-second. I had been down to the harbour to discover if there had been any news of you and when I got back they were inside and their footman was already holding Jon. They said they had news fresh from the battlefield that you had been killed.'

'Impossible—how could they have received any information at that date?'

'Someone they knew was charged with bringing despatches and had seen you, they said. And if you were dead then they were the fitting guardians for Jon. I was not his mother. I tried to persuade them to give him back, but they refused and he was growing frightened. I thought if I told all the staff to wrest him away—and I think it would have taken all of them—he would have been terrified and perhaps injured.'

'So you simply allowed them to walk out of here with my son?'

Our son.

'I persuaded them that they must let Maud and Mrs Goodnight go with him and they saw the sense of that, thank goodness, so he has his familiar faces around him.'

Ross took two angry, limping strides away from her, then back. 'Why did you not follow them? What did you think you were doing, abandoning him?'

'What could I do? Sit on their doorstep? I have no influence. I wrote to Verity and Will—I thought if a duke did not have the power to do something, I had no idea who might.'

She saw grudging acceptance of that, then his expression hardened again. 'But you abandoned him, left the country on a wild goose chase after me—and they had told you I was dead.'

'I did not believe them,' she said vehemently, then struggled to explain calmly. 'Or, rather, I did not believe they had reliable information. They heard a rumour and turned it into what they wanted to believe. If someone had seen you badly injured and had mistaken that for your death, then I might be able to find you, help you. Jon was upset and confused, but he had people to look after him and he was not in danger, but *you* could have been dying for lack of care.'

'I am a man. I can look after myself.'

'Oh, that bull-headed, *pig*-headed, male arrogance!' She found she had stamped her foot and did not care. 'You were lucky, that was all. Fortunate that your men got you back to Brussels and very fortunate indeed that the professor took you in and that he had some under-standing of medicine.'

Ross waved that aside like a man swatting away flies. 'You are a woman—your place was here, doing what I married you for. I didn't ask you to fancy yourself in love with me. I certainly didn't want you using that kind of sickly sentimentality as an excuse to abandon your duty and gallivant off on some rescue mission.'

Chapter Eighteen

They stared at each other in silence.

Does he realise that what he has said, after all that has just passed between us on the Spectre, *is unforgivable?*

'I was faced with the decision to abandon the man I loved, which might result in his death, or the child that I loved when that would result in him being upset and confused for a little while,' Prue said with what dignity she could muster when what she wanted to do was to be sick. 'Or I suppose you would have me order Jon wrenched from their arms, ignoring his terror and possible injury, and then sit in my parlour sewing my mourning for you.'

'If you had been with him instead of mingling with the raff and scruff down at the harbour,' Ross said, 'they could not have taken him.'

'And if you had used some common sense when you arrived in Ostend, or considered your responsibilities in Brussels before you went off on your military adventure, I wouldn't have been desperate for news of you,' Prue retorted, dignity forgotten.

'I must get after them,' Ross said as though she had not spoken. 'If you would kindly move away from that door, I have things to do.'

'Reading Will's letters might be a useful start.' Prue opened the door and found the hall deserted except for Finedon lurking tactfully at the far end. 'Those letters, please, Finedon.'

'My lady.' He produced a silver salver.

Ross walked past her, picked up the letters and went into the study. The door closed behind him with a thud.

'The doctor is on his way, my lady, and Hedges is preparing your bath. As His Lordship has all the correspondence you might wish to see what Maud wrote to me.' He produced some folded sheets from his inner coat pocket.

'Thank you, Finedon.' This was not the time to break down and weep or to take to her bed and haul the covers over her head, both of which she ached to do. 'His Lordship is understandably upset. I think if you could let him know the minute his bath water is ready and then just send the doctor up without announcing him...'

'Certainly, my lady. I will tell the kitchen to hold breakfast until after the doctor's visit.'

If he does not throw the poor man down the stairs, Prue thought as she went up.

She had expected Ross to be angry—with his inlaws—and anxious about Jon. She could have understood if he had been annoyed that she had not told him sooner, although she could have countered those arguments by pointing out that it would have done no practical use and that he could have done nothing until he arrived back on English soil.

But she had not expected the things he had said to her, his complete lack of acknowledgement of her feelings or the reasons behind her decisions. On the ship he had been tender and gentle and…and wonderful. He had said everything she could have wished for, except that he loved her, and she had never even hoped for that. But now it was as though she was a servant employed for a task who had failed miserably at it— and without excuse.

Tansy was adding cold water to the bath when Prue entered her bedchamber. Tansy looked up when she heard the door. 'Ma'am, is His Lordship…? I couldn't help hearing through the door… He sounded very angry.'

'He is.' Prue began to strip off her clothes. 'I need to bathe and change as quickly as possible, before the doctor arrives and my husband has the chance to send him away. I need you to do the same and then pack for you and me, what we will need for about a week, I imagine. One of the maids can pack the rest, have it sent up to the town house.'

'Are you all right, my lady?' Tansy asked hesitantly as Prue climbed into the bath.

'No. Not really, but that doesn't matter now. Getting Jon back is what matters.'

My marriage may be beyond saving.

* * *

The doctor arrived and, to Prue's huge relief, Ross agreed to see him. She supposed he had recovered his temper enough to realise that he needed to be fit and to show as little weakness as possible when it came to confronting the Gracewells. There could not be any legal problem with getting Jon back, she was certain of that because, even in the event of divorces and separations where the husband was clearly at fault, courts inevitably gave custody of the children to the father. But his in-laws were not going to let Ross walk in and take Jon without putting obstacles in his way and making scenes that could only frighten the child.

Maud's latest note said that the Gracewells had gone to their Norfolk house and that, although Jon seemed confused and was clearly missing his parents, they had allowed Maud and Mrs Goodnight to maintain his routine as far as possible.

Maud had written:

They do not interfere with his routine and they are kind to him. Provided we bring our little lord down before dinner-time they are content to let me organise his day.

By the time the doctor left, breakfast was decidedly late. Prue in a travelling dress, and with a determined smile masking an aching heart, sailed into the dining room. 'No, do not get up.' She waved Ross back into his chair. 'I hope the doctor was able to make you more comfortable. Hedges is packing.'

'Why?' Ross enquired baldly.

'Because I am coming with you.' She poured herself coffee with a steady enough hand, then looked at him defiantly. 'Is there any reason why I should not?'

'No. Come if you wish to.'

Prue dropped a lump of sugar into the cup so suddenly that it splashed. What had she expected? That Ross would apologise for losing his temper, for throwing those hateful words at her? Had she really hoped he would take her in his arms, tell her he forgave her, loved her and had not meant to speak to her as though she was a thieving parlourmaid?

'Certainly I wish to. We will go by sea, I assume? Maud's last note was from Norfolk.'

'Yes. Direct to Yarmouth. Your tame duke informs me that he has had his confidential agents watching the London house. They saw Jon being taken to the parks by his nursemaid and a footman the day after they arrived and they report he appears well. They then followed to Falhaven Park where they were in the process of making local enquiries and following the various rights of way across the parkland.'

'I imagined Will would know competent people.'

'As do I,' Ross said, cutting into a kipper as though it had offended him.

'No doubt, but I do not know them and they do not know me. They would have wasted time checking everything I told them whereas Will knew at once that I was not hysterical.' She made herself eat some eggs and bacon she had no appetite for. It would probably be a long, cold voyage. 'Perhaps next time you decide to go off you could provide me with details of your legal advisors, your man of business and so forth.'

'I have no reason to suppose it will be necessary. The situation is hardly likely to arise again.'

I must love you, Prue thought, *because even though you are being so unpleasant I still feel the same deep down.*

But on the surface she had a strong inclination to tip the dish of strawberry jam over his newly washed hair and then add the dregs of the coffee pot. She was hurt, angry and heartbroken. But, she told herself, telling Ross exactly what she thought must wait until they had Jon safely back home.

He had been a fool to let himself feel anything for a woman. Anything at all. Ross walked the length of the deck of *Night Spectre* and then sat on the gunwale near the wheel. He wanted to pace, but the doctor, who had certainly made the wounds feel considerably less painful with his salves and dressings, had said short walks with rests in between would be best for healing. He was the expert and Ross had respect for experts, so, as much as it chafed, he would follow advice.

He wouldn't have sent for the man if it were not for Prudence, he acknowledged that. He could rely on her judgement for some things, but not, it seemed, for the most important. She should have never let the Gracewells out of the house with Jon and, if she had, then she should have followed them to London, called in the Runners if necessary, had her damned Duke of Aylsham cry *Kidnap!*

She said she had followed him because she loved him, which only proved how poor her judgement was if she allowed sentiment to rule her.

He got up and paced to the other side of the stern. He loved her and he knew it now. He did not want to, but he could not help himself and it hurt because this was not the happiness he had felt so fleetingly as they had sailed away from Ostend. As Prue had slept in his arms, worn out, he had acknowledged to himself that this strange feeling must be love and that once home, in private, he would tell her how he felt.

Hell. He had not expected love to be painful, such a messy business. He had never expected to love, if truth be told. It was all going wrong and, for the first time in his life, he could not see clearly how to make something right again.

He had hurt Prudence. Her face as she had stood there, back to the door, was that of a woman who had been struck. He looked down the length of *Spectre*'s deck to where Prudence sat curled up within a small mountain of rugs. They were both hurt now, but at least she would never make that mistake again of putting him before his son. He was a man; he had a business to run, ships to send out to sea, voyages to take. This emotion he was feeling for her was something he could control, ignore. If he pushed it away often enough, it would shrivel and die.

That conclusion sustained him for about thirty seconds before his conscience nagged at him, pointing out that Prudence had been right to be angry that he had left Ostend and even angrier that he had taken those ammunition wagons towards the battlefield.

Ross shifted uncomfortably on the gunwale and told himself that he would not have done any of it if he had not believed Jon was safe with Prudence. Yes, he had been harsh with her, but he had to be certain Jon was in safe hands, protected by a woman who would put nothing, *nothing*, before the boy. Certainly not put emotions first, feelings that could, and must, be mastered.

The instinct to go to her—tell her…no, *not* tell her he loved her. No, explain more rationally—kindly— why he had been annoyed—was strong, but as he rehearsed the words over in his head he found he kept wanting to tell her he loved her, imagining her face when he said those three words. But why should she trust him enough to believe him now? And if she did, then there would be two of them thinking irrationally.

Get Jon back, bring him home and restore everything to normal and then, if she still seemed to feel something for him, then he would tell her. He wondered if they could build a marriage on that. Or would it be worse when it all fell apart as his own parents' marriage had in the face of hardship: love giving way to recrimination, jealousy, anger and then, perhaps worse, a dragging indifference.

Right. Ross stood up. He was a gentleman; he had lost his temper with a lady and it did not matter who she was, he must apologise. *Let us be civilised, if nothing else*, he thought bitterly as he made his halting way across the pitching deck, cursing the fact that he couldn't even walk to her like a man in command of his own body.

Prudence looked up when he reached her side and he sat down, thankful for the excuse to do so.

'Yes?'

'I have come to apologise. I lost my temper and I expressed myself badly. Harshly.'

Prudence nodded. 'Yes, you did,' she said coolly. 'But I understand. My motives do not weigh with you and you find it impossible to believe that I made a rational decision. And I am sorry that my decision causes you to feel anger and upset.'

'But you would not change it?'

'No.' Prudence folded her hands together on top of the coarse yellow blanket.

They trembled, just a little, and Ross found himself reaching for them, then turned the gesture to brush windblown hair out of his eyes.

'I am not going to lie to you,' Prudence said. 'I do not believe that is the way a marriage should be conducted.'

Ross had thought he had been businesslike at the beginning of this relationship—now it seemed that his wife had either decided to copy him or that she had possessed this cool rationality all the time and it was not until this moment when his heart and soul felt raw and battered that he discovered how it could sting.

'Excellent. We are in agreement then.'

'What is your plan?' Prudence asked.

'We will dock at Great Yarmouth tonight and put up

at the Angel. Then I will hire a carriage in the morning. Falhaven Park is close to Norwich to the west.'

'Is it far? I am trying to picture it on the map.'

'Forty-seven miles from the Angel to Norwich.' He was prepared to make small talk if it meant they could have a civil conversation sitting here in the clean salty wind, his wife curled up at his feet.

'That is very precise.'

'Eleven years ago a certain Captain Dickens wagered a considerable sum of money that he could walk into Norwich from the inn and then return within twelve hours. He did it in eleven and a half.'

Prudence wrestled with the mental arithmetic. 'Just over seven miles an hour.'

'It is very flat and the road is good. I think we will do rather better than the gallant Captain.'

That won him a faint smile. Prudence was not someone who would sulk, but she was wary of him and angry with him, too, and she was trying to find a way to be civil without pretending things were not as they were. *Honest Prudence.* But he found it more and more difficult to believe that she loved him. Surely those words had simply been relief that she had found him alive and likely to heal. They were on their way home and she had let go of the tension and the fear and made a declaration that she was probably bitterly regretting now.

In fact, Ross thought as he got up to go back to the stern to watch the compass, that might be why she was so very tense now, regretting those words.

* * *

Why had she been so reckless last night, telling Ross that she loved him? He had been kind at the time, gentle. Almost tender. But it had clearly embarrassed him and the longer he had to think about it, the more he disliked it, it seemed. At first he must have thought it did not matter too much, then he had concluded she had made the entirely wrong decision about Jon because her mind had been addled by silly feminine emotion, an emotion he clearly did not share.

She was a fool, Prue concluded sadly. But she had agreed to this marriage for better or worse and so she just had to make the best of it, never mention love again and hope Ross eventually put her words down to relief after exhaustion and worry.

Sitting here huddled up like an invalid was not going to help. She stood up, folded the blankets except one that she wrapped around her shoulders like a countrywoman, and began to walk up and down the deck. Tansy was sitting with Jacob nearer the bows, talking and laughing softly together. Yes, that was definitely a romance in the making.

Gulls swept by on outstretched wings and she could see no land, only a few other sails, none close. She felt more confident about being at sea now. If she had not been so miserable about Ross, this would be delightful. Jon would love going to sea when he was a little older.

The thought plunged her back into anxiety. How much would a child of his age understand absence? Had he noticed that several days had passed without his parents or would the constant presence of two peo-

ple he knew, and who would keep his routine regular
and loving, be enough to keep him calm and happy?

There was nothing to be done until they found Jon
and she was simply borrowing trouble, she knew that,
just as she knew Ross was watching her. Prue went
back to her nest of blankets, dug out her notebook and
pencil and began to work on the fragments of verse she
had translated days before in Ramsgate.

> *My heart trembled with love as the leaves of the*
> *grove of oak trees are disturbed by the moun-*
> *tain winds*

That was Sappho and *of course* she had to be writing
about love. Prue turned a page, looking for something
considerably less inflammatory than the long-dead
woman's elegantly erotic words.

> *My heart trembled...*

Something about Odysseus, that would be better,
provided she skipped all the fighting, the love affairs,
the gruesome parts. Or perhaps some stolid Roman
biography. Anything but love and death and loss.

Chapter Nineteen

The approach to Yarmouth was strange compared to sailing in to Ramsgate. They had missed the tide the evening before and instead of staying the night at the inn had spent it riding out at sea away from treacherous sandbanks. Prue had shared a cabin with Tansy, had enquired the next morning whether Ross required any assistance with the dressings on his wounds and had refrained from nagging when he had said that nothing needed doing. The very politeness of his refusal stung far more than an impatient ejection. Ross was being too careful; it was like being strangers again.

Yarmouth was 'right tricky' according to Gregg. There was a long spit of sand stretching south and the ship, under much reduced sail, had to enter the narrow mouth of the River Yare and then turn sharply north to negotiate two miles of river before they arrived at the quayside.

'Even I can see the importance of coming in on the

tide so it carries us up,' Prue said as she joined Ross, up at the bows.

He nodded, eyes scanning the waterway that lay between sand dunes on the seaward side and rough, marshy grazing on the landward.

'It feels as though the sea could wash over all of this at any moment,' she added with a shiver.

'And does from time to time,' Ross said absently. 'There's the town now.'

Wide quaysides opened up, lined with warehouses, rows of smart brick double-fronted houses which must, she supposed, be home to the merchants of the town, and then the sail came down, the men ran to the side and began to heave ropes and *Night Spectre* glided elegantly towards the quayside, then settled with a bump.

'Stay here and be ready when I return with the carriage,' Ross said. 'Less than an hour.' He put one hand on the gunwale and vaulted down to the dockside, then strode off towards the town.

Prue, Tansy and Jacob were waiting on the quayside, the two women perched on the small trunk, when Ross returned with what Prue guessed must be the best carriage the Angel had to offer. It was going to have to accommodate six adults and a small child. She hoped.

Now they were within striking distance Prue could feel the tension in Ross that made her own almost unbearable. He gave no outward sign, but she could feel it in his very stillness as he sat beside her in the faintly musty gloom of the elderly coach.

A lady was raised to maintain a flow of light, pleas-

ant conversation. Prue contemplated commenting on
the landscape, then thought better of it and watched the
rich, undulating fields, the woodlands and the areas of
marsh and scrubby heath pass by in silence.

'Acle,' Ross said after an hour and, she supposed,
eight or nine miles. 'Another five miles and we will be
at the Black Horse, the inn where the Duke has based
his watchers.'

So Will had done all she asked and more, Prue
thought, wondering whether seeking help from a high-
ranking nobleman on her husband's behalf had been
precisely tactful. Then she decided that she did not care
if Ross resented it. She would have gone and begged
the Prince Regent himself if she had thought that would
have been of any use.

'There are three of them,' Ross went on. 'One at the
house, one at the inn and one working between them,
carrying messages and relieving the watcher. If the
Gracewells have left, then one will remain behind at
the inn with the others sending messages back to him.
You did well to turn to Aylsham, Prudence. The man
has a head on his shoulders and the resources to put a
solid plan into place.'

So, Ross was not above taking help, which was a
relief.

'He wrote that his legal advisors said he could not
remove Jon himself, having no rights in the matter beyond a letter from the stepmother.' He saw Prue's expression. 'Yes, I know, the law is unfair in that respect.
He said he contemplated kidnap, but that he could not

be certain of being able to take Maud and Mrs Goodnight at the same time and, even if he succeeded, if I was dead then the courts would take a very dim view of the matter and it would count against you.'

For the first time since they had arrived back at the Ramsgate house Prue saw a flicker of a smile on his lips. 'I would have purchased tickets to see Mrs Goodnight being bundled into a coach by masked men.'

'I would have every confidence in her borrowing one of their pistols and making her feelings very clear to all concerned,' Prue said, breathing a little more easily.

The Black Horse was small, neat, and even had roses around the door. Prue was charmed and, at any other time, might have begged to stop there a while and have something to eat and drink on one of the benches outside.

But a swarthy man, dressed neatly like a superior head groom, was watching the coach with sharp-eyed attention and when Ross got down from the coach he walked across.

'Excuse me, sir, but are you the gentleman expecting a message about a small missing object?'

Ross took his card case from his breast pocket and offered the man a card. 'I am. You are the Duke of Aylsham's man?'

'Perkins, my lord. And he told me the first thing to say to you was how the young gentleman was doing, to put your mind at rest. He's in fine fettle and I saw him myself this morning. His nursemaid takes him out for an airing first thing. A fine set of lungs he has on him, my lord.'

Prue released a long breath and suspected Ross did, too.

'Is there a way into the grounds without passing through the main gate?'

'There's an overgrown drive to what looks like an abandoned walled garden. That's how we've been approaching the place, my lord. You can drive up, or ride, and leave the horses hidden by the walls, then it's no distance at all to the back of the house through the shrubbery.'

'We will go that way,' Ross said after a moment's thought. 'Then I will go round to the front door and hope to take them by surprise—we might as well try and be civilised about this,' he added. 'I want to do everything as calmly as possible so as not to frighten my son. But my wife and her maid and one of you will approach from the back, just in case they try to spirit my son away.'

The old track was easy enough, even in the big old coach, and when they reached the gate of the abandoned garden they could see the roofs of the house close by. Ross turned to skirt around to the front.

'Good luck,' Prue called softly and he looked back, then raised one hand in brief acknowledgement.

Prue and Tansy followed their burly guide through the shrubbery.

'There's the back lawn, my lady. And there's the nursemaid now.'

And not only Maud. Prue pushed through to the edge of the bushes and saw that Maud was standing a little apart from the rug on the grass where another woman sat playing with Jon.

It took a moment before Prue recognised her, hatless and in a light morning dress. 'Lady Falhaven,' she whispered.

Then Jon crowed with laughter and she could not bear it another moment. 'Stay here.' She pushed through the branches and walked across the grass.

Maud saw her first, but made no sound, only smiled, her wide, happy grin making her freckles seem to dance.

Prue, feet silent on the soft turf, reached the rug and knelt down as the older woman looked up, then recoiled.

'You!'

'Yes, me. Oh, Jon, how I've missed you.' She scooped him up and kissed him as he laughed and patted her face with both chubby hands.

'Mama.'

'Yes, Mama is here now, darling.' Somehow she kept the tears under control. 'Have you been a good boy for your grandmama?'

'Gramma!' His grin revealed two teeth.

'Why are you here?' Lady Falhaven demanded. But her usually assertive tone had deserted her and her voice broke in the middle.

'To tell you that Ross is alive and well. You were misinformed, Lady Falhaven. He was wounded, not killed, and he very much wants his son back.'

'He is not a fit father—the man is a pirate.'

'No, he is not and never has been,' Prue said gently. There was real distress here, she realised. Not spite. 'You know perfectly well that Ross was a properly licenced privateer attacking French shipping when we were at war.'

'He is in trade.' Lady Falhaven's hands were trembling.

'Is that such a bad thing? He supports himself and his family and the many people he employs. It is honest trade. He is a fine man. Why do you hate him so?'

'Our daughter...'

'He was a good husband, was he not? He was faithful, protected her. He was not responsible for her death.'

'He hated her. She told us.' Lady Falhaven would not meet her eyes now.

'I think, perhaps, Honoria had her faults,' Prue suggested. 'She loved the title more than she loved Ross, is that not so?'

'We were shocked when she wanted to marry him,' Lady Falhaven said. 'The East End Aristocrat, they called him. And he is so ugly—that scar, that ruthless face... We told her how it would be, that he would not be her match in education or culture or refinement, but she insisted.'

'She wanted to be a marchioness,' Prue said. 'And once she had the title and she had a son, then she saw no point in being married to him any longer.'

Perhaps I have gone too far, she thought.

Then the older woman gave a sob and buried her face in her hands. 'She said she wished he was dead, he was so unkind to her. She said…she said she would not go to his bed any longer because he was cruel to her.'

'You do not believe that, do you?' Prue demanded, her sympathy wearing thin. 'The man does not have a cruel bone in his body.'

'The man does not have a cruel bone in his body.'

Ross stood just outside the glass doors on to the terrace, Lord Falhaven by his side, and listened to his wife's impassioned voice. He put out his hand to warn the Earl to silence and stillness and let Prudence's words wash over him like a caress. She could say that after what he had said to her in Ramsgate… She must love him.

'He married me because he needed a mother for Jon. He could afford any number of nursemaids, but he wanted the child to have a mother to love him. He does not love me, but right from the start he has been kind to me, tolerant of my needs and my wishes. Ross is a *wonderful* father to Jon.'

'He left you, went to Belgium looking for loot on the battlefield, I suppose. There's always a profit in war,' his mother-in-law said bitterly.

'That is not true and I think you know it. He went out of duty to bring back those of his men who had been unduly influenced, had gone to join up, despite having no experience of a battlefield. And then he stayed to help take ammunition to the front line. He left Jon with me because he believed he could trust me and I failed.' Her voice cracked, then she composed herself. 'I should have stopped you taking Jon. Somehow.'

Ross took an abrupt step forward, but this time it was his father-in-law who reached out and stopped him.

'Yet you let Jon go without a struggle,' Lady Falhaven said, her voice accusing.

'Because that would have frightened him and I knew he would be safe with you, even if he was a little confused. But he had Maud and Mrs Goodnight and I knew they would do anything for him.

'I did not believe you when you said Ross was dead, you see. I love him, and I loved him then, and somehow I would have known if he had ceased to be. But if he was wounded, then he might die for lack of care lying out there on the battlefield, in pain. What should I have said to Jon in ten years' time? "I have no idea if I could have helped your father because I did not dare to try."'

'Cranford will be angry with you now.'

'He was not pleased,' Prudence agreed with what Ross thought was admirable understatement. 'And I was angry and hurt by what he said, but I understand because Jon is the most important thing in the world to him, far more important than I am. He would never have hurt your daughter, Lady Falhaven.' Prue reached out and touched his mother-in-law's hand. 'He might have loved her if she had given him the chance. He only wanted a family of his own.' She handed Jon back to the other woman who reached for him, hands trembling. 'I hope he will let Jon have his grandparents as well. Will you try and believe what I tell you—if only for Jon's sake?'

Lady Falhaven took Jon and then burst into tears.

Jon began to howl, Prue put her arms around both of them and Ross could see her shoulders shaking, too.

'Oh, hell,' Lord Falhaven said beside him. He was already beginning to back towards the house. 'Best leave them, never know what to do with weeping females.'

'Neither do I, but one has to try, as Prudence says,' Ross said and limped down the terrace steps, lowering himself painfully on to the rug.

'Give me Jon,' he said and Prue turned, smiling through her tears, and handed him his son.

Jon took a great gulp of air, ready for another howl, then hiccupped and broke into a beaming smile. 'Dada! Dada!'

Ross told himself that his face was wet because it was pressed to that of a very soggy little boy, but he scrubbed his free hand over his eyes, then wrapped that arm around Prudence, finding he had hauled his mother-in-law into the hug and braced for the explosion.

It did not come. 'Now, now, Florence, stop that— you'll upset the boy.' His father-in-law had summoned up the nerve to come and join them and lowered himself stiffly on to the rug, too. 'I think perhaps we have all been…er…somewhat prejudiced in our opinions and that has led to some unfortunate…er…misjudgements.'

Prejudiced? *Is that what you call it, you old—*

A small, warm hand landed on Ross's and squeezed. 'Grandparents,' Prudence whispered. She settled against him, tipped her head back until it rested on his shoulder, and together they watched Jon dribbling happily all down his grandfather's handsome neck-cloth while he tried to steal the fobs on his watch chain.

From inside there was the distant chime of a clock. Noon.

Lady Falhaven blew her nose briskly. 'You will be wanting to return home, I dare say. You girl, Maud, help me up and we will go and pack the young master's things.'

The ramrod is back down her spine, Ross thought, but the severe mask had not so much slipped as fallen away altogether. She was an unhappy woman, he realised. One who had not understood her own daughter and who had done everything she could to pretend Honoria was not the selfish, ambitious woman that she was.

Something very strange seemed to be happening to him, he realised as Maud bent to take Jon and carried him away, his face appearing over her shoulder and one hand waving. Something inside him that had been knotted and hard felt as though it was dissolving, unravelling, leaving him feeling curiously naked and vulnerable.

'Our daughter was…difficult,' Lord Falhaven said abruptly, levering himself up and brushing down his breeches as though he was amazed to discover himself lounging on a rug in the middle of his garden. 'Not an affectionate girl, I regret to say. Ambitious. Our fault, I dare say. You do what you can, you know, but sometimes… I'll just go and see if my wife needs anything. Er…' Lord Falhaven set off to head inside.

'They did not want to believe anything bad of their

daughter, so you had to be the villain,' Prudence said. 'They began by having a snobbish prejudice against you and she never allowed that to break down. And when she died they could not accept it was her fault.'

'So it must have been mine,' Ross concluded.

'And they were perishing of love for their grandson.' She hesitated. 'They do love him, you know.'

'I know. I was on the terrace. I heard the two of you talking.'

'Oh.' Prudence sat up, then got to her feet, face averted, as she stooped to gather up Jon's discarded rattle and toy dog. 'How embarrassing.'

'Revealing,' Ross said. Somehow he had to get them all back to the ship before whatever was happening to him rendered him completely incapable.

What he could see of Prudence's face was pink and tear-streaked. Ross stood up, managed not to swear out loud, and found a large handkerchief. 'Here. It is clean.'

'Thank you. I must look— Oh, there is Maud waving. They must be ready to go. That man of Will's has vanished. I suppose he went to bring the carriage round.'

You look…you look like a woman I have reduced to tears. You look like happiness and heartbreak.

'Prudence.'

'Yes?' She looked round. 'Do you need a hand?'

'No,' he said abruptly and the warmth vanished from her eyes. 'And, yes, I expect he fetched the carriage.'

I do not need a hand, I need a heart. I need words I do not have. I need, somehow, to make all this right.

Chapter Twenty

As the coach turned out of the gates towards Great Yarmouth, Prue put Jon into his father's arms and turned to talk to Maud. She wanted to hold him very badly, but Ross needed him more.

'He was a wee bit grizzly at first, my lady,' Maud said. 'There was rather a lot of travelling for him and unfamiliar places and I think he could sense that no one was very happy. But then Lady Falhaven seemed to relax a little and Mrs Goodnight and I did, too— we could tell she wanted to do the right thing for him even if she was wrong to take him. After that Jon liked all the attention.'

She glanced across to where Ross and Jon were deep in an incomprehensible conversation which seemed to be giving them both a great deal of satisfaction. 'He'd look round, now and then, and say *Mama* or *Dada* and screw up his face as though he was going to cry, then we'd distract him and he was happy again. He was puzzled about where you had gone, I think.'

'Not a happy lady, his grandma, if I might express an opinion, ma'am.' Mrs Goodnight waited for Prue's nod. 'I found her crying once or twice. She'd poker up when she saw me, because she's a deal of pride, but our little man made her sad and happy, too.'

'She and her daughter were not close,' Prue said. 'She loves Jon, but she wishes her daughter was alive and that they could all be happy together and I do not think that would ever have happened.'

Jon had fallen abruptly asleep on Ross's chest, worn out by excitement, she supposed. She met Ross's gaze above the child's head and he smiled, not with his lips, but with his eyes, warm and calm and dark.

Had he forgiven her? Was that smile for her, or was he simply deeply relieved to have his son back safe? At least they were together again, a family. She had to trust in love—hers for Ross and Jon, Ross's for Jon—to make the glue that would bind them together.

Her head was on something hard and warm, silk was brushing her face and something tapped on her arm.

'My lady, we are at the ship.'

Tansy was patting her arm and Prue blinked herself awake to find she had fallen asleep with her head on Ross's shoulder and Jon snuggled against them. She sat up carefully, brushed his tousled hair and found Ross watching her, expressionless.

Ah well, that moment of shared warmth had gone cold again and it seemed she had to build his trust again before they could even get back to friendship.

Ross handed Jon to Maud before he got down and strode to the *Night Spectre*, leaving Jacob to put down the step and help the women out.

'What time is it?' Prue looked around and saw the face of the large clock on what seemed to be a warehouse. 'Goodness, three o'clock and none of us have had anything to eat since breakfast.'

'Jon has,' Mrs Goodnight said. 'But he'll be hungry again now. We'll take him down to a cabin, settle him down there, shall we, my lady?'

'Yes, excellent, thank you. I should say to both of you that Lord Cranford and I both felt greatly reassured knowing that you were with Jon. I can only apologise for the upset and for keeping you for so long from your own little girl, Mrs Goodnight.'

'She's in safe hands and it's a pleasure to do what we can for this family, my lady,' the wet nurse said with a decisive nod of her head. 'Now, off we go, my little lord. Up the gangplank and down to your cabin.'

'I'll take your bag below, ma'am.' Tansy went up the plank, too, and Jacob offered his hand to steady Prue.

'I'm quite at ease with it now, thank you,' she told him. 'And besides, the tide is high so the slope is less.'

'There is more to finding your sea legs than not being seasick,' Ross remarked, holding out his hand to help her as she reached the top. 'You are growing in confidence, Prudence.'

'Thank you, Captain. I am a sailor's wife so it is only right that I place my confidence in his ships.'

She said it lightly, but it seemed Ross took it seriously. 'Admirable. Although cramped cabins, wind-swept decks and smelly bilges were not in the marriage agreement, as I recall.'

'I married a man and I took all of who he was, not simply the parts that might suit me.' Prue surprised herself with her own vehemence, but it was the truth.

Ross seemed surprised, too. He stood looking down at her, an arrested look in his eyes. 'You took on a testy, autocratic devil, then.'

'We all have our faults.'

'Some more than others. Come,' he said, suddenly brisk. 'Find somewhere to sit while we make our way downstream. The tide is falling and I do not want to miss it. The cook will send up some food shortly.'

It felt as though she was balancing her way along the top of a narrow wall. Prue swayed and stumbled and every now and again she thought she had her balance. Then Ross's mood would change or he would say something that gave her hope, only to dash it with coolness or impersonal practicality.

Prue walked past her usual seat under the main mast and went forward to the bows where there was a small cask she could perch on to watch the river as they wound their way down to the sea.

How rapidly things changed from what she had *thought* she wanted to what she actually wanted, needed, now. At first all she desired was safety from scandal, a kind haven for the child she might be carrying and the opportunity to fulfil her part of the bargain. Then she found she desired her new, unfathomable husband and that desire had been reciprocated. But now she loved him and that was a burden for both of them to carry after she had so rashly told him how she felt.

Prue sighed and then jumped as a voice beside her said, 'Bread and cheese, ma'am?' It was one of the seamen, offering a platter and a tankard. 'And there's a nice piece of pickled herring if you fancy that. Or some ham. And Cook says, he's sorry, but it is ale or ale to drink, ma'am.'

'This will be delightful, thank you. No, nothing else.' She might be getting her sea legs, but pickled herring was a challenge too far.

She ate her crusty bread and very strong cheese, washed down with ale as they cleared the mouth of the river. More sails came rattling and flapping down, then *Spectre* leaned away from the wind and scudded out away from the treacherous sandbanks as Prue leaned back against the tarpaulin-covered mound behind her and closed her eyes.

When there was a thump she did not turn her head. It would be another seaman. 'Am I in your way here?'

'Not at all,' Ross said and she turned to find that the thump had been him shifting a crate beside her. 'You are exactly where I want you.'

There was something in his voice that had her turning fully to face him. For a second she thought it was sarcasm, then she realised it was bitterness edged with... With sadness?

'Ross? What is wrong?'

'So much that I do not know if I can repair it because it is my fault in the first place,' he said and reached out his hand.

'You are frightening me now.' Her fingers closed around his and he shifted his hand so they were interlocked.

'I brought a great deal into this marriage.'

'Certainly. And I am very grateful—'

'No. That is not what I mean. I brought cynicism and suspicion and—' She saw his throat work as though he swallowed hard. 'Fear.'

But you are not afraid of anything except losing Jon, she almost protested. Then bit off the words. If Ross was making this painful confession then she would not trivialise his feelings. 'Tell me. What did you fear?'

'Letting you become important.' His gaze was downwards on their linked hands, but he looked up sharply then, his expression almost angry. 'If I did not let myself have any feelings for you, then I could not be hurt, not be disappointed.' He looked out to sea as though it was difficult to meet her eyes. 'I have been thinking a lot about that since we sailed into Ramsgate the night before last. I have no experience of caring for someone as you want to be cared for. Deserve to be. No experience of the happy marriages your friends seem to have.'

'So you had no expectation of happiness when you married me,' Prue said, understanding all too well. 'Your parents' marriage was difficult and you were probably far too young to comprehend what was happening between them. Then your marriage proved a painful mistake. But you understood enough to know what you wanted for Jon, to try to give him what you had missed as a child growing up.

'It was probably very sensible of you to have no expectations of finding anything with me beyond an amiable arrangement.' It was a struggle to keep her voice steady.

'Then I found I desired you and, by some alchemy, you seemed to want me back.'

'I did.' Prue found she could smile. Just a small, cautious lift of the lips. It would not do to hope too much. 'I do.'

'And you came for me when for all you knew I was dead. You came into what might have been the middle of a war for me and you told me that you loved me.'

'Yes,' Prue agreed when Ross stopped abruptly. 'I did. And I do.'

'It is not easy, this business of loving.'

'No,' she agreed. 'I am not finding it so. It is very easy to make mistakes and the more someone cares, the more it hurts.'

'I had not comprehended how that would be,' Ross said. He still held her hand, he still looked out to sea, his eyes narrowed against the wind and the occasional drift of salt spray. 'It is so damnably easy to hurt someone you care for.'

I do not understand, she wanted to say. *What are you telling me? That you accept that I love you and you are sorry that you hurt me? Or...*

No, she did not dare put that hope into words. You could not go on for ever in the face of rejection, she found. Best to accept what was possible and not yearn for more.

'When I discovered that you had let Jon go, had not told me, then that hurt.'

'I know. I—'

Ross held up his hand to silence her. 'Hush. Let me finish,' he said as he turned from the sea to look at her. 'It was painful. I was angry because I did not understand your motives and so it hurt that I felt betrayed. If I did not care about you I would have been angry, but not hurt, but I did not realise it then.'

'I know you care,' Prue said, picking her way through the words as though they were sharp knives that would stab one of them if she got this wrong. 'We are lovers and, although I know you find it strange, friends.'

Somewhere behind them someone called an order, a man was whistling, there was a splash as though a bucket of something had been thrown overboard. No one came near them.

'I have never had trouble with words before,' Ross said, his voice harsh. 'And I do not think I have ever been a coward. Damn it, I can say this.' He closed his eyes and she held her breath. 'Prudence, I love you. I am in love with you and if you tell me that you have changed your mind, that what I have said and done these last days have made you fall out of love with me, then that is only just and fair. I deserve that and I will respect it.'

'Oh.' She had not really believed he would say it, mean it. Yes, she had hoped. But not this, this painful, truthful confession. Prue lifted her free hand to touch Ross's scarred cheek, spread her fingers to feel the strong bone structure beneath the skin, feel the blood pulsing through his veins. 'It is not easy to fall out of love, I think. Of course, I have never loved anyone before, not like this, so I may be wrong. When you were so angry I was hurt, I thought I would love you less because you said harsh things to me. But I did not. I cannot.'

And finally, *finally*, he pulled her into his arms and kissed her and all the words fled and all the doubts vanished and there was simply the all-enveloping realisation that she was where she was meant to be, in this man's embrace. Her heart beating against his, his mouth warm on her wind-chilled lips. There was the familiar taste of him, the strong, battered body under her hands, the certainty that she was safe where she belonged, always.

'There is an empty cabin below decks,' Ross murmured in her ear. 'It is very public up here.'

'We can't! I mean...everyone will know what we are doing.'

'What? You think that the crew will be shocked to discover that a husband makes love to his wife?'

'You are wounded.' She tried to sound sensible and only managed to sound flustered and eager. 'It is not sensible.'

'The relevant parts of my anatomy are perfectly sound,' Ross said, taking her hand and placing it so she could check for herself.

'Oh. Yes.' *Goodness.* She snatched her hand away,

convinced that she was blushing so much the steersman would mistake her for a lighthouse. 'But... You might strain your legs.'

Ross stood up, her hand in his so she had to rise, too. 'I am going to rest,' he announced loud enough for the nearest deck hands to glance around. 'I shall lie on my back on my bunk for a while and hope my dear wife will tend to me.'

Yes, it was possible to blush this hard and not spontaneously combust.

'I do wish I had some nice gruel for you,' Prue said as Ross climbed down through the hatch. 'Perhaps the cook could make some. That is just what you need. *Deserve*,' she added as she climbed down after him and he silenced her at the foot of the companionway with a kiss.

Ross propelled her into the cabin and closed the door, dropping the wedge in the catch to lock it. 'That is a cruel threat.' He began to undress and her mouth became dry.

'Just because I love you and I think you are a hero does not mean I would not enjoy spooning a pint of gruel down you. Cold, thin gruel.'

'A *hero*?' Ross froze, his shirt in one hand.

'A hero. I want to box your ears for it, but, still, there it is. You went after your men, you walked towards danger because it was your duty.' She unbuttoned her pelisse.

'No, leave it. I want to undress you, Prudence.' He dropped his shirt on to the deck and reached for the pelisse, slid it from her shoulders and down her arms.

'How can you think that when I broke my word? I am not certain I will ever understand women.'

'Excellent, that is as it should be.' She smiled at him in the gloom of the tiny space, teasing a little so as not to cry out of sheer happiness. 'Women, of course, have fathomed the depths of the male mind for centuries because it is a much simpler mechanism.'

Ross made a sound suspiciously like a growl as he worked on the fastenings of her gown. 'I suppose you would object to me tearing this off in my simple, male way— Ah, there we are.'

The fabric, gown and petticoat together, fell to the deck as he spun her round, began to work on the laces of her stays, his lips moving on the nape of her neck, the nip of his teeth making her shift restlessly as she kicked off her shoes.

Then Prue was naked except for her stockings and Ross kicked free of his trousers and pulled her down to the bunk.

'It is narrow and hard,' he warned as he lay back.

'You cushion it for me.' Prue straddled his hips, gasped as heat met heat, softness nestled against hard flesh. She needed him so much and it seemed he needed her the same way.

'Always,' Ross said as she rose up and took him in. 'I swear I'll never leave you, never break my word to you again,' he said. Joined, they both stilled. Then, as Prue sank down and met his dark, hot gaze, he whispered, 'I love you.'

It was hard to think, to do anything but feel, but Prue felt an urgency, a need that she had never felt before when they had lain together. Their rhythm stumbled, they were both too eager, too desperate, then they had it, a perfect unison of give and take, yield and demand. The sounds of the waves slapping against the side of the ship, the creak and groan of the timbers, the pitch and toss that they became part of as Ross drove her higher, higher towards that peak, that crashing, towering wave of feeling.

As her vision blurred and she felt the tension twist to the point of no return, Prue fell forward on to Ross's chest, felt his heart thunder under hers as their mouths met, their cries heard only within them as they spiralled up together, broke together, sank into rest as one.

Ross lay with his sleeping wife cradled against his side and made a sleepy inventory of how his world felt. Mildly uncomfortable—his wounds ached like the devil and the wooden side of the bunk was digging into his hip bone. Utterly exhausted—making love three times at that intensity was perhaps only to be recommended to eighteen-year-olds. Smug—that he could still manage it, almost thirty or not. And over all of it, he was totally, profoundly, bone-deep happy. He did not deserve to be, he knew that. He could only hope that Prudence never came to the same conclusion.

Love. This was something to be nurtured, tended like a fragile bloom, never to be taken for granted. He would raise his son to be strong and resilient to weather whatever life threw at him and he must work with Prudence at making this resilient, too, because there would be storms and misunderstandings and uncertainties ahead in their marriage. But they would overcome them, he was determined on that. This unexpected, undeserved love was too precious to hazard.

'You are thinking so hard I can hear it,' Prudence said sleepily and wriggled up until she was sprawled across his chest. 'Ouch. This bunk is not made for two. Never mind, you are very comfortable to lie on.' She blinked at him like a contented cat and he watched her wake fully, saw the feeling come into her eyes, saw them turn blue.

All that, for me.

'What were you thinking?'

'How fortunate I am. If he was not such a swine, I would like to shake the hand of the man who treated you so badly because without him we would never have met.'

'I agree. If it were not for him... It does not bear thinking about. Yes, I would tell you his name so you could shake his hand, if it were not for the fact that I suspect you would break his arm immediately afterwards.'

'True. Break both of them, shave his head and drop him in warm tar. How very well you know me, Prudence my love.'

'I warn you, not as well as I will come to over the next eighty years,' she said, stretching up to kiss the point of his chin.

Ross felt the welcome tug of the scar as he smiled.

'That seems like a threat that only a man as deeply in love as I am could relish.'

She moved a little further up his body and he felt her lips curve as she kissed him. 'That was not a threat— that was a promise,' Prudence whispered.

* * * * *